Mistakes and Opportunities

MYRNA K. BURKES

DEDICATION

For my mother Laura…who taught me to reach for the stars.

CONTENTS

IN APPRECIATION

My profound appreciation to Rosie Cortinas. Without your marvelous mind and technical skills, *Mistakes and Opportunities* would never have come to fruition. Thank you Miss Rosie.

ACKNOWLEDGMENTS

The process of writing this book brought back many wonderful memories of excellent teachers, outstanding students, supportive friends, and my awesome family. I wish to express my heartfelt appreciation for letting me participate in your lives and ask that you will forgive me if you feel I may have taken some liberties with our relationships. I would like to thank my daughter Elizabeth and her husband Matt, a Homicide Detective, for assisting with technical information. Thank you to my children, Amy, Elizabeth, and Doug and their spouses, Thomas, Matt, and Patti, for allowing me the freedom of integrating many humorous and happy family memories in my book. Thank you to my wonderful grandchildren, Maddie, Walker, Taylor, Heidi, Ryan, Holden, Hannah, and Hadley, who make their Mimi proud. Thank you to my beautiful sister Laronda for her continuing love and support. Finally, thank you to my husband, Jim…whose patience, encouragement and love sustains me, and makes every day
"Another Day in Paradise".

PREFACE

What creates a killer? Are they naturally born to kill, or as children, are they cultivated and developed from that little seed that makes them different? Does it begin with the kid whose eyes never reach yours, or who is alone in a room full of people? Is it the girl who pulls the wings off a grasshopper, uses a stick to poke a bug on the playground, or takes that same stick and runs it through another child's arm? Perhaps the one who is abused emotionally or physically? It's impossible to know for sure, but we suspect there is something "off" about them. They are always a little odd, rarely fit in, are never remorseful, and one day, when we hear about their crimes, we say, "I'm not surprised… there was always something not quite right about him or her."

April 20, 1999, midway through my teaching career, the Columbine High School massacre occurred. That day forever changed the false sense of security that existed in the public school environment. Schools began locking doors, putting up bars, and establishing an emergency code that would be used to announce a lockdown. Bullying was blamed for the assassins' behavior, and schools immediately implemented instructional videos and lesson plans to assist the system in developing more caring and compassionate students. We created a safer and more secure environment for our children…or so we thought.

America and the World were stunned on December 14, 2012, when in Newtown, Connecticut, a twenty-year-old shot his mother, then drove to Sandy Hook Elementary and shot his way into a LOCKED school. The media and our government immediately jumped on a bandwagon of blame for this unconscionable act and attributed it to video games and guns even though it was determined that the killer was autistic and had a history of being socially different, as is the case with many troubled students.

My experience as an elementary teacher has given me first-hand

1

knowledge of children who are damaged as a result of physical, emotional, or medical abuse. Experiences that nightmares and novels are made of. It has led me to believe that today's classrooms are filled with outstanding students who impact our society in a positive way, and yet those same classrooms include children with Sociopathic tendencies. The latter may have parents who can add to an illness or actually create one by refusing to accept that their child is different and needs help. Unfortunately the result becomes society's problem.

So. Is there anything we can do to truly be safe? The Columbine and Newtown tragedies are names that make our hearts weep, now and forever, but our tears will not end there. As a former educator I believe we can care, we can take precautions, but we can never be totally safe from the senseless behavior of others. Our compassion and concern may assist and possibly influence their behavior, but ultimately we have no control over the choices they make.

PROLOGUE

The intruder entered the school playground and the teacher watched in horror as the gun was raised…bullets everywhere…screams…blood…and she could do nothing. Mimi stood paralyzed as her little ones began dropping one by one and still…she could do nothing. She tried to run, but her body would not respond. All she could do was watch the carnage and hear her student's terrified screams. Oh God. Her children. Mimi Bradley awakened in a panic, sobbing uncontrollably.

"Is it the dream again?" asked her husband Mack, as he pulled her into his arms.

"Yes," she replied shaking her head. "I just don't get it. I haven't had it in such a long time. Why now?"

"It's probably because of all the hype surrounding the anniversary of Sandy Hook. The media has to dredge up every horrible event that has occurred involving school massacres."

"You may be right," she said. "We have been discussing the lockdown code and procedures in the last two staff meetings. I'm a little upset because we still haven't practiced and we are half way through the school year. I guess we can thank the media for at least reminding us we need to."

"Well, seems like the media likes to give their opinion on what causes society's problems and of course what we should do to fix them."

"All I know is schools are filled with dangerous personalities that can sometimes develop into real complications. Some of these kid's problems are doozies and I constantly worry about them. You know, Mack? Teaching isn't just about reading, writing and arithmetic. It's about the whole child and the baggage that comes with them. It is so easy to overlook these kids even when in your heart you know some go home to God only knows what."

"I understand hon, but you have always given your students

3

encouragement and they know you are available if they need you. You shouldn't let it get to you."

"That's not as easy as you make it sound. I try to make them feel valued, safe and secure, but sometimes it's so hard. The problem is I don't always know what is going on in their head…or their homes."

"You take on way too much. It is not your job to make sure kids come to school with healthy minds and bodies. That should be their parents' job."

"Right. So do I ignore them if no one else cares? Besides, how do you teach children the skills they need to survive if their tummy is empty or if they don't have a place to sleep at night. Someone has to care."

"Okay. You're right and you will always care. You look for the best in everything, especially in your kids. I understand you want to make life better for them and provide opportunities they may not have otherwise. Teach them that a "mistake is just an opportunity to learn". Right?" Mack said chuckling.

"You and Julie really love to tease me about my little mantra, don't you? But, it is true, you know."

"I know hon. I know. Now can we get some shut-eye?"

"I guess, but it helps that we have talked. The helplessness of my nightmare still leaves me with a sense of foreboding. I hope it's not a premonition of things to come."

"Nah. We'd have to have a killer and where would you find one in Caradan?" Mack laughed as he turned out the light.

1
MAY 22, 2013

"Bats in the cave." "Bats in the cave," school secretary Melinda Fox screamed into the intercom. "NOW... EVERYONE...GET IN YOUR CAVES!"

"Good grief," said Mimi Bradley. The auburn haired, hazel-eyed, fifty-year-old Second Grade Teacher unfastened the worn room key from the lanyard hanging around her neck.

"I can't believe they didn't give us any warning," she mumbled to herself as she locked the door. Her usually cheerful smile frowned in disapproval. "We've almost completed the entire school year and we haven't had any kind of lockdown practice," she said, turning toward thirteen pairs of anxious eyes. "Why didn't we do it last December when we talked about it during the staff meetings...why now?"

Although her kids were just as surprised at the unexpected announcement as she, Mimi did her best to explain what they were supposed to do.

"Boys and girls," their teacher said. "Do you remember the fire drill practices we have every month? Well, "Bats in the cave" is the code for a different kind of practice. It's called a lockdown drill and is used when we have an emergency. When we hear the code, teachers close and lock the doors, turn off the lights and students are supposed to hide in a corner, or under a desk or table. You can even go into the supply closet as long as you leave the door open and be sure to stay back from the window. Principal Garza will come down the hallway to check the classrooms and if we hide good enough, she won't be able to see us," Mimi said, glancing around the room as her adorable crew nodded their heads in understanding and waited patiently for further guidance.

Her eyes quickly traveled to the colorful bathroom tags dangling from their hooks on the wall and she gave a grateful sigh. "Thank goodness."

None of the tags were missing so she knew her students were safe in her classroom. She glanced at several empty desks and realized almost half of her students had left to go to their pull-out program classrooms. The teacher's secret fear was that one of her kids might be alone in the restroom during a catastrophe. Even though this was just a drill, she was relieved all were accounted for.

Mimi hoped her brief review of the rules would help her children understand what to do. Although she knew this exercise was necessary and long overdue, the teacher was irritated at the untimely interruption as her Second Graders were in the middle of a lesson and would quickly lose focus. The lesson coincided with the timing of her pull-out children's programs. She had forty-five minutes to give her regular education students some one-on-one time. Mimi would not have an opportunity to do a reteach after the lockdown drill was over. This was frustrating for her because every minute counted if they were to complete the day's work and accomplish the required result.

"Oh well," she said to herself. "It's hard enough to find time for the mandatory fire and tornado drills, so is it any wonder we have become so lax about practicing the lockdown drill? And don't get me started on the pull-out programs."

Mimi knew the programs were necessary, but it was one more factor in slowing down the smooth transition of the day.

Cautiously raising his hand, freckled-faced, red-haired, and totally precocious Cameron Jones blurted, "I need to go, Mrs. Bradley."

"I'm sorry sweetie, but you'll have to wait until the drill is over."

"Aw right," the little guy muttered. "But, I hope I don't have an accident."

Giving him a hug and clapping her hands, Mimi encouraged her students to get quiet and locate a sneaky hiding place.

"Be sure to get out of sight of the window," she reminded them.

"My hiding place is best, Mrs. Bradley," said clever little Jade Salisbury, peeking out from under one of the computer tables, her blue eyes shining and a big grin covering her face.

"Look, Mrs. Bradley. Can you see me?" asked brown-eyed, diminutive Celia Sharpe.

"You are all doing a great job of hiding, but we need to be quiet," said Mimi.

"It's just like playing hide and seek, Mrs. Bradley," timidly whispered one of her tiny charges. Her response surprised Mimi, as blonde-haired, brown-eyed Marguerite Hudson did not usually verbalize her thoughts.

"That's right, honey," Mimi gently answered her. "Just like the game of hide and seek."

"Okay everyone," said the teacher as she hurriedly switched off the lights. "Be as quiet as itty, bitty mice and no squeaking till I say so."

"Squeak, squeak, squeak," said hefty, but jovial Kolin Marshall. "I am a little squeaker."

"Yes you are Kolin, but be a silent squeaker, okay?"

The children, thinking it was a game, continued to scurry under desks, into corners, and behind chairs. When the giggling and whispering persisted, she admonished them to be silent.

Holding back her own giggles, Mimi pretended to sternly remind them, "Now children, Principal Garza will be checking the rooms and if she sees or hears us, we will all be in big trouble and we might even lose recess."

"Or sit at the time-out table," solemnly added Marguerite, again surprising the teacher with her participation.

The room was filled with heavy breathing, punctuated periodically by soft voices and a few sounds from scraping chairs and shuffling bodies as students selected their hiding places.

Suddenly, those sounds became starkly silent when Melinda Fox screamed over the intercom.

"Oh Dear God. Please. Get in your caves. NOW."

The secretary's voice and what sounded like a gunshot indicated this was not a practice drill after all. Mimi could literally hear the frantic beat of her heart as she viewed the pint-sized learners hiding so faithfully and whose very lives she was responsible for. She cautiously sneaked a peek out the glass window that opened into the hallway and observed an intruder dressed in black, ski mask and all, pausing at the end of the hall.

"Children," she whispered softly. "We must be very, very quiet and stay in your hiding places. Do not come out...shhhhhh."

The frightening interloper hesitated at the first room in the hallway and tried the door. Of course, it was inaccessible.

"Okay," she thought. "Calm down. We will be all right. The doors are locked and he can't come inside."

She slipped further into the shadowed corner by the door, monitoring the intruder's casual approach down the hall toward her location. It was impossible to ignore the twisted grin that radiated eerily through a hole in the dark mask.

The trespasser stopped at her door and removed a shiny ring with a set of lock picks attached. Selecting a pick from the ring, the intruder quickly inserted it into the keyhole and the knob began to turn. Mimi was panicking as her mind and heart started racing.

"Do you think he will find us?" asked Cameron Jones nervously fingering the space in his mouth where his tooth used to be.

"No, we're hid too good," said Marguerite Hudson solemnly.

"Squeak, squeak, squeak," uncertainly whispered Kolin Marshall, pretending to be a mouse as his green eyes darted nervously.

"We need to be real quiet," said Marguerite tensely. "Teacher says."

Mimi was aware of her children's apprehensive whispers and of the frightening piece of work outside her door.

"What could this stranger possibly want with us?" she thought to herself. "And where did he get a key?"

Suddenly, before she could determine a motive for the trespasser's arrival at her door...so quickly...so unexpectedly...before she could comprehend or develop a plan...the door was thrust open and the room quickly filled with screams of terror as the masked individual stepped in, casually flipped on the light, and turned toward them with a gun.

Amidst the terrified cries of her students, Mimi bravely stepped forward. "Please, don't hurt my children," she pleaded, as she eyed the gun.

Her heart was hammering and a second later, when she looked into maniacal eyes filled with such hate and hostility, understanding dawned on her. This was no accident. This disturbed creature was here, in her classroom, at this moment, for a reason. He was here for her. Mimi found herself zoning out and briefly becoming detached from the circumstances, as the small handgun was raised deliberately toward her chest.

Thoughts of Mack, her husband of thirty-two years and her beautiful daughter Julie, flew through her mind and unconsciously brought a fleeting smile to her face.

"What will they do without me," she whispered softly without thinking.

"Did you say something? Are you grinning?" scowled the perpetrator. "Do you think this is funny?"

"No. No. I...I don't think any of this is funny," Mimi said, stumbling over her words. "I don't understand what is going on. Why are you here?"

Then finally, with a sober face, she murmured the words the intruder wanted to hear.

"Why me?" she asked.

"Why you? Why you? Oh, Mrs. Bradley. You don't remember?" was the tortured reply. "You taught me that a mistake was just an opportunity to learn and I have had many opportunities to learn. You taught me well, Mrs. Bradley. You know I loved you. I did. And you tossed me aside. I let you into my heart and that was one of my many mistakes. But, not to worry. I plan to take care of that right now."

Suddenly, Mimi knew. Those eyes. That voice. Oh my God. It can't be. Why? After the flicker of recognition, she watched as the killer gently squeezed the trigger. At the last minute, Mimi Bradley reached out her arms and closed her eyes, so she didn't see the bullet as it sped rapidly toward her heart. With the gun still raised, the killer turned toward the teacher's rug rats.

2

EARLIER

Unable to still my trembling hands, I sit nervously in my newly-purchased pride and joy. The sleek sports car is idling just inside the locked and gated entrance to Caradan Elementary School. I take a few minutes to inhale the fresh air as I peruse the time-worn building and its boring surroundings, as common to me as the mole on my left pinkie. I look at the sand-colored brick structure that is slowly decomposing and showing its age, and notice the St. Augustine grass that has turned brown from lack of regular watering.

The marquee at the front of the school arrogantly announces it as a State Recognized School and the italicized motto "Children are Special" is proudly displayed.

"Liars. Hypocrites."

I find myself staring at the gently waving flag. I am reminded of the many years spent at this small campus so long ago, and terrible pain endured at the hands of my recently departed parents, as well as uncaring teachers, who were never there for me. The many hours spent with people who tried to figure out what my problems were. Like it was all my fault. It seemed only yesterday and I was immediately transported back to the dark place that pulled me into the grave where I died over and over again.

"Please, don't hurt me. Please. Please, I love you. Please."

I could picture the weeping child in my mind as I recalled the punishing response and felt the hand that crushed my heart. I witnessed the pain over and over. So many memories and all of them bad. No one had cared. No one had helped. No one had remembered.

"Well, they would remember me now," I said. "I would make them all remember."

Slapping the steering wheel with the palm of my hand, the frustration and resentment began to build and a slight tear leaked from the corner of my eye, as if it were a drop from an irregular faucet.

Gripping the wheel and squeezing so tightly, my hands became numb.

"It should have ended here, at this school. She ought to have made a difference for me like she had for so many others. I lived through so much heartache because she hadn't cared. Mrs. Bradley had been indifferent to that person who needed her so. I just wasn't as important as the favored students. It was all her fault. I should have made her pay for it back then. They all should have been made to pay those years ago. Well, they would pay now. I would take care of my mistakes, as well as my opportunities to learn. Now was the time. They would all pay, but especially the wonderful Mrs. Bradley."

Earlier that morning, I had carefully removed the black knit ski mask from my dresser drawer. It had been purchased to coordinate with the long sleeved, black cotton t-shirt and well-fitting black polyester parachute pants, as well as my skintight black gloves. The ultra-suede, black-on-black Reebok jogging shoes completed my ensemble.

I practiced stashing my gun in different pockets of the pants and finally settled on the left hand pocket pouch. The compartment was large and would accommodate the mask, as well as allow easy access to my 9mm Glock handgun. There was a smaller pocket located directly above it that would hold the newly purchased shiny key ring and the awesome set of lock picks attached.

"Pretty cool," I chuckled to myself as I slipped out of the vehicle, making sure I had tucked the mask, gun, and key into the designated pockets. Then I casually began sauntering to the entrance of the building.

The skies were a Texas blue, with wispy clouds floating like feathers. I stopped briefly when I spotted a small group of buzzards catching a thermal and spiraling in the air. It was peaceful and quiet and I did not encounter one other soul as the worn and cracked sidewalk guided me toward the donor brick area.

"What a stupid name," I said.

I remembered the first year the school opened and the campus Parent Teacher Association came up with the idea to create a unique bricked entrance, paid for with contributions from parents and staff members. The donor's names were inscribed on the brick. The flag pole was perfectly located in the center of the bricked space and surrounded by three large mountain laurel trees, now heavily laden with fragrant purple clusters. A meticulously hedged row of boxwoods bordered flower beds sprinkled with colorful snapdragons. It all helped to create an attractive outdoor location that was used for a variety of activities and was often referred to as the donor brick area.

A small sprinkler rained on the spot, trying to maintain some visual beauty, as it welcomed parents and visitors to the building's entrance.

"Thanks for welcoming me with so much splendor," I said sarcastically.

My eyes were drawn to the front entrance with the massive, latched and heavy black iron gate, which denied entry into the school. I moved toward the office and it's standard issued door. This door represented safety to the inhabitants of the building. Visitors could only enter the school through this door after 8 a.m. All the other doors were locked and could only be opened from the inside in the event of a fire or other emergency. I knew the routine by heart and frequent observations reassured me I could walk right in. Oh, they thought they were safe and secure, because what other choice did they have?

Yes indeed, there was only one way in.

"Well," I said to myself. "Their false sense of security is about to be shattered."

I hastily ran the scenario through my mind. I would enter through the door and shoot anyone who got in my way. I knew sweet little old school secretary Melinda Fox would be in the outer office. I wondered if she would announce my presence to the school and if so, how? Well, if she stayed out of my way I would let her live.

Just outside the business office immediately to the right, would be Counselor Katie Larson's office. I had spent many hours in that room. If I didn't see her, she would live for a few more weeks. Then I would head past the Kinder and First Grade Halls until coming to the Second Grade hallway.

I picked up my pace to the entrance and just thinking about my goal got the adrenalin going.

"On this beautiful Spring day I would be changing so many lives. Perhaps someone will do a write up about me. It was about time for me to get noticed."

Just before entering the building, I prepared myself by pulling on the mask and gloves, slipping the Glock out of my pocket, checking for my key ring, and then grabbing the knob of the office door.

"Let's get this show on the road."

3

THE PERPETRATOR

Opening the door, I leisurely walked into the administrative workplace. Soft music was playing on the secretary's radio. Melinda Fox, with her eyeglasses perched on the end of her nose and her gray hair pulled into a tight bun, was inputting information into her computer.

"May I help you?" she asked without looking up. When I did not respond she glanced up, then jumped up from her desk, spilling the large mug of coffee sitting near the radio.

"My God. What do you want?" she squealed as she observed me in my black clad glory. I ignored her and headed out of the office and into the hallway. She began yelling at the top of her voice for me to stop. I turned indifferently and showed her the gun. Smart woman that she was she ducked behind her desk.

Smiling, I exited the office and began walking down the hall. Lo and behold, there she was. One of my not so favorite people.

"Stop. Stop." Counselor Katie Larson was hollering as she ran out of her office.

This was perfect. I was going to save her for later but, oh well. It was an opportunity and she was on my list. I calmly shot her through the head. Spot-on.

"One down with a clean shot," I said, as I continued my journey toward Mrs. Bradley's classroom.

Melinda was a quick one. After I left the office the secretary had immediately rushed to the intercom and announced the lockdown code to the entire school. She was going crazy, screaming and yelling over and over that "Bats should get in their caves."

"Oh Man. The famous code," I said with a snort. "Let's see how well that works."

"People were scrambling to get into rooms and lights were being turned off everywhere. Just because of me. All because of me."

I stopped at the Second Grade Hallway and observed the windows and doors that lined the corridor. I took in the school's scent for a moment. The slight trace of pencil shavings, Lysol and floor polish brought back memories. Unhappy memories.

Pushing those memories away I turned toward the door on the left. Just for the fun of it I tried to open it. I could feel the panic coming from inside, even though I couldn't see anyone.

"Wow. They sure knew how to hide. Hmmm. What would happen if I did open the door?

Ha. Ha. They would certainly get a surprise. This was more fun than I had anticipated."

Suddenly, the predator stopped. There she was. Watching from her classroom.

"Doesn't she know I can see her peering out the window? Does she think she is safe in her corner by the door? What a coward," I said to myself as the trembling returned. "Will she recognize me? Will she remember that child who needed her so? No. Of course not. That child wasn't important to her. Never had been."

Hatred made my blood boil and the terrible trembling rapidly turned into rage. I stopped at her door. The campus was unusual in that the windows looked into the hallway instead of the outdoors. It kept the kids from getting sidetracked by what was going on outside.

"No watching the birds, bees, or butterflies at this school, children," I said.

My eyes shifted to the decorated area under her window. Student work dominated the space. The window itself had huge yellow stars with student's names written on them and also the motto "Reach for the Stars!"

"Oh, sure. Right. Reach for the Stars," I said. 'She never helped me reach for any stars."

I tried the door and of course, it was locked.

Well, a locked door would not stop me. Nothing would ever stop me again. Taking my recently acquired shiny ring with the lock picks attached and keeping my gun handy, I watched her move further back into the recesses of the darkened corner. I slowly inserted the correct pick into the lock, turned it gently and pushed the door open. Calmly, I stepped into the room and switched on the light. Mimi Bradley just stood there, staring at me like a deer in the headlights.

"Please, don't hurt my children," she pleaded.

That's right. That's where her heart always went. Always to the children. Never to me. Those rug rats didn't deserve my special attention right now. This was for her. All for her. Suddenly I thought a smile had crossed her face.

"Did you say something? Are you grinning?" I scowled. "Do you think this is funny?"

"No. No. I...I don't think any of this is funny," Mrs. Bradley said nervously. " I don't understand what is going on. Why are you here?"

Then finally, with a sober face, she murmured the words I wanted to hear.

"Why me?" she asked.

"Why you? Why you? Oh, Mrs. Bradley. You don't remember?" Was my tortured reply. "You taught me that a mistake was just an opportunity to learn and I have had many opportunities to learn. You taught me well, Mrs. Bradley. You know I loved you. I did. And you tossed me aside. I let you into my heart and that was one of my many mistakes. But, not to worry. I plan to take care of that right now."

She looked into my eyes and for a moment, just a moment, I thought she "saw" me.

But, no. That was not possible. Again, I wasn't someone she had ever cared about.

Carefully, I caressed, then pulled the trigger. I experienced an overwhelming sense of power as I saw red blossom on her chest.

"I'm the one in charge. I'm the one making the decisions. It's my show. Killing is such a high and I am becoming very good at it."

Amidst the shrieks, I turned toward her kids.

"You're bad. You hurt my teacher," shouted Kolin Marshall as he ran at me from the closet. I went to school with the boy's Father, who was always the popular jock. I couldn't stand him. So...I shot the kid.

Behind him came Marguerite Hudson, so I shot her too. Her Mom was a popular cheerleader when we were in high school. Didn't like her either.

Bit by bit, I calmly and indiscriminately emptied my gun. I hadn't planned that, but what the heck. I'm the one in charge. They were like sitting ducks in a shooting gallery. The distant sirens warned me it was time to hurry, so I guess Miss Melinda had called the police.

My anger and hatred had been released amidst the howling and screeching and I would carry those images and expressions with me forever. The huge pleading eyes. The frantic bodies hurling under desks. The stark terror I had just created. What a catharsis. I rapidly spun, left the classroom, threw an unconcerned glance at the lonely body of Counselor Larson as I passed by her in the hallway. I briefly observed the crimson stain leaking from her head wound as I hurried from the building.

Counselor Katie Larson wasn't important. Never had been. Hence, the head shot. But dear Mrs. Bradley. The awesome Mrs. Bradley had hurt my heart and so the shot to her chest.

"I am so cunning. Everyone will see that after today. Yes, they will remember me."

I quickly departed the building and walked to my waiting vehicle. I had purposely parked near the exit for a quick getaway. I pocketed the gun and key, ripped the mask off, jumped into my ride and carefully began the drive home. I needed less than an hour to get there and change into different clothing before returning to the scene of my crime. The place where all of my troubles started. The place where all of my struggles were discounted.

Calming myself, I exited the campus and glanced into the rearview mirror. I could barely make out the flashing lights as the first black and white began pulling into the school parking lot.

"It is time to execute. Ha…no pun intended…the next part of my plan. Hold on to your horses, Caradan. I'm about to turn your world upside down."

4
TEACHER OF THE YEAR - 2000

"You deserved it. Everyone knows you are the best," said green-eyed Katie Larson. The thirty-something young lady would turn heads if you passed her on the street. Lazily reclining in Mimi's rocker, the slender woman pushed back her shoulder-length blonde tresses as she said, "I mean, look at what you have done in just ten years. As a member of the Caradan Elementary Campus Improvement Group, you made some important changes for the kids. I remember when you and some of the other members of the group worked with the staff at Region 5 and brought the new Math Program to the school. The program was so successful at our school, that other schools were asking how they could apply the same curriculum. You were terrific."

"Thanks Katie, but I didn't do it by myself. It was a team effort."

"What about the year you were the Reading Curriculum Planner? For years we had tons of kids on the playground and all the teachers had to monitor them every morning before the school day began. It was such a free-for-all. Kids fighting and running. So crazy. Then you came up with the great idea of implementing a Morning Reading Program in the school hallways. It worked like a charm by eliminating all the chaos and it was so much better than having the whole school on the playground at one time. Not only that, it helped that it took only two teachers to monitor each hallway so the other teachers had time to get ready for their day. You know, the fighting stopped, the kids were reading and the teachers had more time to prepare. Just another one of your little successes that other schools began to emulate."

"Oh come on, Katie," Mimi said. "Nita Stone helped me implement the program and besides, you are giving me a big head, girl."

"Doubt it," said Katie, her green eyes sparkling. "Your achievements are many Mimi and you never toot your own horn. You are one of the best

16

volunteers we have in this school. The fact that you received both the Texas and the National PTA Life Membership Awards speaks volumes for what you have done for kids in our school community."

"I have loved every minute of it Katie and look forward to continuing to serve my school and this community. Now stop embarrassing me."

"Nope. There is such a long list of accomplishments I can embarrass you with. For example, how about your performance when you led the Science Team? Initiating the Science Fair and encouraging our kids and teachers to get involved in Science has been great. Your after-school projects for kids and workshops for teachers have gone far to increase our scores. What a superwoman you are and would you just look at this classroom?"

Katie's eyes lit up as they traveled around the colorful, print rich environment of Mimi's room. Her eyes moved from the Science area that was filled with rocks, tortoise shells, snake skins, microscopes, weights and measures, and NASA Space Shuttle posters.

The Counselor's gaze continued traveling to the Reading area which included the chair she was rocking in, a huge life-like tree, bookcases filled with reading books and several comfortable floor pillows.

She paused at the Computer Center. The area held five computers and also displayed a huge bulletin board filled with technological information to help guide the students in their studies.

Moving on to the Math Center, Katie observed the colorful variety of unifix cubes, dominoes, chess sets, and place value materials. All had been carefully chosen by Mimi to help her children learn and develop problem-solving skills.

Finally, Katie's eyes were drawn to the Writing area. It contained a variety of materials used to educate and challenge budding authors. The wall in this area displayed an assortment of student-produced work. Gold stars adorned the chosen work which was exhibited for all to view. This was done to support and encourage students to always do their best, take pride in their work and the goal was to excel.

"Mimi, I always wondered why you put so much of your energy into displaying your kids work. It takes so much time and effort."

"Oh gosh Katie. How can I expect them to do their best if I don't value their work? It's the least I can do to show them my appreciation for their efforts. Besides, sometimes that is the only recognition some of these kids get."

"I love this room Mimi, and everyone knows you are fantastic because of your commitment to education. You also have taken on new teachers to mentor and train and you even earned a Master's Degree as a Reading Specialist in your spare time. Man, is there anything you can't do?"

"Come off it. You are beginning to sound ridiculous," said Mimi.

"You come off it. Everyone at this school knows you are a Master Teacher and I just don't understand why it has taken so long for you to be made Teacher of the Year. It should have happened a long time ago."

"I don't care about that, Katie. Not that I don't feel honored, because I do. I appreciate your wonderful accolades, but the truth is I'm still listening to my husband grumble about the fact that I've never used my Master's Degree to get out of the classroom. Mack doesn't get that I didn't go to graduate school to become a Specialist in Reading. It wasn't for more money, or to move up and out of the classroom. I did it to help my students become better readers."

"Oh, Mimi. Mack gets it. The man thinks you are the best thing since sliced bread and he knows as well as everyone how much teaching means to you."

"Well, for some reason it appears climbing the career ladder is what our society values and I sure didn't become a Reading Specialist to gain a title. You know I never intended to leave the classroom, but it seems like most people think being a good educator is not nearly as important as being a principal, a vice-principal, or even a counselor. No offense. I mean just think about it. You, Cheryl and I went through the Graduate School Program at Lake University on the same teacher scholarship program and received our Master's Degrees at the same time. Hers, in Administration, yours in School Counseling, and mine in Reading. Cheryl saw her salary go up $7,500 a year as a Vice-Principal and it's even more now that she is a School Principal; your salary as a School Counselor increased $6,000 a year; and of course mine, because I chose to stay in the classroom, went up a measly $1,000 a year. Sadly, even if I had decided to leave the classroom and become the school Reading Specialist, I would have only made $5,000 more a year. What does that say about how valued educators are? I know how hard an Administrator's work is, but come on. It's almost like you are penalized for wanting to stay in the classroom and become a better teacher."

"Hey, you know you are preaching to the choir on that one, but we both know how lucky these kids are when they get a teacher like you who cares about the whole child."

"Well, as much as I appreciate the honor of Teacher of the Year, or TOY, this gift means more to me."

"What gift?"

Smiling broadly, Mimi gave Katie a framed picture of students in caps and gowns with a High School Banner waving in the background that congratulated the Seniors of 2000.

"These students recently graduated from Caradan High School and they were in my very first Second Grade Class my first year at Caradan Elementary. Do you recognize Carrie James? Her Mom took the photograph at graduation last week and had it framed for me. Carrie dropped it by this morning as a congratulations gift on being selected as the District TOY. Read the subtitle Katie."

Her friend carefully caressed the 16 x 20 inch frame of ten smiling students pictured with a caption that read, "For Mimi Bradley - Teacher of the Decade - 1990-2000".

Katie's eyes moved over the picture of the young people and she said, "I think it is cool that the Seniors have already completed their graduation ceremonies and are finished for the school year. I wish we were done."

"We will be soon enough," said Mimi, as she looked over Katie's shoulder. "Only one more week left."

"Yeah. I can't wait. My Mom and I are taking a two-week Alaskan Cruise," said Katie as her eyes came to rest on Carrie James. The girl's azure blue eyes twinkled as if she had a secret she wasn't willing to share with the observer. Her stunning shoulder-length, white-blonde hair, gently flipped about her chin and the angular face with the pert little nose accompanied by a luscious, pouty mouth, gave Carrie an unusually appealing appearance. She wasn't beautiful, but she was an eye-catching young lady. Add to that her petite, curvaceous figure and there was no doubt she would be fending off the boys when she attended Texas Tech University in Lubbock this coming Fall.

"Carrie has always been such a sweetheart," Katie shared. "And it's obvious you hold a special place in her heart."

"And she in mine," said Mimi. "How is your Mom doing after losing your Dad last year?"

"Oh, she is doing okay I guess. I tried to get her to come stay with me, but she insists on staying in their hometown. That is where her friends are, but I do think she is looking forward to our cruise."

"You will love it. Mack and I are still talking about our Alaskan trip last summer."

"Yeah. I have been trying to convince Cheryl to join Mom and I, but we are running out of time to purchase her ticket if she decides to go."

Katie's eyes moved on to Carter Westin. He had also turned into a good-looking young man. His long, curly blonde hair, cobalt blue eyes, slightly chubby cheeks, straight white teeth, and wide grin, drew people to him. He stood approximately five feet, ten inches tall and weighed about one hundred sixty pounds. He was in excellent physical condition, with a sturdy body that he apparently kept in shape.

"This one always made me uncomfortable," said Katie as she touched Carter's face. "He was a nice boy, but I always felt there was a side to Carter that was not very likable. He had such a short fuse and was so moody, that even though I tried to counsel him on several occasions when he was much younger I could never get him to open up. He was an odd one and had a really mean streak."

"Well, I would agree with you on that. Carter could be in a room full of people and still be alone," said Mimi. "He comes by to visit with me off and on, but I have never been able to get close to him. Do you remember when we first met Laronda Steelman?"

"Yeah, I remember," said Katie. "That was a long time ago. Laronda told us to keep an eye on him because she thought there was something off about his behavior. She felt sure he had abusive parents, even though she couldn't prove it. Her years of experience, or maybe it was just her intuition, led her to believe he had the tendency to hurt others or maybe even himself."

Katie continued her appraisal with red-haired, brown-eyed, freckle-faced Eric Madison. He looked out at the photographer with the infectious grin he had carried throughout the years Katie had known him. He had come to her for counseling when he was in the Third Grade. His Father had died in a hit-and-run accident and Eric had gone through a difficult time. However, he was a good kid and she hadn't had to counsel him for anything other than his grief during the years he had attended Caradan Elementary. It was hard to believe this awesome young man was well over six feet tall.

Her eyes moved to handsome, athletic Zachary Marshall whose sparkling green eyes and wonderful mischievous smirk made you wonder what he was up to. He had also been a great student and never got into trouble. Until recently.

"I feel so bad for Zach," Katie said. "I hear he may not be able to use his athletic scholarship for college since he got the Wright girl pregnant."

"No. That isn't correct," said Mimi. "I just hate gossip, especially when it is wrong. Just so you have the correct information, Zach came by last week and told me he and Jenna Wright are going to get married soon. She plans to get her GED and will join Zach when he goes to A & M on his football scholarship this fall. The baby is due around the holidays and they will live in College Station."

"Well, I'm glad to hear that. They are good kids. Are their parents being supportive?"

"Yes. They are living with Jenna's parents this summer and Zach's folks are helping too. I think it will work out for them. He is actually excited about being a Father and they already know they are having a little girl."

"Shouldn't he be worried instead of excited?" asked Katie.

"You forget he's eighteen years old. He's happy and enthusiastic about everything right now and they have already decided to name their daughter Kelly."

"Cute name. He and Jenna are lucky they have such great parents."

"I agree with that," said Mimi. "By the way, have you noticed that seven out of ten of these kids are wearing National Honor Society drapes? I know they are responsible for their own success, but I'm so darn full of pride and just knowing I had a small impact on their lives makes me happy."

"Well, God knows you have made a difference for lots of kids and it is true you seem to get more visits each year from former students than any teacher I know. I see Carrie around a lot, but I've also noticed Tori, Eric, and of course Carter, come by too. By the way, why isn't Tori in this picture?" Katie asked.

"Good grief, girl. Don't you remember? Tori is Julie's age. She won't graduate for two more years. How many counseling sessions did you have with Tori when she was a little girl? All those times you met with her to try to help her deal with the problems she was experiencing and you can't even remember how old she is?."

"Okay. Okay. Sue me. I forgot. I don't have the super memory you do, and besides, that girl was another odd duck. I never got close to her either and Laronda was always concerned about her because of what her sicko father did to her."

"Life wasn't easy for Tori that's for sure," said Mimi.

"Well, I guess she has turned out all right," said Katie.

"She's become an awesome young woman in spite of the trauma of her early years and I am proud of her," said Mimi as she found herself frowning at Katie. She had never understood how anyone who interacted with kids on a daily basis had so much trouble remembering them. Especially concerning to Mimi was the fact that a large portion of Tori's elementary days were spent in counseling sessions with her friend. Mimi adored her pal, but felt Katie had a capricious nature that was not always very attractive as a character trait.

"So," Katie said. "Tori is the same age as Julie? God, I feel so old. I can't believe your Julie is already a High School Sophomore."

"I know what you mean," Mimi said. "But time does fly by when you are happy and having fun. I am glad I have my kids, as Julie calls them, to keep me busy though. I know it is going to be hard when she leaves the nest in a few years. I always wanted more children and Mack and I even toyed with the thought of adopting, but life has just seemed to slip by. Sometimes, I think about what would have happened if we had been able to keep Steven Barker. Do you remember him?"

"Yeah, I've wondered about Steven and what might have happened to him."

"Do you remember a few years ago Laronda told me Steven was living with his Dad and Step-Mom and had a younger sister?"

"Vaguely."

"Well, the family went through some counseling and Laronda said he seemed happy and well-adjusted in spite of the things his Mother had put him through. His Father was given full custody and took Steven to live with them in a small town in Illinois. I guess I've never felt comfortable contacting him, but I do hope one day he will want to get in touch with Mack and me. I'd like to know what he looks like and what kind of person he turned out to be. If he had stayed in Caradan, he would have been in the graduating class of 2000 and would have been in that picture too."

Without warning the door flew open and a whirlwind engulfed them. The brown-eyed, dark haired, pocket-sized Latina hugged Mimi. Principal Cheryl Garza drew attention anytime she entered a room. She had that kind of charisma and did not do anything without exuding tons of energy.

"Congrats on being our new TOY Mimi. I am so pleased for you," she said squeezing the teacher tightly before falling into the nearest chair.

"Thanks Cheryl. I appreciate it."

"Look at this Cheryl," Katie said, as she grabbed the photograph to show their friend. "One of Mimi's former students gave it to her."

"Well, Mimi always gets the good stuff, don't you girl?"

"Yeah. I guess that's why I get paid the big bucks, huh?"

The veiled sarcasm brought a smile from both Katie and Cheryl. Mimi's lively friend regarded the photograph and commented on what a pretty girl Carrie had turned out to be. She remarked on Eric and Carter and pointed out a couple of the other students she remembered and the three friends began a dialogue about the years that had passed since they began their careers at Caradan Elementary.

"Hey girlfriend. Mimi and I were just discussing that little boy she and Mack took into their home so many years ago. Do you remember him?"

"How could I forget the morning she brought Steven to the conference room because he had hurt Julie's dog. Steven. That was his name, right?" she asked.

"Yes," said Mimi quietly. "His name was Steven."

"I remember Mimi didn't want to send him away, but you and our CPS lady convinced her he might be dangerous," said Cheryl.

"I still think it was an accident, but he just didn't seem to understand the consequences of his actions. I couldn't take a chance that he might hurt my little girl," said Mimi.

"He was in the Fourth Grade, wasn't he?" Cheryl interjected and continued. "That means he was old enough to know what he had done was wrong. You did the only thing you could do. You had to protect your family. Julie was only in the Second Grade after all, and in the long run everything worked out for him, because the CPS lady contacted you and said he was with his Dad and he was happy. Isn't that so?"

"Yes, but I always wondered, you know, if it could have been different," Mimi said. "By the way, you know her name is Laronda, so stop calling her the CPS lady."

"You know I do that just to get your goat," said Cheryl.

"Well, it works. We have all known Laronda Steelman for years and shame on you for making fun of her."

"Oh, come on Mimi. You know we love Laronda," said Katie.

"It's just that ya' all's sense of humor sometimes escapes me. Must be the age difference," chuckled Mimi as she stood up.

"Oh sure. You are so much older than us," said Katie.

"I was thinking so much more mature," said Mimi as she turned and started walking to the door. "Okay girls. My conference time is up and you know some of us have real work to do. Thanks for your good wishes and I'll see you later for my Celebration Party, and hey," Mimi smiled at them as they joined her at the door. "You know I love you guys."

The three pals exited the classroom, walked to the end of the hallway, and then went their separate ways. Mimi collected her students from the Art Teacher, grinned and sang out, "It's another day in paradise," and with her little entourage mimicking her, headed toward the water fountains and restrooms for their afternoon bathroom break.

Later that day, after her kids had been dispersed, Mimi relaxed in her Reading rocking chair and held the framed picture. Where had the time gone? It seemed only yesterday she was beginning her career and was so excited about the future.

Her memories gently drifted back to her first year at Caradan Elementary, her first Second Grade Class, and those youngsters whose lives had somehow intersected with her own and become interwoven like the silken threads in a spider's web. Mimi closed her eyes and remembered.

5

FIRST DAY OF SCHOOL - 1990

Mimi and Mack were enjoying a cup of coffee as they sat on the front porch swing and observed the sky open the day with a gorgeous sunrise. They experienced the dawn's beauty as pink and lavender rays developed on the horizon. It was Mimi's first day of teaching at Caradan Elementary. She had recently received her Master's Degree in Reading, and was eager to start the year at a brand new school. It would be their Julie's first day of school as well, and she was so excited about Kindergarten. It was perfect. Julie would be able to come to Mimi's classroom after school and she wouldn't have to leave her in daycare. It had always been such a conflict for the Mother. She loved teaching, but she also loved being with her little girl. Every extra moment was precious.

"You seem to be a lot more enthusiastic about heading back to school this year. Is it because you will be working with your new friends, or is it the new school, or is it because Julie will be at the new school with you?" asked Mack.

"All of the above," said Mimi happily, as she stood and took one more look at the morning view. "It will be great not to have to drive so far for my work. I liked my former school, but this year is going to be so wonderful. I can't wait to use the new Reading strategies I've learned and I love my classroom floor plan and just to have Julie close to me. Oh Mack. I am so blessed and every day is just another day in paradise."

"It is good to see you so happy, Sugar. Well, I guess we had better get moving."

Mack and Mimi hurried into the house, and as Mimi packed Julie's lunchbox, Mack called for their daughter to come downstairs. Julie had selected her outfit the night before, and she insisted she was going to get dressed and ready on her own. She was a big girl now.

"Mommy, can you tie my ponytail for me?" she asked as she came into the kitchen. "I can't do it."

"Sure sweetie, and my don't you look just perfect. What a great job you did getting ready."

"I remembered to brush my teeth too and I even made my bed. I can't wait to see my new teacher and my new classroom."

"Wow. Aren't you the responsible one. I am anxious to see your new teacher and classroom too," said Mimi.

This was her first year at Caradan and she didn't know the other teachers very well, thus didn't know much about Julie's teacher. She had met Miss Jones at their school in-service and talked to her a bit during the teacher workday last week. The Kinder Teacher seemed like a good fit for Julie and it was good to know her friends, Cheryl Garza, the new Vice-Principal and Katie Larson, the new school Counselor were there for any moral support Mimi might need when she left her baby with Miss Jones later.

"Have a great first day you two," said Mack as he hugged them both. "See you this evening."

"Okay. Be safe, hon," said Mimi.

They piled into their vehicles and went their separate ways.

Mimi quickly got Julie settled in her new classroom and then hurried to her own room. A group of parents and children were waiting by her door.

"Good morning everyone," she said. "Come on in."

Mimi visited briefly with parents, passed out student nametags, got the children settled at their desks and began organizing their school supplies.

After the first bell rang, the school's intercom system crackled as the Principal made the announcement that parents must leave the school building immediately.

"Boys and girls. Please stand as we recite the Pledge of Allegiance to our country's flag, followed by the Pledge to the Texas State flag," said the Principal after the second bell rang.

"Stand up straight and tall everyone, and recite with me," said Mimi.

Following the pledges she instructed the children to write a story about themselves while she continued checking her class roster. She was still missing a few students.

"Perhaps I will have a smaller classroom this year," she thought as she realized only twenty of her desks were filled with students. Of course, she also knew that often some of the children didn't show up on the first day of school.

"It's a good start," she said.

6
CARRIE

Later, after the second bell had rung, the door abruptly opened and a harried young Mother entered the room with a little girl in tow. The seven-year old with gorgeous blue eyes, and lovely blonde hair, was crying hopelessly and her sweet face was filled with red blotches. The child was absolutely terrified as her eyes scanned the room and she finally turned toward her Mother and tugged at her skirt.

"Momma, I wanna' go home," the little girl said as she sobbed. "I don't know this place."

"Come on Carrie, please. It will be okay. Just give it a chance," said her Mother.

"I wanna' go home. I want my Daddy."

Carrie James's family had recently moved from West Texas when her Father was hired by the Caradan Police Department. They hadn't really made any friends yet. The struggling Mother tried to reassure her daughter, but Carrie clung to her.

Mimi approached the pair and gently put her hand out. "Hello. I am Mrs. Bradley and guess what? I know just how you feel. This is my first day at Caradan Elementary too, and I'm kind of nervous because I haven't met anyone yet. Will you do me a favor? Will you take my hand and help me get through the day and maybe even be my friend?"

The glistening blue eyes held hers and a small hand cautiously reached out to Mimi. "It's aw right," her soft voice whispered, pausing as she touched Mimi's hand.

"What is your name sweetie?"

"My name is Carrie James and you don't have to be afraid. I can be your friend, I promise, and you can be my friend. Okay?"

"Okay Carrie. Thank you so much. Would you like to help me put some of your school supplies away and put your name tag on your desk?"

"Yes Ma'am."

"Oh what wonderful manners you have and Carrie, you can call me Mrs. Bradley."

"Yes Ma'am, Mrs. Bradley."

Thus began a special bond that would endure over the years. Carrie struggled with Reading, becoming frustrated and tearful whenever called upon to read orally. She also had trouble copying from the board, reading orally from books and her writing was very disorganized. She was extremely shy and had low self-esteem. Fortunately for Carrie Mrs. Bradley, a Reading Specialist, was familiar with the signs of Dyslexia and Dysgraphia. After evaluating her, Mimi decided the little girl probably suffered from Dyslexia, a learning disability affecting reading, writing and spelling and referred her for psychological testing. Carrie was officially diagnosed with Developmental and Visual Dyslexia which is characterized by number and letter reversals and the inability to write symbols in the correct sequence. Mimi knew with encouragement and support as Carrie matured the Developmental Dyslexia should diminish. She urged Carrie to stay after school and had her write on the chalkboard with a water paintbrush to practice words and numbers, as well as doing little odds and ends. These exercises and continual repetition improved her skills. The little girl showed a talent for writing, so even though it was difficult for her to form her words, Mimi helped her practice and persuaded her to write short stories. When Carrie finished a story she would design a construction paper cover and staple it together with her story. She was thrilled to add her books to Mimi's library for the rest of the class to read. Carrie's self-confidence grew with each passing day.

Fortunately, the child's mother supported and appreciated the time given to her daughter and in no time Carrie had settled comfortably into the classroom. Several days after school started the child came to her teacher and shared the concern she had for her Father.

"Mrs. Bradley," she said. "I am so scared for my Daddy. I don't think he is safe."

"Oh honey, your Daddy is a smart, brave policeman and I am sure he is fine, but if you would like to meet with the Counselor, perhaps you can talk to her about your fears."

"I think I would like that Mrs. Bradley."

Katie was the new School Counselor and Mimi referred Carrie to her. Miss Larson met with her and apparently the little girl's mind was put at ease, because she didn't mention her concerns again, at least not to Mimi.

Carrie continued her education at Caradan Elementary and later in Middle School found her love for basketball. She was a corker and her love for the sport was obvious to everyone. When she began Eighth Grade she was diagnosed with hyperthyroidism, a health problem that kept her from participating in sports. She was devastated, as was her father, who was her biggest fan. Did Carrie give up? Oh no. At the early age of thirteen, applying her optimistic attitude toward life, Carrie turned her energies toward band. She laughingly referred to herself as a band geek, and the clarinet became her instrument of choice. The young lady did surprisingly well considering the problems she had when she was younger. As the years progressed Carrie's academics became stronger and over the following years Mimi attended several UIL or University Interscholastic League functions in which Carrie performed as part of the band, but also as an outstanding soloist. Her former teacher was not surprised when, in her Sophomore year, Carrie was elected by her peers to be the section leader over the Freshmen through Senior clarinets and Mimi was reminded of the following year when Carrie came running into her classroom with so much pride and excitement in her voice.

"Guess what Mrs. Bradley? I just made drum major for my Senior year. I can't believe that out of all the people who tried out, I got chosen."

"I can believe it. You are such an awesome girl and it is not a surprise to me that the teachers and students all love you and know you will do the best job," Mimi said.

Under Carrie's leadership during her Senior year, the band placed first in the UIL State competition and the band directors insisted their achievements were directly related to Carrie's positive work ethic and responsible attitude. Carrie was enrolled in advanced honors courses and despite the difficulties she encountered, had done well. Mimi had been thrilled at the end of the school year when Carrie came by her classroom.

"Mrs. Bradley. Mrs. Bradley. Guess What? I got my letter of acceptance to Texas Tech and can you believe it? It looks like I am going to get an Academic Scholarship. I am so excited."

"Oh Carrie. I am happy for you. You should be so proud of yourself and oh my goodness, Texas Tech? Do you have any idea what you are going to major in?"

"I think I want to be a journalist. You know I attribute my love of writing to you. All those years you spent with me. You just can't know what a special part of my life you are, Mrs. Bradley," said Carrie as she gave Mimi a big hug.

"Oh Honey, you are like a second daughter to me and I am so proud of you."

Mimi knew the girl's Developmental Dyslexia had diminished and she was on her way to a successful future. Of course, the teacher was especially tickled that Carrie had applied to Tech because it was her and Mack's alma mater and both were thrilled she would become a Red Raider in the Fall. Although she would miss the young woman's frequent visits, she knew Carrie would continue to keep in touch through texting and when the holidays arrived, could be counted on to spend some time with Mimi and her family.

Carrie and Julie had become good friends and Julie planned to attend Texas Tech when she graduated. The girls were already talking about becoming roommates in college and the Bradley's were okay with that. Carrie was a terrific person and would be a positive role model. She was obviously one of those children who became an important part of Mimi's life, but there was another who would join her in that very special place in the heart.

7

STEVEN

Mimi's mind immediately gravitated to the image of a pint-sized boy named Steven Barker. Her Steven was one of those special few. She remembered how on her first morning of teaching at Caradan Elementary she had noticed a poorly dressed young boy, clutching a shabby lunchbox and standing at the door to her classroom.

"Would you like to come in?" she asked tenderly, as she moved toward him.

"Is this Second Grade?" he asked. "Cause I'm supposed to be in Second Grade."

"Yes, this is Second Grade. Can you tell me your name?"

"I am Steven," he said proudly, standing tall and pulling his delicate body up to its full height.

Mimi checked her class roster and found she actually had three Stevens. "Hmmm… must have been a popular name that year," she said.

"It's nice to meet you Steven. Can you tell me what your last name is?"

"Yeah, it's Barker and I am kind of small, but I am seven years old and I am supposed to be in the Second Grade."

"Well, Steven Barker, my name is Mrs. Bradley and guess what? Your name is on my class list, so I will be your teacher this year. Is your Mother here with you?"

"Naw," the little one said shaking his head. "I walked to school by myself."

This concerned Mimi because even though their school was located in a great community, it seemed wrong for a seven year old to show up the first day of school unaccompanied by an adult. She was even more shocked when she found he had walked five blocks to get to his school.

"Well, Steven, what a smart boy you are that you found your classroom and your teacher all by yourself. You should be very proud."

30

The boy stood a little taller and his face glowed with pride. This started their extraordinary relationship for the next two years.

The first three days of school required teachers to lunch with their students. Somehow, on the first day Steven and Carrie ended up sitting on either side of Mimi at the lunch table. She couldn't help but notice the contents of Steven's lunchbox when he opened it. The meager sandwich of two slices of white bread with cheese and a cracked blue thermos of water, brought an ache to her stomach. It was amazing. This undernourished, but upbeat little man, proudly told her he had prepared the lunch himself.

"Why didn't your Momma do it for you?" asked Carrie.

"I can take care of myself and I don't like to bother my Mom, because she doesn't feel good most of the time. And besides, sometimes when I ask her for help or something to eat, she gets mad and yells at me."

Carrie, as young children often do, accepted his answer without further questions.

"Does your Mother make breakfast for you, Steven?" asked Mimi.

"No," he murmured under his breath. "But I make all kinds of good things for breakfast."

"What did you make this morning?" Mimi asked.

"Well, I put some sugar on some bread," he said. "It was pretty good."

Mimi felt a need to help this little boy and so made it her goal to provide a nourishing lunch for Steven. Each morning, when preparing a lunch for Julie, she would add a variety of lunchbox food items, including juice and a snack for later in the day for Steven. She slyly slipped them into his lunchbox when he went to P.E. or during her conference time.

One day he came to her and whispered reverently. "I need to tell you something Mrs. Bradley. We have a lunchbox fairy in our classroom and she is getting into my lunchbox every day and leaving me goodies. I just don't know how I could be so lucky Mrs. Bradley."

He was such a smart little guy and so precious, but obviously had not experienced a lot of lap time early in life. He needed some extra help with phonics and his reading skills were weak. Mimi contacted Steven's Mom and asked for permission to tutor him after school. His Mom readily agreed and it seemed to Mimi the woman didn't show much interest in where her son went or how he spent his time, whether it was in school or after school. Steven enjoyed staying for tutoring and his skills improved and Mimi always sent him home with a snack box and juice, just in case he couldn't find anything for his evening meal.

During the week, it was Mrs. Bradley's practice to display her students' work on the hallway wall and on Fridays she would take it down to be sent home. She noticed Steven always threw his work in the trash when leaving for the weekend and one Friday she asked, "What are you doing, Steven? Why don't you take your work home to share with your Mom?"

31

He looked at her solemnly and said, "Oh, she doesn't want to see my stuff, Mrs. Bradley and besides, you put it on the wall for everyone to see. You know, Miss Garza told me she loved my art work the other day. Sometimes I just don't know how I can be so lucky, Mrs. Bradley."

Mimi's heart always melted when this little guy said anything and it was hard not to love him. He and Carrie seemed to be kindred spirits and appeared to relish their time together. Of course, it could have been the popcorn, crackers, hot chocolate and/or the fruit juice the teacher provided, that drew them in. All she knew was that for two hours after school, most days, they would bond and became an after school family and she didn't know who looked forward to it more. Mimi or the kids.

When the school year ended and summer came, she lost him. The Principal had suggested, and Mimi had agreed, to participate in the Summer School Reading Program. She hoped to utilize her Reading Specialist Certification to help those students who were still behind. She maintained contact with Carrie, who participated in the Program and was able spend time after school with Mrs. Bradley. Mimi tried contacting Steven's mother to inquire if he would attend the Program and learned their telephone line had been disconnected. One day after school, Mimi found herself driving by his house and it appeared to be empty. Out of concern she talked to one of the neighbors and the lady told Mimi that Steven's mother and her boyfriend had been arrested on drug charges. Child Protective Services had been contacted and Steven had been removed from his home and his Mother's care.

"Those two are bad news. Just a couple of druggies," the neighbor told Mimi. "The little boy's Mother and the dude she lives with are both in a Rehab program. The guy's Mother owns the house and she told me they would be coming back when they got clean, so all their stuff is still there."

"Do you have any idea when they will be coming back to the house?" asked Mimi.

"I don't know anything about them, but I did tell the owner if they do come back they need to straighten their lives up and take better care of the boy. They was abusing that boy big time and always locking him out of the house. That's why I finally called 911 on them and I'll do it again."

"It was good of you to think about the little boy," said Mimi. "Do you know where he is?"

"No, but this here card has the phone number of the CPS lady that the police called to take the boy away."

She looked at the name on the card. It read, Laronda Steelman - Case Worker.

She was pretty sure Mrs. Steelman was the Caradan School liaison, so she called to see if she had any information on the family. The caseworker informed her that Steven had been sent to a Boy's Town Shelter, located near Austin, Texas.

"I went to visit Steven and a neighbor told me she had called 911 and turned his mother in for abusing the boy," said Mimi. "The neighbor also said Steven's mother would lock him outside all the time and make him sleep on the front porch night after night. He wasn't being fed and when the police arrived they found his mother so strung out on drugs she didn't even realize what she had done and she couldn't tell them where Steven was. After a brief search of the neighborhood, the authorities located him hiding in a nearby culvert and he was immediately taken away and put into protective custody for his own safety. I was wondering if you have any other information about him or if I can call him?"

"I'm sorry, Mrs. Bradley. You're not a family member and contact is not allowed. But, please try not to worry about the boy," Laronda said. "He is in a safe place and is being cared for, and please feel free to call me if you have any questions about Steven's status and I will try to tell you as much as I can due to the circumstances."

"I can't tell you how much I appreciate that. He is very special to me."

"That is obvious Mrs. Bradley," said Laronda as their conversation concluded.

When the fall school year began, Carrie returned to Caradan Elementary and Third Grade, as well as the after school visits to Mimi's classroom. Steven did not and Mimi felt the need to know what had happened to him, so she called Mrs. Steelman and was informed Steven's Mother would soon be released from her court-ordered drug rehabilitation program. A few weeks later, Mimi once again found herself driving by Steven's house and was surprised to see the little boy's Mother standing in the front yard.

She stopped, got out of the car, and walked up to Steven's Mother.

"How are you Mrs. Barker?" she asked.

"I remember you. You were Steven's teacher."

"Yes. My name is Mimi Bradley," replied Mimi. "I was wondering how you were doing?"

"I am trying Mrs. Bradley. I am trying so hard."

"I am sure you are. How is Steven," Mimi asked. "Is he here?"

The nervous, emaciated woman was twisting her hands and refused to make eye contact with Mimi. She said, "No. I'm not sure where he is, Mrs. Bradley. CPS took my boy away, but I'm finished with rehab and I'm getting him back. I have to do some Counseling and stay clean for a few months. I got to get a job and then I can get him back."

"Is your husband with you?" asked Mimi.

"He gets out of rehab in two weeks."

"You know the neighbors will be watching you Mrs. Barker. If you get Steven back you must try to make a better home for him. You owe it to him."

33

"I know, I know and you done a lot for my boy. I know you care about him and I am much obliged to you for that."

Mimi was overwhelmed and with tears in her eyes said, "It's okay. Your son is a sweet boy and I know you care about him in your own way. I hope he is able to come home soon and if I can do anything to help you or Steven, please just call or come by the school."

"Thank you. You are a good person," said Mrs. Barker as Mimi walked back to her car.

Fall moved into winter and after the Christmas holidays Mimi was thrilled to see that Steven had returned to school and been placed in the same Third Grade classroom as Carrie. He seemed no worse for wear; however, after talking with his current teacher, it was agreed the lunch box fairy would be promoted to Third Grade and each morning Mimi would bring lunch items to be placed in Steven's lunchbox before he went to the cafeteria.

Mimi had developed an uneasy but somewhat comfortable relationship with Steven's Mom and was able to once again keep him after school for tutoring. The after school family was reinstated. The teacher spent much of her time with Steven and Carrie, mostly listening. According to Steven, when his Mom got tired of him, she would call the police and tell them bad things about him. His mother would say he did things that he hadn't done, but they still believed her and that is why they would send him away.

"What bad things did you do?" asked Carrie.

"Once, my Mom said I tried to set the house on fire, but that wasn't true. Her husband did it and then blamed me."

"You're not supposed to play with matches," Carrie said.

"I wasn't," he said angrily.

"What else did she say you did?" asked Carrie.

"She told the police once that I hit her husband with a bat, and I didn't. He tried to take it from me and just got in the way when I was practicing my swing."

"Did you tell him you were sorry?" asked Carrie.

"Nah. He should have been careful. It was his fault he got in the way."

Mimi remembered the chill that came over her when she heard those emotionless words.

"The police don't like me and so they come whenever my Mom wants me to leave."

Mimi tried to reassure Steven and told him she thought the police just wanted him to be safe and that is why they took him away from his Mother. It was for his own safety, and obviously, his Mom loved him because when she got healthy, she always brought him back home.

Sadly, Mimi thought to herself, that's how the system works. Apparently, Mrs. Barker attended counseling after drug rehabilitation, and things would be good for a while, then she would begin doing drugs and the cycle would start over. Mimi was sure Steven's Mother loved him, but she loved her drugs more. She just couldn't give up her addiction, not even for her son. This became evident the next year when CPS was preparing to put Steven back in a Boy's Home. The neighbors had contacted 911 to report they found Steven sleeping on the front porch at night and that he had been locked out of the house once again.

Laronda Steelman, Steven's CPS caseworker, recalled Mrs. Bradley's continued interest and compassionate concern for the child so she contacted Mimi at her school and informed her of the situation.

"Mrs. Steelman, is there any possibility you could place Steven with a family?" Mimi asked. "I just don't think putting him with a bunch of troubled boys is a good solution to the problem. In fact, it may cause more problems for him."

"Of course we place children with families if they are deemed suitable and are able to take immediate custody of the child. However, the child's parent must give permission in writing and sign them over to the family. Did you have a family in mind, Mrs. Bradley?" asked Laronda.

"Yes. I do. I was thinking perhaps Mack and I could take temporary custody of Steven. Let me talk to my husband about it and I will get back to you as soon as I can."

"If you are really suggesting you and your family might take this boy, Mrs. Bradley, you need to know that in order for you to get custody of the young man his mother will have to agree and it needs to happen right away."

Mimi quickly called Mack and explained the situation to him. She pleaded with him to agree to take the boy in and Mack, already aware of his wife's compassion and growing love for the little boy, agreed.

Mimi then called Mrs. Steelman back and told her she and Mack were in agreement and would like to take Steven home if his Mother approved. The caseworker said the Bradley's would need to be in her office within the hour and she would have the necessary paperwork ready, assuming Mrs. Barker was agreeable.

Surprising everyone, Steven's mother immediately agreed, saying, "If someone needs to take my boy, I want it to be this lady."

Although she had talked with her many times, this was the first face to face meeting Mimi had with the case worker. Bright red hair that was spiked with an excess of mousse, sparkling verdant eyes dressed with tortoise shell eyeglasses, flamboyant attire, and at five foot two inches, the turbulent Mrs. Steelman exploded into the meeting like a rocket, with a police officer trailing in her smoke.

The paperwork for temporary custody was signed and Steven went to live with the Bradley's. It was quite a shock for Julie when her parents picked her up after school with an unexpected addition to the family.

For some reason the boy didn't want to socialize with Julie, and sensing his detached demeanor she stayed out of his way. It was obvious they didn't like one another. Steven enjoyed games and particularly interacting with Mack. He was the son they had always wanted and Mimi knew Julie would come around eventually. Their daughter just wasn't used to sharing her parents' love and attention. Steven helped them paint and decorate his room and spent a lot of time in it reading, playing games, and enjoying his privacy.

"Sometimes I can't believe how lucky I am, Mrs. Bradley," he said. "Sometimes I miss my Mom, but I love this room."

Each morning the drive to work was a special time and on one occasion Steven asked Mimi if there was a place called Illinois. When she told him yes, he said he thought he used to live in a town called Carrollton…in Illinois.

"I'm not sure, Mrs. Bradley, but I think I had a Dad and maybe even a Grandma and Grandpa," he said. "But their names were different from mine. I don't understand that. Wouldn't my name be the same as theirs?"

"Well, of course it would be the same," said Julie, interjecting herself into the conversation.

"I can't believe you wouldn't know if you had a Dad."

"I guess you're right about that," Steven said.

"Do you remember their name, Steven?" Mimi asked.

"I heard my Mom talking once and she called them Amos. She was talking on the telephone and I heard her yelling the name Amos."

"I think you're just making this all up," Julie said as she gazed out the car window.

"I'm not. I think I have a real Dad and really I think he loves me."

Mimi's heart went out to this little boy who she thought was probably creating stories about his life. Still, she called Laronda and gave her the information. Stranger things have happened and perhaps there may have been some truth in his musings.

After a few months they had all settled into a comfortable pattern when late one Sunday afternoon, Steven walked into the back yard carrying his baseball and bat. Winston, the Bradley's dog, followed closely at his heels. It was such an exquisite evening. The sun was just getting ready to set and the vista was streaked with a variety of gorgeous hues in reds, yellows and oranges.

Mimi was in the kitchen, making dinner preparations and observing the youngster at play. Mack was in the garage helping Julie with a birdhouse she was building for a 4-H project.

"Be careful, Steven," Mimi called from the open window. "Winnie will try to get the ball when you throw it in the air. Do not swing the bat at the ball if the dog is in the yard with you. We can put him in the garage if you want to practice hitting the ball with the bat."

"Okay Mrs. Bradley," Steven said with a wide grin.

Mimi had turned away for just a second when Steven called out, "Watch this Mrs. Bradley."

She looked out the window and watched in horror knowing what was about to occur. Steven was tossing the ball up, and swung the bat and just as the bat connected with the ball, it also connected with the dog's head. Winnie had jumped to catch the ball just as Mimi had told Steven he would and Steven had swung anyway. Mimi screamed and Mack and Julie came running from the garage. The dog's head was bleeding profusely. Mack carefully picked him up and carried him to the car. He gently placed Winnie in the back of the SUV and hurried into town to the veterinarian. Julie was inconsolable, fearful for Winston and angry at Steven for hurting her pet.

"What is wrong with him Mommy? He hurt my dog. I don't want him here. I don't want him in my home," wailed Julie as she ran into the house and upstairs to her bedroom. Mimi followed and tried to comfort Julie. It was impossible and as her daughter exhausted herself with tears, Mimi laid her down to rest then went to talk with Steven.

She found him in his room relaxing and calmly reading a children's novel.

"What were you thinking?" she questioned, as he looked at her wide-eyed.

"I just wanted to hit the ball," he said.

"I told you we could put Winnie in the garage if you wanted to hit the ball. I specifically told you not to use the bat as long as the dog was in the back yard with you. Don't you realize what you did?" Mimi asked as she searched his eyes. "You hurt Winston."

"But the dog shouldn't have tried to get the ball," a confused Steven said. "It was his own fault."

Frustrated, Mimi told him to stay in his room until Mack came home and she went to check on Julie, who was lying on her bed, sniffling and whimpering into her pillow.

"He's mean Mommy. You need to make him leave. I don't want to see him again."

Her mother held her tight and hushed her as she kissed her forehead and rocked her until both of them fell asleep. Thirty minutes later, Mimi awoke and left the sleeping Julie on her bed.

She went downstairs to complete her earlier dinner preparations and heard Mack's car in the driveway awhile later. She hurried outside to meet him.

"How is Winnie?" she asked as they walked to the front door. "Will he be all right? Where is he?"

Mack gave her a hug and said, "I had to leave him with the veterinarian. He needed some stitches in his tongue and the doctor had to wire his jaw shut because of the damage from the bat. Winston will have to stay at the animal hospital for several days. He is on an antibiotic that can only be given intravenously because of the wired jaw. Fortunately, he should have a full recovery, although he will need some special care for some time."

"Thank goodness," said Mimi.

Following Mimi into the kitchen, Mack reached into a kitchen cupboard, took down a glass, got some ice from the refrigerator dispenser, took a pitcher from the refrigerator and poured himself a sweet tea.

Returning the pitcher to the refrigerator, Mack took a sip from the glass of tea then sat it down on the granite countertop. Tiredly turning toward Mimi, an austere Mack asked, "Where is Julie?"

"She is resting in her room and Steven is reading in his room."

"I will check on both of them."

Mack went upstairs to look in on his girl and to see if she needed anything. He left a sad and silent Mimi behind.

Opening the door to his daughter's room, he found Julie sitting up looking small and forlorn. Her face was a picture of distress with eyes swollen from the tears she had shed.

"How is Winnie, Daddy?" she asked.

"Your dog is going to be okay Julie. He will be staying with Dr. Canon for a few weeks, but then he will be coming home," Mack said as he hugged his little girl.

"I don't want Steven here, Daddy. I don't like him. This is my house, too. I want him to leave."

"I understand how you feel sweetie and I am going to talk to your Mother. I hear what you are saying and you are right. This is your home, too."

Mack left Julie to go to Steven's room. The boy was sitting on the floor bouncing a ball from one hand to the other. Mack took the ball from him and sat down.

"What do you have to say for yourself, Steven?"

"What do you mean?"

"Do you even want to know how Winston is?"

"I guess."

"You really hurt the dog, boy, and you don't even want to know how he is?"

"Well, it was the dog's fault. He shouldn't have got in the way of the bat."

"Yes, you are probably right, but you should not have swung the bat as long as the dog was in the backyard. I went over all of the rules about using the bat and the ball when I bought them for you. I told you how important it was that you be careful whenever the dog was around and I am sure Mimi reminded you about those rules when you went into the backyard.

"Sure she did," said Steven. "But the dog should not have got in the way."

"Actually, Winnie should not have even been in the backyard if you wanted to use the bat and you knew that. Perhaps you didn't know what would happen, but that doesn't change the fact that you are the one who hit him and hurt him. How does that make you feel?"

"I don't know."

"You don't know, or you don't care?"

"I don't know what you want me to say," Steven said angrily.

After spending some time with the boy the grim, unsmiling man exited the room shaking his head and walked downstairs to the kitchen.

"Mimi, we have a problem," Mack said. "I am genuinely concerned about the situation. Julie thinks Steven needs to leave and I am inclined to agree with her. The boy does not seem to comprehend that he has done anything wrong."

"Is that any wonder," Mimi cried, wiping the tears, as she turned from the kitchen sink. "Think of what his life has been like, and our daughter is spoiled. Julie likes being an only child. She doesn't like sharing us."

"That's not fair to Julie and you know it," Mack said.

Putting her face in her hands, Mimi cried, "Oh, listen to me. I know what a wonderful child Julie is. I love her. Oh, Mack what are we going to do? It had to be an accident. He didn't mean to hurt Winston."

"No, honey, I don't think he did mean to hurt our Winnie, but what bothers me is he did hurt our dog and yet he showed no remorse at all. He didn't ask about the animal, didn't shed a tear. Not one. That is not normal. Julie made the comment that this is her home too and you know, we never included her in the decision to have Steven come to live with us. I think maybe we need to give her that consideration now."

"Oh my gosh. I feel so awful. I didn't even think about Julie because I got so caught up in helping Steven. What kind of mother am I?"

"You are the best and Julie knows it. But, Sugar, one thing is for certain," Mack said as he put his arms around Mimi. "When you said we don't know that much about the boy's background or what he has been through, you were right. We don't know how the abuse from his mother has affected his behavior. We can't trust him and I don't think we can let him stay in our home any longer. Steven needs help and we don't have the kind of training necessary to help him. I refuse to jeopardize our family's safety with a child who doesn't seem to understand that his actions hurt a defenseless creature, and he shows no compassion whatsoever." Mack paused for a moment and asked, "What if it had been Julie and not Winston?"

At that moment, Mimi's mind snapped back to the conversation she had with Steven when his mother told the police that he had hit her husband with a bat. Steven had insisted it wasn't his fault. It was the husband's because he got in the way. Just like Winnie. Mimi was reminded that Steven had seemed remorseless about that incident as well.

Mimi and Mack sat down at the kitchen table to discuss what to do about Steven.

"I guess you are probably right Mack," said Mimi. "We have to let him go. He can't live with us anymore."

"I just don't think it is safe to have him here, Sugar. I'd like for him to stay, but I'm afraid for Julie," said Mack. "I also think it would be best for Steven. There is something wrong with that boy and he needs professional help."

They agonized over the decision to send Steven back. They had both loved that little boy. He was such so cute and he desperately needed love. In her mind Mimi pictured eight year old Steven with his adorable chocolate brown eyes, uneven black hair, and a personality that shone. His positive attitude toward life, even after living in a house with a mother who was on drugs most of the time and a tattooed teenager whom she referred to as her husband was amazing. But that wasn't the little boy who had stood in her backyard, ignored her instructions, and uncaringly injured a defenseless animal. She and Mack had tried to make a difference, but they had to think of their daughter and what was best for her. Hopefully, their decision would not send Steven back to his mother, or to a Home, but to a place that would help him and benefit him in the long run.

"I think our decision is made, Sugar. Why don't you give that caseworker a call and let her know what happened. Hopefully, she can tell us what to do about Steven."

Fortunately, Mrs. Steelman had given the Bradley's her personal cell number when they took custody of Steven. Mimi left a message on her voice mail and asked the lady to call her back as soon as she could. That it was important. Mrs. Steelman called back immediately and after Mimi filled her in on what had transpired, suggested they meet first thing in the morning. She knew Mimi was friendly with the school administrators and asked if she would mind letting them know about the meeting. Mimi agreed to call her friends.

It had been a long night and Steven ate a late dinner with Mimi and behaved as if he didn't have a care in the world. Earlier, Julie had refused to eat with the family so Mack had placed dinner on a tray, took it upstairs, and ate with Julie. After dinner Steven took his bath, jumped into his flannel pajamas, brushed his teeth, and went to bed as if nothing had happened. Mack and Mimi had hoped for an apology or some kind of reaction from Steven, but the boy didn't say a word.

The next morning Mimi tearfully packed Steven's belongings and told him he would be leaving them. His biggest concern was whether he could keep his new clothes and the baseball and bat. He didn't appear to be upset at all, just reticent, almost like this was what he expected from adults and life in general. Julie refused to ride to school with them, so Mack drove her to school in his vehicle.

Upon their arrival at school Mimi took Steven to the conference room where Laronda was waiting with Katie and Cheryl. After saying hello, Katie took Steven out of the room.

"The boy's Mother will not be getting custody, because she's completing yet another rehabilitation program. Steven also won't be going to the Boy's Shelter," said Laronda. "Instead we are sending him to an excellent facility near Houston where he will undergo a complete psychological evaluation. I appreciate your trying to help this child, Mrs. Bradley. Not many teachers would have done what you have done. I am so sorry it didn't work out and I hope your dog will make a complete recovery."

Mimi was silent. She simply had no words.

The adults left the room and Mimi joined Steven. She took his hand and walked him outside where Mrs. Steelman was standing by her car. Mimi gave Steven a hug and the boy held onto her so tightly…it broke her heart.

"I am so sorry Steven, but you need to understand you hurt the dog. Whether you thought it was your fault or not you hurt him and you must understand that.

He just nodded his head.

"You do know why you can't stay with us anymore, don't you?"

Mimi wanted so badly to hear him say that he was sorry and he didn't mean to hurt the dog.

That he knew it was his fault and that he had done something wrong. That he was sorry.

Instead, Steven said. "Bye Mrs. Bradley." He turned and walked to the car. Suddenly he stopped, turned around, and ran back to Mimi. She knelt down to him as he put his arms around her and he asked, "Do you still love me?"

"With all my heart, Steven. Now and always. I believe you are a good boy, sweetie and try to always remember that "a mistake is just an opportunity to learn". I hope you can learn something from what has happened and Steven know that you are always in my heart and I will always, always love you."

"Love you too," said the little boy, and finally, unexpectedly, Mimi saw the moisture in his eyes.

That was the last time she saw Steven, but the social worker kept her informed of his progress. Steven wasn't allowed to write letters, but he could receive them and so Mimi wrote to him and Mrs. Steelman delivered them when she made her monthly visits to the Houston facility. One day, Laronda sent Mimi an e-mail with the news that they had actually located Steven's Father and as it turns out, the child did have grandparents in a small Illinois town. Apparently, his Mother had kidnapped Steven when he was two years old and his family had been searching for him all this time. His Grandparents and Father would be coming to Houston to meet with him and the entire family would be undergoing counseling. Steven's psychological testing showed he had experienced some emotional trauma resulting from living with his mother and her addiction, but the doctors felt through counseling, they could work that out.

Finally, one day out of the blue, Laronda called Mimi to let her know Steven was going to live with his Father, Step-Mother, and his little half-sister in Illinois.

"You know Mimi, you went above and beyond for this boy, and he has a lot to be grateful for. I will let you know if I have any updated news on Steven, but it looks like we have a happy ending for everyone," she said.

Mimi thanked her for the call and said, "Yes, a happy ending for everyone."

Laronda said, "You are a very special person Mimi and I would love to get to know you better. Perhaps we can get together sometime."

"Thank you for the compliment Laronda. How would you like to meet for coffee about 9:00 a.m. at the Starbuck's on Chula Vista this Saturday?"

"Sounds like a plan," said Laronda ending their conversation.

The following Saturday they got together and after sharing information about their families Laronda asked, "Mimi, would you like to continue writing to Steven? I can make sure he gets your letters in Illinois and perhaps he can write you back."

Smiling wistfully, Mimi said, "No thanks Laronda. Steven will always be a part of me and I hope one day I will have the opportunity to see him again, but remember, after you told me about his Father and Grandparents coming to Houston I wrote him a letter and informed him I would not be writing anymore and I wished him the best. I want Steven to have a new beginning with his father and his new family and maybe one day he will take the initiative to write a letter, or even visit. It will be up to him."

Laronda understood and over the next few years she and Mimi continued to work together for children, but they also became great friends and even after Laronda's retirement, they tried to get together often.

Suddenly, as Mimi's memories continued, without warning and unbidden, the little soul that haunted the pathways of her mind called to her. Tori, Tori, Tori. Just the sound of her name could bring tears to Mimi's eyes and her heart would weep.

8
TORI

Mimi's third year of teaching Second Grade at Caradan Elementary brought seven-year old Tori Roberts into her life. In fact, that was the year Steven Barker came to live with the Bradley family.

Mimi had known Tori since she began Kindergarten at Caradan. She observed her as a happy, energetic little girl who engaged in many recess activities and seemed to enjoy everyone around her. The tall, slender girl, with a shy smile had a sprinkling of freckles across her petite pug nose and her face was surrounded by a mane of dirty blonde hair that cascaded past her waist in beautiful waves. Her gifted personality endeared her to teachers and classmates.

At the end of each school year, teachers would fill out pink or blue sheets for each student, also referred to as pinks and blues. Pink for girls and blue for boys. This practice aided educators in gaining pertinent information and insight into their new student's needs. The pinks and blues updated and informed the next year's teacher if a student needed assistance in a specific area of learning, had behavior issues, a medical condition, or wore glasses. This data was annotated on the sheet. When Mimi received Tori's pink slip two weeks before the new school year began, it had no information about the child. Her previous teacher had written only one comment on the pink sheet…SEE ME!

Mimi met with Mrs. Markham, Tori's First Grade teacher and asked, "Why did you write this comment on Tori Robert's pink?"

"Because I wanted you to know what was going on with her last year, but I didn't want to put it on paper," said Mrs. Markham.

"Why not?" asked Mimi.

"Because I didn't want a record of my comments. When Tori came to my First Grade class she was making decent grades in academics and conduct, but by the end of the year she was failing."

"Did you meet with the parents to discuss her problems?" asked Mimi.

"No. The Father visited school regularly and often had lunch with Tori, but I did not like the man. In my opinion he behaved in a very inappropriate manner with Tori and he always had the little girl on his lap and was hugging and kissing on her," sniffed Mrs. Markham, as she shuffled items around on her desk.

"Did you call the Mom, or talk to the school Counselor? How about Tori?"

"I didn't talk to the child or to her parents. I did refer her to the Counselor," the teacher responded with distain.

"Why didn't you meet with her parents? That was the first thing you should have done."

"I didn't see that as my job." said Mrs. Markham.

"Well, who's job do you think it is?" an angry Mimi asked. "A child doesn't change like that unless something traumatic is going on in their life."

"I was not going to get involved in something that required so much of my time. You know if I had written any of this on the pinks or blues, I'd be in trouble for not doing any follow-up. I am telling you this now just so you know why her report card grades are low and why I decided to promote her to anyway."

"I don't understand why you would promote Tori if she is not ready for Second Grade if you haven't even tried to work with her or her family."

"I didn't want to deal with repercussions from failing her. You are the miracle worker around here, at least that's what everyone thinks. Maybe you can figure out what to do about her."

With that bit of information, Mrs. Markham turned back to her desk, dismissing Mimi.

Mimi headed straight to Katie's office, walked through the open door and said, "Katie, I know you there is a confidentiality requirement with the students you work with, but I need to talk to you about Tori Roberts. I just finished visiting with her former teacher and I understand there may be some problems with Tori and I would like to help her in any way that I can."

"You know Mimi," said Katie. "I requested Tori be put in your classroom because she needs a lot of help academically, but also emotionally."

"Yeah, because I am the miracle worker. Right?"

"What are you talking about?"

"According to Mrs. Markham that is why she left Tori's problems up to me to solve. She told me she was too busy to get involved and I was the miracle worker around here, at least that's what everyone thinks."

"Okay. Okay," said Katie. "Let me give you a little background. I started seeing Tori after she began First Grade when Mrs. Markham came to my office to discuss her. She told me the child was happy at the beginning of the school year, but recently seemed sad and cried a lot and was often hostile toward classmates...even to her teacher on a few occasions. She used to play with friends, but lately seemed to lose interest in everything."

"I told Mrs. Markham to write-up a referral request and I would see Tori. She referred the child to me and I was a little surprised, because I remembered Tori as having a pleasant, active personality and the child I saw seemed to be turning inward and had become a loner."

"I don't understand why no one talked with the parents about this," said Mimi.

"I conferred with Mrs. Markham and she assured me she would speak to the parents," said Katie.

"Well she didn't, because apparently that is not her job."

"Okay. I screwed up. She dumped it on me and it became my job."

"Yeah. You did screw up."

"Well, I started seeing Tori on a regular basis. I know I should have followed up with the parents, but I really believed Mrs. Markham would do what she said she would do. I saw some improvement in Tori's behavior when I met with her, even though she never completely opened up to me and I'll continue to see her. I really believe you will make a difference for her this year. I mean after all...you ARE the miracle worker," Katie said with conviction.

"Hmmph. Last time I checked, being a miracle worker was not part of my annual teacher evaluation."

"Maybe it should be," Katie said with a laugh.

Mimi was not sure what to expect when the school year started, but was pleasantly surprised when the engaging Tori showed up for the first day of Second Grade. Her long hair was in braids, tied with red ribbons and she wore a cute, plaid corduroy jumper, red knee socks, and a big smile. The little miss seemed thrilled to be at school and spent most of the day attached to Mimi's side.

The first month of school began smoothly. Tori's father would have lunch with her at least three times a week. One day, as he was leaving, Mimi said, "You know, Mr. Roberts, Tori is really getting too old to be sitting on your lap. The other kids may start making fun of her."

"I don't see that as any of your business, or theirs Mrs. Bradley."

Although she was a little offended, Mimi had to agree and left it at that. However, the October morning when Tori came to school wearing a mini skirt, tank top, dangly earrings, blue eye shadow and red lipstick, she changed her mind. Classes had not begun and the children were doing their silent reading in the hallway. Mimi called Tori into the classroom for privacy.

"Tori, I'd like for you to visit with Counselor Larson. Is that okay with you?" Mimi had asked.

"Am I in trouble, Mrs. Bradley? Have I done something wrong?"

"No dear, but I think the Counselor might want to talk to you about a few things. Would you meet with her?"

"Okay. Sure," the little girl responded indifferently.

Mimi filled out a referral slip requesting that Katie talk to Tori about her apparel and any other personal problems she might be having and immediately escorted Tori to the Counselor's office.

Katie discussed proper clothing attire and the fact that Tori was too young to be wearing make-up.

"Where did you get your make-up Tori?"

"It's my Momma's."

"Okay. Are those your Momma's earrings?"

"Uh huh."

"Okay. That is a pretty skirt you are wearing. Is that your Momma's too?"

"Huh uh."

"Okay. I need you go into my bathroom and wash your face, but before you go I have something for you."

Katie searched through her clothing surplus box, kept on hand for a purpose such as this, and pulled out a cute little dress in Tori's size. She handed it to the girl.

"Oh. It's pink. My favorite color. Thank you Miss Larson."

"No problem sweetie."

Katie sent Tori into the bathroom and had her change, then escorted her back to the classroom and asked Mimi to step into the hallway for a moment.

"Do you want to call the parents or do you want me to?"

"I guess I can call, but I'm calling the Mother. I wanted to talk to her about after school tutoring for Tori anyway," said Mimi.

Mimi telephoned Tori's mother and requested Tori be allowed to spend time with her after school and when her mother agreed she took the opportunity to communicate her concerns about Tori's manner of dress and the change in her behavior.

"I am a nurse, Mrs. Bradley and often work a 24-hour turn around. My husband is an accountant and works from our home so he is generally responsible for getting Tori dressed, dropping her off, and picking her up after school. I was not aware there was a problem with Tori's attire, but I can assure you I will certainly talk to my husband about it," said Mrs. Roberts. "Do I need to bring her some different clothes?"

"No. The school keeps extra clothing on hand. She is fine right now."

"All right. Do you think staying after school will help my daughter with her self-esteem? That is one thing I have noticed lately about my girl. She seems to get down on herself a lot."

"I'm glad you brought that up, Mrs. Roberts. Has anything occurred in her life or your family's lives recently?"

"No, not really."

"Well, her grades are dropping and she has really become a loner of late. For that reason I recently referred her to our School Counselor. I hope giving her the opportunity to meet with Miss Larson and spending time with me after school will help to build up Tori's self-image."

"Thank you Mrs. Bradley. I wasn't aware that Tori was seeing the School Counselor, but I know she loves being in your class and I have heard wonderful things about you as a teacher and also as a person. If you think it is helpful for her to see Miss Larson, then it is fine with me. Thank you again and let me know if you need to talk to me. I am always available if Tori needs me."

Tori joined their after school family. Unfortunately, Carrie and Steven didn't gravitate toward the little girl. Perhaps because she was younger, but more likely because she was just so different. Julie was usually there and the two girls would spend time coloring or reading, but not together. It was obvious Tori resented Mimi's daughter and didn't like Julie receiving any attention. Julie, on the other hand, was happy entertaining herself with activities she most likely would have done had she been at home. Mimi spent her time moving amongst them and giving them individual attention.

Tori spent some time talking with Mrs. Bradley, but still was quite a loner. It was terribly frustrating at times, but Mimi reassured the child that she was always there if she needed to talk to someone.

Often, Tori's father would show up to take her home early and it was obvious he disliked Mimi and the closeness she had established with his daughter.

As time progressed, Mimi noted that Tori began to suck her thumb, complain of stomach aches, and began scratching her arms and legs with opened paper clips. This was not the same child who had entered her classroom in August. Tori seemed to fall into herself and spent much of her time sitting alone or she insisted on being near Mimi.

Finally, one day after school Mimi consulted with Katie about the changes in Tori's behavior and Katie shared some of her observations about the child.

"I think it is time to call in CPS," said Katie. "I will do it first thing in the morning."

The next morning, Tori showed up after the tardy bell had rung. She was dressed, in Mimi's opinion, like a little hooker. There was no other way to put it. The child was referring to herself as Kandi and even signing her name with a K. Tori's bizarre behavior compelled Mimi to buzz for the

Counselor and Katie came to the classroom immediately. Mimi stepped into the hallway to meet her.

"Katie, I don't know what is going on, but Tori Roberts came into the classroom this morning dressed inappropriately and is insisting she is another person. I really can use your expertise right now."

"Hey Tori," Katie said as she walked into the classroom. "Can you come with me for a moment?"

Tori did not respond, so Mimi said, "Kandi. Can you go with Miss Larson for a moment?"

"Certainly," said Tori.

Katie lifted her eyebrows as she took Tori and they left the room. Mimi turned toward several surprised faces.

"What is wrong with Tori," asked a student.

"I am not sure," said Mimi. "The Counselor will help her and we will continue with our morning work."

Later, Katie buzzed Mimi over the intercom and asked her to meet with her during the teacher's conference time.

When they met, Katie said, "I think something really bad is going on in the Roberts' home."

"I know what you mean," said Mimi.

"I went ahead and reported our concerns to the local CPS office and just finished talking with Laronda Steelman, the school liaison."

"I noticed you didn't let Tori come back to the classroom."

"Right. I think it is best she stay with me today."

"What is happening with CPS?"

"Mrs. Steelman is following up on my report. I told her about Tori's behavior and how you and I have been concerned for some time and after monitoring the situation we decided to involve CPS. I mentioned to her that the Father may be the problem so she may want to contact the Mother, as she seems to be the more suitable of the two."

"Okay."

"She thanked me for our input and said she would come by the school as soon as possible to talk with us."

When Laronda Steelman arrived an hour later, she asked to meet with Tori, who had been with Katie. After visiting with the child she met briefly with Katie, Cheryl, and later with Mimi to discuss information regarding Tori. Finally, just before the school day was over, Mrs. Steelman asked Cheryl, the Vice-Principal in charge of behavior issues, to call Tori's mother. Cheryl left immediately, returned to her office, looked up Tori's student identification card, located her Mother's work number, and made the call to Mrs. Roberts at her place of employment.

"Mrs. Roberts," said Cheryl. "Would it be possible for you to come by my office and meet with me when you pick Tori up after school?"

"Well, normally my husband picks our daughter up, but I can probably get off work a little early and come by. Why do you need me to pick her up? Is she okay?"

"I am sorry Mrs. Roberts, but it is better if we talk to you when you get here."

"Is she in trouble? Let me call my husband."

"She is not in trouble, but it is better if you do not call your husband. We need you to come to the school today."

"Okay. I will tell my husband I will be picking her up today. Can she wait in the office until I get there?"

"Certainly," said Cheryl. "I appreciate your willingness to come in and meet with me."

"No problem," said Mrs. Roberts. "I just hope everything is all right with my daughter."

"We will talk when you get here," said Cheryl. She hung up the telephone and rejoined Katie and Mrs. Steelman to prepare for the meeting.

Mrs. Roberts arrived at the end of the school day looking exhausted. She had not been to sleep in 24 hours, and came alive when she saw her daughter's appearance. The Mother was absolutely shocked at her child's get-up. She said she now understood why her husband had been extremely upset when he found out she would be collecting their daughter from school and that she didn't want him to accompany her.

"I suspected something was not right, but I just didn't want to believe it. I work such long hours and I come home physically and emotionally drained, go right to bed, and sleep for several hours. It's just easier to let my husband take care of Tori's daily routine," Mrs. Roberts said, as she lay her head on her arms. "Most of the time I only have dinner with Tori once or twice a week."

The Administrators, Mimi, and Mrs. Steelman talked over Tori's disturbing behavior, her emotional imbalance, and her physical appearance with Mrs. Roberts and after discussing their concerns, Mrs. Steelman decided to call in local law enforcement. They allowed Tori's Aunt to get her from school and made arrangements to take her to her house to spend the night. The next day Tori's Mother, with Mrs. Steelman's assistance, filed a restraining order against her husband and hired a lawyer.

Later that evening, Mimi and Mack were sitting on the front porch enjoying a glass of wine and discussing the day's events.

"Mack. Can you believe Mrs. Roberts told us she never really wanted children, but her husband insisted. That's why they just had one child. She said she loved her daughter, but it sounds to me like she didn't even want Tori," said Mimi. "In my opinion Tori was actually being abused by both of her parents, just in different ways."

"Take 'em both out and shoot 'em, I say," said Mack. "Especially that so-called father."

"It makes me so sad, Mack. We would have loved to have had more children and it isn't fair that people who don't always deserve them are blessed with them."

Putting his arm around his wife's shoulders Mack said, "If anyone can help that little girl, you can Sugar. You care so much for these kids and that is one of the reasons I love you."

"I wish it was that easy."

The ensuing investigation proved that Tori's Father had been repeatedly molesting her for some time and the Mother was totally unaware of it. It was incredible, because the child was only seven years old, and yet the evidence collected by her doctor substantiated that Tori's Father was playing pretend with his little girl when he was supposed to be caring for her.

The doctor also conducted an emotional evaluation and suggested she be sent to an adolescent psychiatrist on a regular basis. It was also recommended that she and her Mother meet with a local Family Counselor for therapy. Tori and her Mother would have a long, hard road ahead and hopefully would get through it emotionally intact.

The Roberts' family was shattered. Tori's Mother was granted a divorce and after a lengthy trial, her father was found guilty of Rape and Child Molestation. He was sentenced to prison for thirty years and would have to serve a minimum of twenty years before he was eligible for parole.

Mimi noticed as time went on that Tori was miserable and missed her Daddy. The child blamed herself, as many children of divorced parents do, and thought she was the reason her Daddy left. She wasn't told that he was in prison or that her Mother had filed for the divorce. She was led to believe her Daddy had divorced them and just didn't love her anymore. Mimi spent many after-school sessions listening to her and trying to comfort her and didn't understand why none of the so-called "experts" told Tori the truth about her Father. Mimi knew the situation, but as an educator she was not at liberty to divulge confidential personal information. Her concern for the child 's emotional welfare became so great one day, she went to Katie's office.

"I am really upset."

"Okay. What are you upset about?"

"Tori Roberts is seeing all of these specialists, including you and yet none of you seem to think it is important to tell her about her Father. Every day I have to console this little girl because she thinks she's responsible for her parents' divorce and doesn't have a clue where her Father is or why he left."

"Look Mimi. Tori isn't aware that her Father molested her, so you need to continue comforting the child and let the specialists treat Tori. That's their job and if they need us to intervene in any way they will let us know. We don't know how circumstances affected Tori, but when Tori took on the Kandi personality it was probably her way of asking for help."

"Well. Okay. I guess it makes sense when you put it that way."

Slowly, as time went by, Mrs. Bradley began to see the happy child she remembered return and thought the resilient Tori appeared to have dealt with the difficult events in her life and had moved on without Daddy.

Mimi never saw Kandi again and Tori never appeared to be the broken little girl she could have been, or should have been. Mimi watched her develop back into a happy, energetic and confident young girl and although she never excelled in academics she seemed to have become a well-adjusted individual. Her former teacher was so proud of Tori for standing tall and never feeling sorry for herself.

Later, when Tori moved into Middle School, she unexpectedly dropped by Mimi's classroom one afternoon. She was in an extremely agitated condition.

"I hate my father, Mrs. Bradley," she blurted as she paced around the room. "And I actually hate my mother too. She allowed the abuse to happen."

"What are you talking about, Tori?" Mimi asked.

"Last night my Mother finally told me where my Father is. After all these years of thinking he had run off and left us I find out he has been in prison for what they say he did to me. I always thought it was my fault, Mrs. Bradley. I know the doctors have tried to help me understand what happened to me, but the truth is, he was my Daddy and I'm confused, because sometimes I think I liked the way he loved me. All I have thought about today is getting here to talk to you, so I walked over right after my last class. What kind of person am I if I could let my Father do those things to me?"

"Tori," said Mimi as she grabbed the young woman and hugged her tightly. "None of what happened to you or your family has been your fault. You didn't do anything wrong, and I don't ever want you to blame yourself."

"But my Mother says my Dad did bad things to me and he's in prison for it and I don't remember...why can't I remember and why didn't anybody tell me about it before."

"Tori, you were just a little girl. You wouldn't have understood and it wouldn't have changed anything."

"So you knew about everything that happened to me, Mrs. Bradley?"

"Yes Tori and I am so sorry. I knew, but I was not allowed to talk to you about it. I want you to remember one thing. Your Father was the grown up here and he is the one who did wrong."

Mimi spent an hour talking with Tori once she had calmed down. They discussed a lot of things and Mimi answered a lot of questions…at least the ones she could.

"I guess you were just following the rules and I understand now what the doctors were telling me.," said Tori.

"It wasn't your fault, Tori. None of it was," said Mimi. "Are you okay?"

"Yes, but there is a part of me that hates my Father and my Mother, too. How could she have let that happen?"

"I can't answer that sweetie. I'm not sure anyone can give a satisfactory answer to your question. I do remember how upset your Mother was when she realized the truth and she immediately got you away from your Father. Perhaps she was trying to protect you in her own way by not giving you more information earlier. Only she can answer your questions."

"Guess you're right Mrs. Bradley. I just am so angry with her."

In her heart of hearts Mimi felt the same way, but knew it wouldn't help Tori if she shared her true feelings. Instead, Mimi just held her tight and later called Mrs. Roberts and asked if Tori was still seeing someone for counseling. Her Mother assured Mimi that Tori was being helped and expressed her gratitude to the Mrs. Bradley for talking with her daughter earlier that day.

Tori apparently worked things out, because although she and Mimi talked often, she never mentioned her feelings about her parents again.

Mimi had always hoped Julie and Tori might become close, but it never happened. They were courteous to one another, but while Julie had many friends Tori remained a loner. Mimi maintained a special bond with Tori and the girl visited her often. Mimi knew she had not become involved in many extra-curricular activities, other than 4-H where she unexpectedly outclassed her peers in the shooting arena. In fact, Julie was quite jealous of Tori's proficiency with a gun. As a Sophomore, Tori was a quiet girl who spent much of her time reading or at the shooting range.

One afternoon during one of her visits to Mimi's classroom she said, "Mrs. Bradley, when I get ready to go to college, I've decided I want to be a teacher."

"Oh Tori, there isn't anything more gratifying. You are such a special person and should be proud of your accomplishments."

"Sometimes I wish you had been my mother," she said.

"Oh Sweetie, I will always be here for you. You know that don't you?"

Tori just smiled and Mimi reached out and pulled her close.

9

CARTER

Then there was Carter Westin. A small, blonde, blue-eyed, fragile-looking imp who seemed afraid of his own shadow. Mimi remembered how hard she had worked hoping to find that boy's strength and to encourage him. It had been so frustrating, because no matter what she had done, and no matter how hard she had tried she couldn't get through the defensive shell he had created to keep people at arms-length.

Mimi asked his parents if their son could stay after school and help in the classroom. She had hoped to get to know Carter better and after repeated requests his peculiar parents gave their permission. Unfortunately, Mr. Westin often interfered by interrupting Carter's time with Mimi by observing them from the hallway or asking her unnecessary questions. Anything to annoy or intrude upon their time. He would also parade up and down the hallway attempting to impress the attractive young teacher next door. The other teachers laughed behind his back and made fun of his appearance. Mr. Westin wore red suspenders, a bowtie, and at 5'6", thought he was God's gift to women. He walked around like a little bantam rooster. He was an annoying little man, figuratively and literally, who spoke in an abusive tone to and about his son. His favorite comments were "that boy can't put two words together" or "he's just an ignorant little cuss".

Mimi knew Carter was embarrassed by his Father's behavior and did her best to shield him from the sometimes malicious comments expressed by her colleagues. She could also never figure out why Mr. Westin was not at his job at 3:30 in the afternoon. He never told her what he did for a living and of course, she never asked.

One time Carter showed up in class with bruises on his face. By law, she had to report it to CPS, and after discussing it with Katie, Mimi decided to contact the local office. Mrs. Steelman, the CPS school liaison scheduled a conference the following day. Counselor Larson, Vice-Principal Garza, Mr.

and Mrs. Westin, Mimi, and of course Carter, were in attendance. Mr. Westin was extremely offended that he was being questioned about his son's face. He insisted the boy had run into a door, because he wasn't paying attention, and nodding her head, Carter's mother, a nervous, mousy lady, agreed with her husband. Of course, it was obvious she deferred to him in just about everything, at least in Mimi's opinion.

Poor Carter…that is how she always saw him…would sit pitifully on a chair, fidgeting and looking at his hands. That little boy never made eye contact with any of the adults. Not once. He just mumbled that his parents were right and Mrs. Steelman had no choice but to close the file with no further investigation.

However, Laronda had paused and turned to the Westins, narrowing her eyes and said, "If that boy of yours should meet with any more doors, your case will be reopened immediately. Mark my words Mr. and Mrs. Westin, I will make every effort to find a different avenue to investigate the cause of the bruises on his face. Believe me, I know he didn't run into any door."

"I shall be contacting your supervisor Mrs. Steelman. You are a rude woman and your behavior is totally unacceptable. Let's go," Mr. Westin said as he stood up, all 5'6" of him, and regally walked out of the room. His wife and child followed him fearfully out the door.

"Feel free, Sir. By the way, would you mind telling me the name of your supervisor in case I need to contact them?"

"I am self-employed," huffed the little man.

"I'm sure you are," said Laronda.

Later, after Carter and his parents left, the Social Worker considered the file remaining on the table. "We need to watch that one," she said. "With folks like that, Carter is bound to have a lot of emotional problems."

"Well, it is pretty obvious he already has some issues. His previous counselor referred him to me at the beginning of the school year. I see him twice a week, but I have to admit most of the time he just sits and refuses to even make eye contact with me. It's pretty challenging," Katie said.

"I understand, but I'm just saying you need to watch him," said Mrs. Steelman.

Everyone knew Carter had been hit in the face, most likely by his Father, but again more proof was required if they wanted to prove that abuse was going on. It was so maddening. Teachers were expected to report these things, but often there were no consequences. At least none until something bad occurred and then it was too late.

You also had to worry about retaliation from the parents, but Mr. Westin decided to stay as far away from the school as possible and didn't pose a threat to anyone. If Carter had any more bruises they were hidden where teachers wouldn't see them.

A few weeks after the meeting with his parents, Mimi discovered Carter taking things from other children's backpacks. She caught him red-handed and yet he insisted he had found the items and was just putting them back. He was so furious that she didn't believe him and started kicking desks and throwing books, chairs, and anything else that was within his reach.

"I found these things by the door and I was just putting them back," he shouted at her as she was trying to talk to him. "I'm not lying Mrs. Bradley, and you better not tell my Dad," he said.

"Carter," Mimi said calmly. "I watched you from the window. You were taking those items out of the backpacks and putting them into your pocket."

"You're just a sneak, Mrs. Bradley," he said, shifting the blame and making her the heavy.

He was even more furious when she marched him into the Vice-Principal's office, where he was put on three days of after-school suspension.

Carter's visits after school were infrequent and he began to change from a shy, insecure individual into a bully, with a small following of other bullies. He would never apologize for his behavior, always blamed others, and reacted with anger when he was given directions or rules to follow. He was a very smart boy who knew how to manipulate, and his goal was to be the winner, the one in charge, always.

Mimi shared her unease about the shift in Carter's conduct with Katie, who attempted to address them during her sessions with Carter. Unfortunately, the Counselor said Carter would generally just sit in a chair...and ignore her. Wander around the office...and ignore her. Or look at a book...and ignore her.

He also spent a lot of time with Cheryl, who was in charge of campus conduct and citizenship. The Vice-Principal often saw Carter in her office for fighting, damaging property, or hurting other children. Mimi once caught him using an opened paperclip to pin the class goldfish to the bulletin board. Most of the children were grossed out by the action, but his small following thought he was really clever.

"What were you trying to do?" Mimi asked.

"I just wanted to see how long it would wiggle around before it died," he said.

"But you killed it Carter."

"I guess I did," he said.

Another time his teacher referred him to the Vice-Principal because Carter had taken a sharp stick he found on the playground and rammed it through another student's arm.

"Why would you do such a thing," Vice Principal Garza asked.

"Well," Carter said. "He got in my way so I wanted to stick him and make him bleed. It was pretty cool. He sure has a lot of red blood."

He got into trouble for sneaking matches into the boy's restroom and starting a fire in the trash can. When he was caught and questioned about his behavior, he didn't understand why everyone was upset.

"I didn't set the fire. I was just putting it out. You just want to get me in trouble, Mrs. Bradley," he said.

"But three other students saw you start the fire, Carter."

"Whatever. When I found it, I wanted to watch the fire burn. It's pretty when it gets hot," he said.

"But you could have burned down the school or hurt yourself or another student," Miss Garza said.

"So?" Carter casually responded, obviously showing no remorse for his actions.

He seemed to do okay in school, academically, and was popular with a certain kind of follower. Carter appeared to be charming when he wanted to, but his charm was superficial, and Mimi got the impression he didn't care much about anyone but himself.

Over the years, he dropped by to visit with her occasionally, but for the most part she really didn't know Carter. She had never been close to him even though she had tried. Perhaps that is why she was so surprised when he became a frequent flyer visitor to her classroom during his Senior year in High School. On one of those visits he disclosed his plan to attend classes at the local college when he graduated. He planned to major in Criminal Justice.

"I want to be a policeman, Mrs. Bradley," he said. "And maybe become a Homicide Detective."

"It will be great to help people, Carter. That is such a worthy vocation," said Mimi.

"Oh, I don't care about helping anyone. I just like the idea of carrying a gun, looking good, and being in charge. That and seeing dead people."

It took Mimi a moment to realize he was serious. His comments validated why she felt a little uncomfortable around Carter and really thought there was something genuinely wrong with him.

There had been so many youngsters who moved through her life and her heart had expanded like a balloon with each and every one. Some you wanted to hold on to forever, and others…well, you weren't so unhappy when they moved on. She had never seemed to click with Carter and he was one she had not really missed when he continued on with his life.

10
JULIE

The Bradley's lived on two acres in a suburban community five miles from Caradan. They had moved into their brick colonial when Mimi was expecting Julie, and the family loved their home. They raised chickens, had a horse and enjoyed country living.

Mimi grinned as she thought of her Julie. What a charmer. From the time she was small, Julie had been, as her Daddy put it, a tall drink of water and the family comedian. Their girl walked with such grace and everyone just knew she would choose modeling, acting, or ballet as a career. Who would have believed that as a High School Sophomore, their five foot ten inch Amazon had already chosen law enforcement as her career. Mimi and Mack had often wondered where their daughter's genetic makeup came from, because although she had inherited her Mother's outgoing personality and her Father's sense of humor, they had produced a child that looked nothing like her parents.

"Definitely takes after my Great-Grandmother," said auburn haired, hazel-eyed Mimi.

"Well, I don't know," replied her green-eyed, blonde-haired husband. "Her black hair comes from my Irish Great-Grandfather and she gets those beautiful eyes from my Great-Grandmother."

"Nonsense," said Mimi. "My Grandfather was French and his wife was a member of the Potawatomi Indian Tribe. She gets those good looks from my side of the family."

"No, those eyes came from my Great-Gramma," said Mack.

"Okay, okay. At least we know she got her features from both our family trees," said Mimi.

Julie was a coffee-black brunette with eyes that shifted from shades of black to gray and she was perpetually happy. Their Julie was at the center of everything. It was almost as if there wasn't enough action to keep her lively brain and body satisfied and busy.

She remembered how in Elementary School, Julie participated in ballet. Her parents had watched as the six-year old practiced for weeks, dancing around the living room; jumping, pirouetting, and spinning with such grace. Julie was so excited on the evening of her first dance recital because she had the lead role. Mimi spent an hour styling her hair and helping her into her pink tutu, tights, and slippers. Mack and Mimi watched with anticipation as their little pink cloud floated onto the stage. Suddenly, their gregarious little angel froze, stopping dead in her tracks, as she faced the audience. On the sidelines her instructor whispered to her softly, then louder and louder. The audience and her parents held their collective breaths which they released with a group sigh when Julie began dancing. After the show she informed them she wanted to keep taking ballet lessons, but she wasn't ever going to perform again. With a serious voice she said, "I nearly had a heart attack and it just isn't worth the headache." Her parents stifled their laughs and gave her hugs.

When Julie was nine years old she was in Girl Scouts, after having passed the Daisy and Brownie years. Mimi was the Girl Scout Troop Leader and Mrs. Mathis, one of the Mothers, had volunteered to be the troop's Cookie Captain. Unfortunately, Mrs. Mathis fell ill, so Mimi agreed to perform her duties and she didn't think it would be such a big deal. All she had to do was accept and store boxes of cookies in her garage until the girls in her troop were ready to pick them up. Her mouth and Mack's, dropped to the floor when the semi pulled into their driveway, and oh my gosh… trying to get all those cookies to the right people was a complete fiasco. Her little girl told them, in a serious voice, "Mommy, I don't think you should ever volunteer again. It just isn't worth the headache." Mimi had to agree with her.

As Julie reached Middle School, volleyball, basketball, and baseball became the focus for their daughter. Mack and Mimi spent countless hours attending games and watching their child compete. If a sport involved a ball, their Julie wanted to play it. She was a talented athlete and they took such pleasure in her natural ability to excel in sports.

Julie joined the local 4-H Club as a pre-teen. Every Spring she and Mack would select a lamb for Julie to feed, exercise and train over several months in preparation for the local Stock Show and Rodeo. Mimi would never forget the first lamb Julie had. She had named him Acey-Duecy and was so proud of him. He showed well, and when he was purchased by a local business, the little girl was excited. Julie walked her lamb to the truck, hugged her animal, and with teary eyes encouraged him to run up the ramp and into the truck.

"You know what is going to happen to him, right?" asked a little boy standing near her.

"What?" Julie asked.

"They are taking him to the slaughter house to make lamb stew out of him."

An already emotional Julie came running to Mimi, crying, "Is it true, Mommy? Are they going to kill my lamb?"

"Oh sweetheart. That is why we raise farm animals. Your lamb will feed someone who is hungry."

They spent several hours over the following days trying to console Julie and make her understand that she was not a bad person because she had sent her lamb to be...in her words...killed.

It was pretty brutal for a while, but fortunately, although Julie made a point of not getting too attached to her animals after that, she enjoyed the experiences of raising and exhibiting show lambs.

Finally, upon entering High School, their girl continued with athletics, but also became involved in Student Council where she loved working with other students and teachers. She participated in 4-H shooting and became a crack shot. Ribbons and trophies decorated the shelves lining her bedroom wall.

On Julie's fifteenth birthday, the Church's Missionary work called to her, and she, Mack, and Mimi helped build a Habitat for Humanity house. Her parents loved looking at pictures of their daughter wearing rubber boots, nurse fatigues, and a headband, while mixing and hauling wheelbarrows of concrete for the house's foundation. Julie had also spent the following summer in Costa Rica teaching Bible School with a team from their Church.

These interests, in addition to her outstanding academic talents and compassion, made her a well-rounded young lady. She was inducted into the Junior National Honor Society in Middle School and was currently a member of the High School National Honor Society. This year, as a Sophomore, Julie had volunteered as a runner for the local Police Department, and Matt Holden, a Homicide Detective and Mack's best friend, helped her get the position. Thanks, Mack and Matt. My girl now wanted to join the Police Department.

Julie had always been such a good girl and never gave her parents a minute of concern.

Unless you counted the time earlier that year when Mimi and Mack left Julie home alone with Carrie, who was a Senior. Mack had business in Boston, and Mimi went along for a brief vacation.

"I'll be fine," Julie said, "You'll only be gone for a few days and I need to stay home. I promised to help Pastor Witten chaperone the eighth grade girls for the Youth camp and besides, Carrie will be here."

"Well, you have never given us a reason not to trust you Julie," said Mack. "I guess you and Carrie will be okay, but stay safe. Let the Shelton's know if you need anything. They are good neighbors and you can count on them."

Mack and Mimi let Julie stay behind and upon their return, Mack noted some beer cans and cigarette stubs in the grass and in the shrubbery around the pool. After some investigating by Mack, a tearful Julie explained she had only invited a few friends over while Carrie was at work.

"But then, they invited a few friends, and they invited their friends, and before I knew it, there were at least thirty people in the house I didn't even know. Carrie came home and called Mr. Shelton and he got everyone to leave. I was going to tell you. I was just waiting till the right time. Don't blame Carrie. She told me I shouldn't have had a party," a tearful Julie sobbed and began wringing her hands. She couldn't bring herself to meet her father's eyes.

"Well, you are on restriction for a month, and your job is to clean the pool for the next two months. Hopefully, you learned a valuable lesson, young lady," Mack said.

"I know, Daddy, I know."

"Just remember a mistake is an opportunity to learn, Julie," said Mimi.

"Right Mom," Julie said, rolling her eyes.

They spent a lot of time talking about love and trust and their daughter learned from her mistakes. Julie was a wonderful role model for her peers and the Bradley's were grateful God had blessed them with such an exceptional child. Mimi was excited to see what the future would bring for Julie and she looked forward to seeing her child graduate, get married and of course make her a Grandmother one day. She couldn't wait.

11
MEMORIES

Mimi's reveries continued as other names ran through her mind. She thought of Jared, the child who suffered from Tourette Syndrome, an inherited disorder of the nervous system characterized by unwanted movements and noises. Jared was constantly shouting out obscenities during class, so Mimi told him when he lost it she would put her hand on his shoulder and gently squeeze. That was the signal for him to try to still himself. Although it didn't completely eliminate the problem, Jared did develop better control and there was less disruption to the classroom.

Or what about Angel, who had been diagnosed with Autism, a developmental disorder that appears in the first 3 years of life and affects the brain's normal development of social and communication skills. Her parents didn't believe there was anything wrong with their daughter, and refused to give Angel her medication. The child's outbursts made it impossible for her to concentrate and learn, which then interrupted Mimi's teaching, and inevitably kept Angel's classmates from learning as well.

There was also Henry, who suffered from Kleptomania, an inability to refrain from the urge to steal items for reasons other than personal use. Mimi would greet Henry's Dad every morning and give him the little boy's backpack so he could empty it of coffee cups, the family's television remote, his brother's miniature cars, and once even a mixer, along with other miscellaneous items he had taken from home. At the end of the day Mimi emptied an assortment of items, such as pencils, rubber bands, library books, stuffed animals, paperclips, and the class stapler from his backpack. It was a bit humorous, until the day he decided to use his scissors to cut a piece of fabric from the blouse of the girl sitting next to him. Or a few days later, when he found the scissors which Mimi thought she had hidden and tried to slice a piece off a little boy's ear simply because he liked the way it looked and wanted to take it home.

Or what about the beautiful, precious Joy, who was a high achieving autistic student, as long as she received her medication. Mimi recalled the Monday morning Joy celebrated her seventh birthday and the class sang Happy Birthday to her. Her shining face revealed her pleasure at the special attention.

"Did you have a birthday cake or party over the weekend, Joy?" asked Mimi.

"No, but I made cupcakes for the whole class, Mrs. Bradley."

Mimi, thinking they were baked cupcakes told her she could pass them out, but the students couldn't eat them until lunch. Joy solemnly went to her backpack, pulled out a paper bag, walked over to Mimi, took out a construction paper cut-out of a cupcake, and proudly presented it to her teacher. It was carefully decorated with a variety of colorful geometric patterns.

"Should I wait until lunch to give the class their cupcakes?"

"Oh sweetie, this is a lovely cupcake and you know what?" said Mimi. "The entire class can enjoy your treat as soon as you put it on their desks."

The little girl beamed with pride as she carefully passed out her gifts.

Mimi's thoughts moved to a delightful little girl named Michelle, who would spend the remainder of her days in a wheelchair courtesy of a drunk driver. Mimi remembered how she had prepared her room for not only the wheelchair bound miss, but also for the school aide who assisted with the child during the day. Crickett Martin had become one of her biggest fans and a good friend after assisting Mimi in the classroom by caring for Michelle's special needs. Mimi told Katie she wished she had been able to have Crickett all day, every day, all year. What a fantastic worker the woman was.

Yes, Mimi reflected, over the years her supposedly regular education classroom now actually included special education students who were being mainstreamed. Mainstreaming, or the enrollment of students with physical disabilities or learning difficulties in general education classrooms was becoming the norm and it had truly become more and more difficult to teach effectively. Her diverse classroom could be seen as a menagerie and perhaps it was, but it was filled with variety and to her, was a beloved menagerie.

Her beautiful babies. She loved them all. Each one was special and her calling was to touch their lives in the most positive way she could. Her goal was to develop individuals who would have a beneficial impact on society and become lifelong lovers of learning.

Did they know how much they meant to her? Regardless of their abilities or their personalities, did they know how much she had loved and cared about each of them, or had she fallen short somehow? As a teacher she knew she had made a difference for many kiddoes, but she wondered.

What about the ones she had not been able to reach? What about the ones who hadn't felt her touch, or realized her compassion. Her love?

Mack once told her that it would have taken him a lifetime to change as many lives as Mimi was able to reach in one day.

"You have to be content with the ones you have helped. You can't save them all, Sugar."

"But she wanted to," Mimi thought. "She needed to."

Reminiscing at an end, she stood and began preparations for tomorrow's lessons. After completing them she would head for the library where many friends, co-workers, parents and former students would be joining her for the small celebration that had been planned to honor her as the District Teacher of the Year-2010…and there would be food.

"That is always a big draw for teachers," she snorted to herself. It would be good to see everyone. She knew some of the District's Administrators would be there, as well as Julie and Carrie and of course her beloved Mack.

12
HELL - 2013

"All hell has broken loose at Caradan Elementary," yelled Jim Donovan. The slightly obese Duty Officer was puffing from his run up the stairs and he bent over to catch his breath at the entrance to the office of recently elected Caradan Chief of Police, Matthew Holden.

"There are black and whites on the scene and we just got a call for Homicide. About an hour ago a perpetrator entered the school, shot the school counselor dead, then shot a teacher. The teacher is in critical condition and God, Chief, there is a whole classroom of kids who were also shot. It's unbelievable."

Chief Holden unwound his lanky form and swiveled up and out of his chair. He was a tall, thin, rangy man, with graying hair that matched his slightly droopy mustache and seemed to have a perpetual scowl. The Chief grabbed his white Stetson off the nearby horseshoe coat rack and said, "Good Lord. How can that be? A school for God's sake. Can you call for my car please, Jim and let the officers know I am on my way. Oh, and get a hold of Detectives Ames and Bradley."

"You sure you want the rookie on something like this, Sir?" questioned the frowning Duty Officer. "She's only been a detective for a few months."

"Detective Bradley has already got her feet wet. She has been working a double-murder, as well as a suicide-murder, since she teamed with Ames. Julie Bradley is a natural and I know she will learn a lot from Detective Ames."

"I can't believe how young these new Detectives are. Seems like they are getting younger and smarter everyday aren't they, Sir?"

"Yup. They sure are. Oh and Jim, get Detectives Ross and Cortinas there too."

"I will start calling right away, Sir," said the Officer.

"Thanks," said the Chief as he hurried to the exit to the stairwell, bypassing the elevator, rushing down the stairs, and flying out of the recently remodeled building. His car and driver pulled up and the Chief quickly folded his six foot six frame into the backseat of the car and held on as his driver peeled out of the City Lot.

They arrived on the scene about fifteen minutes later, just as Homicide Detective Devlin Ames pulled in behind them. The Detective stepped out of his unmarked vehicle and was ready to go in his light gray pinstriped summer suit, crisp white shirt and black and gray geometric designed silk necktie. His professional appearance was noticeable, as were his brightly polished black leather loafers. Pandemonium ruled and there were several ambulances, the Forensic Specialist's SUV, as well as the Medical Examiner's van parked in the front of the building.

"Where is Bradley?" asked the Chief as he struggled to get his long legs out of the car.

"I think she's on the way. You know Sir, her Mom teaches here," said Detective Ames.

"Oh, man. That's right. I had forgotten that."

At that moment Officer Roberto Gutierrez grabbed the Chief's arm and took him aside. "Chief. The teacher who was shot is Mrs. Bradley. She was shot in the chest and the bullet missed her heart by a fraction. The school nurse called EMS right away and the paramedics began working on her about fifteen minutes ago. They are still in her classroom."

"Apparently when she was shot she fell and struck her head on the corner of her file cabinet. Right now she is not responding and is considered critical. They are going to take her to Caradan Memorial Hospital," added his partner Jeremy Rodriguez. "She's probably our best chance of finding out who did this."

"Oh Lord. I've known the Bradley family for over thirty years. My God, how can things get any worse?"

"Well, Chief, when you see the carnage in her classroom you will know," Jeremy said with tears in his eyes. "It breaks your heart and I don't think I will ever get the picture of those little kids out of my……"

He was interrupted when Carter Westin, who had just arrived on the scene, asked the Chief what he could do to help. Carter was told to join several other officers in trying to cordon off the school parking lot entrance and exit areas. The chaos had already begun, with both police and media helicopters flying over the area. Nearby, neighbors were running into the streets and parents were beginning to congregate along the outside perimeter of the school. Everyone knew it was only going to get worse.

Without warning a sleek, silver Ford Mustang screeched through the gate and into the parking lot, just as an early responder opened the door to one of the ambulances and his crew wheeled a patient from the side exit of the school.

"Oh God. Poor Julie," said the Chief.

Slender and graceful, dark haired Julie Bradley quickly hopped out of her vehicle, pausing to straighten her navy blue blazer over a soft baby blue button-down shirt. She carefully reached up to shift her shoulder holster a tad. Her long legs were encased in a pair of khaki Dockers and she wore comfortable dark brown penny loafers decorated with fringed tassels. Her ears were pierced with diamond stud earrings, a thin gold chain graced her neck, and around her wrist was a slim gold watch that had been a college graduation gift from her parents. The normally cool, attractive, and professional young woman appeared to be troubled.

"What is going on Chief?" she asked as she rushed to the group. "What's happening?"

"Calm down, Julie," her partner Devlin Ames said as he touched her arm.

"Calm down," she whirled indignantly and snatched her arm away. "You calm down and where have you been by the way? I've been trying to reach you for the last hour and then I hear I need to come to the school. Hey, maybe you don't realize it, but my Mom works here."

"We know that Julie," said Dev.

The Chief quietly took her arm and said, "Julie. There have been several shootings. Your Mother…and the kids…and the counselor. Oh Julie. They are bringing your Mom out right now."

Her eyes traveled to the patient being wheeled out of the school.

"Oh no," Julie ran to her mother's side as a paramedic held her back. "Mom, Mom."

"You can ride with us, Ma'am, but you need to stay out of our way. Your Mother is in critical condition."

"Okay. Okay," Julie said as she climbed into the emergency vehicle. Before the door closed, she shouted out, "Chief. Does my Dad know?"

"I'll call him for you," Ames yelled at her.

"No," she said. "I'll just text him."

She grabbed her cell phone and sent her father a text message, asking him to meet her at Caradan Memorial's Emergency Room.

"I'm here Mom. It's going to be okay. I love you Mommy," Julie spoke softly, reassuring her Mother, and then as the paramedic moved her out of the way, she began to pray.

13

HEARTBREAK

"Fill me in on what we've got so far," Chief Holden ordered as he and Detective Ames turned back to his men.

"Rodriguez and I were first on the scene and backup arrived right behind us. The Secretary met us at the door and told us the killer had left. She filled us in on what had occurred while backup canvassed the school," said Gutierrez. "Then we asked the Vice-Principal, who had been in her office during the shooting, to make an announcement and tell the staff and students to stay in their rooms and wait for further instructions. The whole school is pretty shook up, especially the Second Grade classrooms located in Mrs. Bradley's hallway. They heard the shooting and screaming and we have them contained in their rooms at the moment..."

"A bunch of Mrs. Bradley's kids were wounded," interrupted a distressed Officer Rodriguez. "There are dead kids Chief. The paramedics are in her classroom and are working on them now."

"Settle down, man," continued Officer Gutierrez, glaring at his partner. "You aren't making any sense."

"Officer Rodriguez. Perhaps you should take a time out and get yourself together," said the Chief.

"Yes Sir. I think I will Sir," replied the Officer, trying to get his emotions under control as he walked away.

"Chief. We got lucky. According to Mrs. Fox most of Mrs. Bradley's kids were in pull-out programs. We were told she normally would have twenty-four kids in there, but today seven were in Resource classes and four were attending GT, or Gifted and Talented classes. Eight children were wounded and we have seven fatalities, including the Teacher and Counselor. Oh and by the way I got a copy of the school schematic from the Secretary, Sir."

"Thank you Officer," said the Chief as he looked at the blueprint.

"See. Look here," said Gutierrez pointing to a spot on the paper. "Mrs. Bradley's room is located right by an exit door at the end of the hallway and that is how the paramedics took her out."

"Good thinking Officer," said Detective Ames. "You showed good judgment exiting the teacher out that way. Perhaps we can use the same procedure in taking the wounded children out to the ambulances. That way we will preserve the integrity of the crime scene."

"Yes Sir. Thank you Sir," said Gutierrez.

"Now," said the Chief, revealing a haggard and weary expression. "Tell me about the kids."

"There are five dead and eight wounded," Officer Rodriguez said as he rejoined the group, struggling to keep his voice steady.

"Oh Lord. Do we have any witnesses?" asked the Chief.

"Right now, the secretary and perhaps some of the teachers and students in the Second Grade hallway may have seen something. The secretary, Mrs. Fox, was in the office when the killer came in and he threatened her with a gun so she ducked behind her desk. When he left the office Miss Larson tried to stop him and he shot her. The secretary was quick though and used the lockdown code over the intercom, then immediately called 911," said Gutierrez. "She remained hidden under the desk until we arrived."

"He shot the counselor in the head and she died instantly and then the guy made his way directly to Mrs. Bradley's room. It looks like her room may have been the target, but Jeez...the kids," said Rodriguez.

"Get some people in here who are qualified to deal with this heartbreak. We'll have to wait awhile to talk to survivors and we need to make sure these kids are cleared medically and emotionally before we interview them," said the Chief.

"Okay, men. Set up some people to help the secretary begin calling parents, starting with the children who were in Mrs. Bradley's class. I want the children who are wounded and the parents of the homicide victims called first. Have Mrs. Fox inform the parents of the wounded kids there was a shooting at the school and their children will be at Caradan Memorial. Do not give them any more information than that. Then have her call the parents of the murdered children and tell them they need to come to the school. Please. Please, make sure she does not give them any other information. She can tell them there has been a shooting and we need them to come to the school as soon as possible and that's it!"

"What do we do when they get here, Sir?"

"Escort the parents to the conference room at the front of the school. You can bring them in through the office door."

The Chief continued examining the schematic of the school and said, "Let's begin withdrawing the students. Start with the Third, Fourth, and

Fifth graders located on the other wing of the campus, and have teachers exit their kids out the back door to the gymnasium. Inform the officers monitoring the entrance and exits that when parents arrive they can check out their children from the gym."

"Chief, how are the parents supposed to get to the gym. You don't want them coming through the school building. Right?" asked Rodriguez.

"Tell them to enter through the gate that backs up to the cafeteria next to the gym. Post some officers there to assist them and be sure to keep them from any area related to our crime scene. When the upper grades have all been released, we will exit the Kinder and First Grade classes out the door at the end of their hallway and they can also be taken around the school to the gym," said the Chief.

"What about the rest of the kids?" asked Detective Ames.

"Well that leaves us with the Second Graders. The Medical Examiner should have completed her work on the homicides and EMS will have taken the wounded to the hospital. We will take these kids out last, the same way we exited Mrs. Bradley's kids. That should work. By the way. Where is the Principal?" asked the Chief.

"Miss Garza is on her way back from Central Office. She was in a district meeting," said Officer Gutierrez.

"Let me know as soon as she arrives. Have the Vice-Principal make an announcement over the intercom informing the teachers by levels and rooms of the new instructions for evacuation," the Chief said, as he and Detective Ames began walking into the school building.

"Ames, I want you to interview the secretary as soon as she is finished contacting the parents of the children in Mrs. Bradley's class. Perhaps the Vice-Principal can help Mrs. Fox with the calls."

They passed by the Forensics Specialist, George Kwan, who was working the area where the Counselor had been shot. The compact, little man squinted as he acknowledged them through a pair of horn-rimmed glasses. He stood up, tightened his latex gloves and said, "This is a bad one Chief."

"Has the Medical Examiner released the Counselor's body yet, George?" asked the Chief.

"Yes Sir. The Doc is already in the classroom working on the kids, so we can get them moved as soon as possible.

The Chief was glad Olivia Olsen, aka the Doc and the City's Medical Examiner, was in charge. She was always on top of things and he knew he was going to need her expertise.

"Has the removal team taken the Counselor, yet?" asked the Chief.

"Yes Sir. The Doc finished with the Counselor about ten minutes ago and went to the classroom. The removal team took the Counselor out a few minutes ago," George said.

"Okay. Keep things organized and flowing. Detective Ames, since you are short a partner you can work on the homicides with Detectives Ross and Cortinas…at least for the time being," said the Chief.

"Yes Sir," said Detective Ames.

"Sir. Are you ready to hear about the kids, Sir?" asked Gutierrez subtly.

"Yes," the Chief said taking a huge breath. "Yes. Tell me the names of the kids."

Chief Matt Holden felt he had aged ten years in the last few moments. He stood outside Mimi Bradley's room, his fists pushed against his eyes as he did his best to maintain his resolve. His men needed to see him strong, but God, how could this have happened and why? His chest felt so tight, he was afraid it would burst and he was having trouble breathing. He could still picture those five perfect little bodies, with holes in their perfect little foreheads. They looked like they were asleep and yet he knew, in just a few minutes he would be telling their parents they were sleeping with the angels. Four of the children attended his church and he knew their parents well. His radio buzzed and as he lifted it to his ear he was told the parents of the homicide victims Celia, Jade, Kolin, Marguerite, and Cameron were in the conference room…also the Principal had arrived. She wanted to speak with him before they met with the parents.

"Bring her through the exit door at the end of Mrs. Bradley's hallway."

"Chief, I am almost finished and ready to have the children removed," said the Doc.

"Let's hold up for a little bit. The parents are here and I am going to change procedures. I want you to exit the students in the room across the hall to the gym and we will move these babies into that room…away from all the blood. I want to allow the parents to view and identify their children here, before the removal team arrives. This loss will be difficult enough for them. I think that is the least we can do."

At that moment, he saw the Principal, Cheryl Garza. Her normally styled and coiffed hair was in total disarray, as was her entire demeanor. She raced toward him with Officer Gutierrez on her heels. The Chief met her and when she turned to go into the classroom, he grabbed her arm.

"Please, I need to see Mimi," she said.

"She is not in there. Mrs. Bradley is on her way to the hospital and so are the wounded children. Miss Larson has been taken to the morgue and the only ones inside are the five murdered children. I have decided to permit the parents to see their children after we talk with them. I want to give you a moment with the little ones now, so you can be prepared."

"Morgue? Katie to the morgue? Murdered children? I don't understand."

"I'm sorry. I thought you had been told. We had a spree killing and Miss Larson didn't make it, nor did some of the children in the classroom. Do you understand?"

"Yes. No. Okay."

"Take a moment and let it sink in. I know this is difficult for you, but try to pull yourself together."

"All right. So you are telling me that Katie is dead and when I walk into Mimi's room, I will be looking at dead children?"

"I am so sorry, but yes."

"Okay. I can do this. I can do this."

Cheryl Garza turned and walked shakily into the classroom. She began hyperventilating and the Chief placed his hands on her shoulders and told her to calm herself.

"Take some deep breaths," he said.

"My God. My God. Why? How? Mimi? Katie? My babies? Oh My God. Oh Dear God," Cheryl was gasping for air as she tried to follow his directions.

She collapsed against the Chief moaning and bumping her head against his chest. Matt held her tightly for a few moments. He was aware that this young woman had been close to the deceased, but he also knew she needed to be tough right now and get her act together.

"Listen," he said as he took her outside the room and told her firmly. "I don't know who...or why... but I do know what, Miss Garza. I need you to get your chin up and get ready to face the parents of those babies. They are waiting for us in the conference room and we need courage right now."

Cheryl took a few deep breaths and forced her emotions aside. The Chief was right and she knew people were counting on her. She asked him what was being done and he quickly reviewed the situation with the wounded, the plan for evacuation of the students, and the circumstances of the homicide victims.

"I have called Pastor Witten and I am expecting him to arrive shortly. We will try to contact other clergy as soon as possible," said the Chief. "We will have someone contact the Counselor's family as well."

"Katie's Mom lives out of town and her Dad died last year. I will call Mrs. Larson as soon as I finish meeting with the parents. I want to thank you for being so systematic and taking charge in such a positive manner, Chief. I should have been here," Cheryl said turning toward him with a sob in her voice.

"How could any of us know a madman would choose this morning to visit your school?" the Chief said. "Blaming yourself won't change anything and right now we all need to be strong for the parents we are going to be facing in a moment."

"You are right, Sir," Cheryl said as she bolstered herself and suggested they not keep the parents waiting any longer.

Matt Holden and Cheryl Garza bleakly walked down the hallway and entered the Conference Room and the Chief informed the waiting parents that a gunman had entered the school and started a shooting spree. Mrs. Bradley and eight of her students were wounded and were dispatched to Caradan Memorial. Then, squaring his shoulders, the Chief sorrowfully faced the parents.

"Five of her students were shot and killed," Chief Holden slowly made eye contact with each of the parents and speaking softly in as straightforward a manner as possible said, "There is no easy way to tell you. I am so sorry. Celia, Jade, Kolin, Cameron, and Marguerite didn't make it. I am so sorry."

Celia's Mom, a single parent fainted and the Chief barely caught her before she hit the floor.

Jade's Father had not been able to reach his wife, as she was out of town visiting her Mother. He simply stared dumbfounded at the Chief.

The other three couples stared at him in disbelief. "How do you make someone understand something so horrendous and so unbelievable," Matt thought to himself.

"Not my Kolin. Not my Kolin," sobbed the boy's mother as her husband held her in his arms.

"But Cameron is just a baby. He's such a good student and he loves school," Mrs. Jones said with an anguished howl. "It can't be true. It just can't be. He's my only baby."

Cheryl had moved to take the woman into her arms, as her husband just stood there a shell of a man, hanging his head in utter disbelief.

"Well, you are wrong. You need to go check again. Where is she?" asked Mr. Hudson. "My little girl is not dead. Where is she? Where is my Marguerite? Let me see her. She needs me." Then, pounding the Chief on the shoulder, he screamed, "You are just plain wrong. Where is she?"

His wife sat in her chair and put her hands over her ears and began keening. The heartbreak and sorrow was so overwhelming, the Chief was not sure he could contain his own grief.

He didn't know what to do. Matt turned to the principal and she told him she would call their Counselor to come help and then, with a look of devastation, she realized what she had said. It was all she could do to hold herself together but, with tears in her eyes, she calmly told the parents that if they could all take a few deep breaths, in a minute they would go to see their loved ones.

Normally, family members would have to wait to view homicide victims until after an autopsy was performed, but due to the circumstances, the Chief had decided to waive procedure. Mercifully, the Pastor walked in and after a few quick explanations, offered to escort Miss Garza and the parents to the classroom. Matt pressed the Pastor's arm and then softly told Miss Garza he would be talking to her later in the day.

He walked outside and looked up at marshmallow clouds lazily drifting by in the sapphire blue sky, as if this was a day like any other. He knew it would never be the same for anyone in this little community. These murders had touched them all. The Chief walked around the facility, tapping his men on their shoulder, encouraging them to stay tough.

After he completed his rounds, the Chief said, "I'm going to the hospital to check on the wounded children and Mimi Bradley. I'll see if I can get any information that will help us. Detective Ames, you will coordinate the investigation with Detectives Ross and Cortinas."

"Yes Sir," said Detective Ames.

"Okay, everyone. Let's get going. I want this guy."

With a heavy heart, the Chief turned toward his vehicle and immediately became aware of some drama going on at the entrance to the parking lot.

14

CONCERNS

A small, red, late model sports car was parked at the gate of the front entrance and the driver was arguing with Officer Carter Westin. As the Chief watched, he recognized Carrie James, a local journalist and Julie's best friend. The Chief walked toward the couple and realized that Carter was actually consoling the girl.

"Carrie. Mrs. Bradley and some of her students were shot and some of the kids are dead and so is Miss Larson," Carter said as he held Carrie in his arms. She was dressed casually in Texas Tech Sweatpants, a t-shirt and wore red Nikes on her feet and her blonde ponytail was bunched up in a scrunchie. "You can't go any further because we aren't letting anyone onto the premises."

"What are you talking about?" Carrie said. "I was going for a run when my editor called and told me to come to the school to report on a shooting. I had no idea it would be Mrs. Bradley. Good gosh, Carter. This is just crazy and her kids too? Dead? You are scaring me Carter. Who would do this?"

"We don't know Miss James, but Officer Westin is correct. You cannot enter because the area has been secured as a crime scene," said Chief Holden as he walked toward the pair.

Unexpectedly a brand new, flashy, cobalt blue, Honda Prelude pulled up behind Carrie's car.

When Tori Roberts climbed out of the vehicle, Carrie ran to her and threw her arms around her and began crying. Tori, who was also casually dressed in cut off jean shorts, a sleeveless red blouse and matching red sandals, stood absolutely still for a moment and then responded by holding tightly to the girl.

Carrie started babbling, "Mimi was hurt and Katie is dead and the kids. Oh Tori, the kids."

Tori stepped back, extricated herself from her friend, marched up to Carter and the Police Chief and demanded to know what was going on.

Carter responded by grilling her on why she wasn't at the school and Tori snapped back, telling him it wasn't any of his business. Carrie, following the ill-tempered, angry young lady reminded the police officer, with tear-filled eyes, that Tori's parents had recently died and she had taken a brief leave of absence from her teaching position to take care of her Mother's effects.

"What an uncaring creep. I can't believe you would be so hateful to me, knowing what I've been through. But that's who you are, right, Carter? Not a compassionate bone in your body. I can understand why your parents didn't leave you a penny. Here you are working away even though your parents just passed away…"

"What do you know about my parents? For that matter, what do you know about me?"

"I read the newspaper, Carter Westin and everyone knows about your parents and about poor Carter and…"

Chief Holden intervened saying, "Stop this nonsense. What is wrong with you? Ya' all seem more concerned with arguing than with what has occurred today. Let me make it simple. Miss James, you cannot come onto this campus, nor can you Miss Roberts. However, both of you might be appreciated at the hospital and by the way Miss Roberts, just exactly why are you here today? I don't understand if you've been on leave, why you would choose to come to school at this time and on this particular day."

Tori eyed the Chief with hostility and replied indignantly, "Well, even though I am on leave, I am still responsible for my lesson plans. Principal Garza left me a voice mail yesterday reminding me of my obligations, so I just stopped by to drop off my plans for next week. Do you want to cuff me right here Chief?"

"You really have a bad attitude Tori. How can those little kids stand you?" Carter said. "Well, you can't come in today, so get your little butt back in your little car and scram."

"That will be enough of this nonsense. Grow up. Both of you. I am on my way to the hospital and if either of you girls care about the Bradley family, you may want to go as well."

"I'm sorry Chief Holden," Tori said. "Just how bad is Mrs. Bradley?"

"I'm not sure, but it doesn't look good. Julie would probably appreciate your support right now."

"No, not mine," Tori said. "But I'm sure she would want to see Carrie."

She turned to Carrie and said, "You know how much Mimi means to me. Please give my best to her family and could you text me on how she is doing?"

"Sure," a tearful Carrie answered and after giving Carter, a hug got into her car. Tori gave Officer Westin an unladylike gesture as she returned to her vehicle.

Chief Holden headed toward his car and Carter called to him. "Chief, would you let us know how Mrs. Bradley is doing? She's kind of special to a lot of us."

Detective Devlin Ames was turning to go into the building when he heard Carter call out to the Chief and added his request. "Please tell Julie I am here for her if she needs anything."

The Chief nodded to both before getting into his car.

As everyone went their way, the killer gave a leer and said, "Ooh. That was a nice touch. Am I good or what? I could say all this ooey, gooey nonsense is getting to me, but I am kind of getting off on all this pain and suffering. I was a little shocked to see the Chief at the school so quickly and I hadn't realized he was such good friends with the Bradley family, but then, how would I know. Obviously, I'm not a part of the Bradley's inner circle. And besides, how else did Julie move so quickly up the career ladder? Well another opportunity to learn. I can't believe I missed Mrs. Bradley's heart. Maybe she doesn't have one. Ha. And I can't believe I missed so many of the kids. I nailed a few of them, but the rest definitely didn't make it easy for me to take the perfect shot. Still, it was an unexpected high taking them out like that."

"Well, mistakes and opportunities," the killer said. "My plan is working so far, but we'll see if Mrs. Bradley makes it or not. This could get very interesting."

15
GOODBYE

Mack arrived at the emergency entrance right behind the ambulance. He ran up just as the attendants began removing Mimi from the vehicle. He grabbed Julie and immediately demanded to know if she was all right. Julie just pointed to her Mother and sagged weakly against her father. Mack lovingly hugged her before moving to his wife's side.

The paramedics rolled Mimi swiftly into the Emergency Room, where she quickly disappeared behind closed doors. Julie held onto her Dad and as they watched the gurney disappear inside, she fought to hold back the tears.

Mack searched her eyes for answers and she matter-of-factly articulated what she knew.

"A gunman came into the school and shot Mom," Julie sobbed.

"Was anyone else hurt?" asked Mack.

A stunned Julie remembered Chief Holden's words.

"Oh, Gosh. No. Chief said Mom, her kids, and the Counselor, and Mom is here and they called in homicide, so that means. Oh Dad. That means Katie or Mom's kids. The M.E. was there and... Oh, I don't know."

They heard the shrieking sirens outside, as ambulances began pulling up to the entrance. Shouting and noisy clamor was heard in the hallway, as police officers, emergency personnel, and EMS paramedics began bringing victims from the school massacre into the hospital. Pandemonium and panic was everywhere and the madness of the day moved into the hospital.

Mack grasped his hysterical daughter and reassured her everything would be all right, but the terror finding its way from his heart to his brain told him he knew this was not so. He turned as two doors opened.

Through one door walked his best friend and through the other the man who would tell him his life as he knew it was over. His Mimi, the woman he had loved for so many years. His beautiful, wonderful, giving Mimi, was gone.

Mack sat heavily on the seat nearest him and held his head in his hands.

Julie had looked into the doctor's eyes and once again began crying.

"Oh God in heaven. Mack. Julie. What. What can I say?" the Chief stood with his Stetson in his hands and watched his friend fall apart.

"I didn't say good bye," Mack mumbled. "This morning I rushed out because I was running late and I didn't kiss her, and hold her, and tell her she was the best thing in my life. I didn't say good bye."

Through her own veil of tears Julie watched her father, the man she adored, the hero whom she had never seen shed a tear, silently crying as tear after tear tumbled from his eyes. She realized then that her father needed her. She moved toward the broken man and gathering all of her willpower, cuddled him like a needy child. Then, tugging at his sleeve, Julie murmured, "Daddy, Let's go. Let's go say good bye to Mommy."

The Chief watched his Compadre walk away, looking worn-out and beaten, holding onto his little girl's hand and as he viewed the two, he observed the strength of her spirit. Julie Bradley had visibly drawn her shoulders up and Matt could almost see her inner-strength become more determined. Thank heaven for little girls, Matt thought, because this one would take care of his best friend.

The Chief shifted his thoughts to the doctor and quizzed him on what Mimi might have told him. Did she regain consciousness? Did she say anything? Did she suffer? The physician's answer to all three questions, was no.

Matt Holden, Chief of Caradan Texas Police Department, head down and heart heavy, moved toward the reception area to express his sympathy and concern to the wounded children's parents and determine the prognosis of their injuries. Would any of them be able to help him find the answers to his questions? God he hoped so. He truly hoped so.

16
PARADISE?

She was gone. She really was gone. Julie sat on a chair as she watched her Father touch her Mother's cheek and whisper how much he loved her.

The day had begun with so much promise. Julie's mind was spinning as she recalled the delightful, early morning breakfast she and Carrie had shared with Mack and Mimi. Julie rarely came home for breakfast anymore, because she had her own place in town. In fact, she and Carrie James had been roommates for the last three years. A wistful smile graced Julie's lips as her mind speedily recalled her Mother's love for her and also for Carrie, whom she had loved like a daughter. Mimi had met Carrie when she was enrolled as a student in her Second Grade class so many years ago.

It had been so pleasant, with all of them laughing and chatting. Her Mom had talked about this year's crop of students, Carrie about the newspaper article she had recently completed, and Julie about her new partner in the Homicide Division.

"He rubs me the wrong way," Julie had complained. "I know everyone thinks he's such a talented guy because he came from the Chicago Police Department, but in my opinion, he is kind of a jerk, a real know-it-all. He has been in the department for a few months and the entire division already thinks he hung the moon."

"Well, last time I looked Missy, being talented or coming from Chicago doesn't mean the fellow can't teach you a few tricks. Matt says he is an excellent detective and you should work with him and learn as much as you can," Mack said. "That's why the Chief partnered you with him, Julie."

"But Daddy, how do you learn from someone who rarely talks to you," Julie squealed, as she carried her cup of coffee to the table. "And when he does, he won't even look you in the eyes. I think he is weird."

"Well, he may be weird," Carrie said. "But he is a hottie, with those liquid brown eyes, cute dimples, that divine black hair and whew. Don't get me started on that body."

"Oh stop. You only saw him from a distance when we went to lunch last week and besides, he's too short," Julie said. "I mean he isn't even six feet tall."

"Well, my darling. Here is a news flash for you. Your father isn't six feet tall and he is perfect," Mimi said.

"Carter's not six feet tall either, and I like him just fine. Of course, we all know our long, tall, Julie goes for the big guys," said Carrie.

The conversation moved on to the murder-suicide of Tori Roberts's parents. Tori's Father had recently been released from prison and Mimi had really been worried for her former student, who had experienced such a traumatic life.

"Poor Tori. She's been through a lot," said Mimi. "I always wished you had developed a better relationship with her, Julie."

"I know Mom. I remember you discussing Tori's background with me when I was in High School and you really wanted me to like Tori. I was sympathetic toward her but we were never close. I will say we have become a lot more friendly lately and that could be because she and Carrie are friends."

"I am happy to hear that. I just can't believe Tori's Mom was seeing her ex-husband again," Mimi said. "Especially in light of what he had done to Tori."

"Well," Carrie said. "I don't know that much about the circumstances, but Tori told me her Mom insisted he had been rehabilitated. In fact, she told Tori they were planning to get back together.

"Hmph," Mack huffed as he began picking up the breakfast dishes and taking them to the sink. "I know I couldn't believe it when I heard the authorities let that monster out. He should have been kept locked up and the key thrown away and maybe the Mother along with him."

"Hey, Daddy. Why don't you tell us how you really feel," Julie said chuckling. "Anyway none of that makes any difference now, because he is dead and so is Mrs. Roberts."

"It was kind of strange," Julie said. "When Tori called 911 she was really freaking out, insisting her Mother had been killed by Mr. Roberts. When Devlin and I got the call from dispatch, we drove directly to the Roberts's house expecting a murder scene. Instead we found what appeared to be a murder-suicide and it looked like it was Tori's Mom who killed her Father then turned the gun on herself."

"Isn't it peculiar that there was no suicide note?" Carrie asked. "I thought in suicides there was always a note."

"No. Not always," said Julie. "I can't share a lot of the details of the crime, but I can tell you that the gun that was used belonged to Tori. Mrs. Roberts had asked to borrow it for protection when she heard about

Carter's folks being killed."

"That was another shocking incident," said Mack. "It is unbelievable that Carter's folks were murdered also."

"What's unbelievable to me is Carrie is still dating Carter Westin after a whole year," said Julie.

"Yeah, very funny," said Carrie. "By the way, did ya' all read my article? I tried to explain what had happened to the Westins."

"You did a good job covering the robbery-murder of Carter's parents Carrie," said Julie.

"There wasn't much to cover. His parents were murdered when they arrived home in the afternoon and interrupted a robber. Carter told me ya' all thought it was one killer and there was very little evidence left behind," said Carrie.

"That's true," said Julie. "At least that's what it looks like. The case is not closed and it is still an ongoing investigation."

"I was really surprised by Carter's response to his parent's deaths," Carrie said. "He insisted it didn't matter to him, 'cause their relationship had been strained and they hadn't been a positive part of his life for a long time."

"In all honesty, sometimes I wonder how Carter ended up as well as he did considering the parents he had," said Mimi.

"Well, I for one almost feel guilty for passing the detective's test first time around. Carter wants to be a detective and has tried so hard to pass the test, but even after three tries he has never been able to make the cut," Julie said.

Carrie voiced her opinion in her soft West Texas drawl. "Ya' all know. I actually think he was more upset and angry about not being able to pass that exam than he was about his parent's death."

"What about the fact his parents named a local charity as their beneficiary instead of Carter," asked Julie.

"He said that didn't bother him at all, but did you know his Dad essentially called him a loser and a moron when Carter told him he hadn't passed the detective's exam?" said Carrie. "Can you believe that?"

"Yes, I can," said Mimi. "That Mr. Westin is the same cretin he was when I taught Carter in Second Grade. Carter was definitely not brought up in a warm and loving family."

"I guess that explains why Carter seemed so detached when we interviewed him after he found his parent's bodies," said Julie. "He said he had gone home for the day and walked in and found the house a mess and his parents dead. He insisted it was a robbery because a clock was missing. He hadn't talked to his folks in two days, and apparently, even though he lived with them, he came and went as he pleased…often going days without even seeing them."

"Sometimes I feel so sorry for him," Carrie said. "There's a secret part of Carter that I can't reach no matter how hard I try."

"I had the same problem when he was younger. I was never able to truly bond with him and it always made me sad, because he seemed to have so much potential that he never used in a positive way. I hope he will not disappoint you, Carrie," Mimi responded with a worried frown.

They had continued their banter and reminded each other how fortunate and blessed their lives had been, especially in light of the recent violent deaths in the community. Carrie enjoyed her position as a journalist at the local newspaper, Julie was thrilled with her new promotion to detective in the Caradan Homicide Division, and Mack and Mimi enjoyed their vocations and were both healthy and happy.

"I have such a great bunch of kids this year," Mimi said.

"You say that every year Mom."

"I know but these little guys remind me a lot of their parents. I taught the parents of Cameron Jones, Marguerite Hudson, and Kolin Marshall, too."

"I remember Zachary Marshall was a real jock and he had to get married right out of High School," said Carrie.

"Yes," Mimi said. "That's true, but he's been a wonderful Father to Kelly and Kolin and has done well for himself and his family. That little guy is adorable. He has a Knock-Knock joke for me every morning. It starts my day with a smile"

"I know you love seeing your former students and what they have achieved," said Mack.

"Yes, I do and Mack," said Mimi. "Knock, Knock."

"Who's there?"

"Orange."

"Orange who?"

"Orange you glad to see me?"

"Ha. Ha. Very funny, okay? It's time to make the donuts and I'm running late. Love you Mimi and see you later girls," Mack said as he had grabbed his briefcase and jacket and rushed out the door.

"Well, he can make donuts," Mimi had said. "For me, it is just another day in paradise."

Suddenly, reality slapped Julie in the face and she felt the tears slipping down her cheeks as her Father gently laid his hand on the top of her head and then they kissed Mimi good-bye and exited the room.

"Oh Daddy," Julie said. "You may have rushed off to work, but we had a wonderful breakfast together."

"You're right Goose," Mack said, using his pet name for her. "We did have that."

"And Mommy knew how much we loved her. Oh Daddy, everyone

loved her, so how can this be?"

At that moment her best friend ran into the Emergency Room.

"How is she, Julie?"

"Mom is gone Carrie," Julie said, sobbing as she fell into her friend's arms. "Oh Carrie, it will never be another day in paradise…ever again."

17
THE MOURNERS

"How are you holding up girl?" Carrie asked.

Julie sat at the kitchen table, her head in her hands and didn't bother to look up at her friend. "I can't believe Mom's gone, Carrie. Why? Why? Who would do this?" she cried as tears blurred her eyes and she began gasping.

"Take it easy, Julie. Take a deep breath."

Julie slowly began to breathe in and out. Carrie was right. She needed to suck it up and be strong for her Father. Falling apart wasn't going to change anything.

Blinking back the tears, Julie took a moment to get her head straight, just as her Dad and the Chief walked into the kitchen,

"What's going on Goose?" Mack asked. "Are you all right?"

"Oh Daddy, I just needed a minute. There are so many people in the house and everyone keeps asking me if I am okay. I just got a little overwhelmed. I'll be all right."

"Well, I sure understand that," the Chief said.

"Can I get you some water?" her Dad asked.

"Nah," Julie answered, rising from the table. "We need to get back to our guests. I can't believe how many people are here now. There were so many parents, former students, and friends at the service today. I am constantly reminded how loved Mom was."

"It's been quite a day," Chief Holden said.

"Oh, I'd say it's been quite a week," responded Carrie, shaking her head.

The four of them walked into the den and were quickly greeted by a group of people.

Julie and Carrie began wading through the sea of well-wishers and Julie was so touched as each of them shared their expressions of love for her Mother. She heard comments such as:

"Your Mother was an angel on my shoulder." "What a dedicated teacher and so much compassion." "Our town, our school, will not be the same without her." "I'll never forget what she did for my kids." "She was so talented." "She changed my life." "Do you think she suffered?"

Carrie's head snapped to attention as she recognized the individual who had asked the question, "Do you think she suffered?"

"What is wrong with you Carter?" Carrie hissed in a voice filled with anger. "How can you ask such a thing?"

"I'm sorry. What's the big deal," he said as she dragged him onto the front porch.

"It's inappropriate, that's all. Where is your compassion and sensitivity?"

"Well, maybe I should just leave."

"Sounds like a good idea to me," said Julie standing behind Carrie. "I'm sure they all suffered. Carter. Katie, my Mom, those little kids. Your parents probably suffered too. But not nearly as much as we are hurting now. Just go and let us grieve."

"I didn't mean anything Julie," he said. "I was just making an observation, but I do need to go anyway. Call me later Carrie?"

Carrie just stood with her mouth open as he sauntered across the yard to his car.

"The nerve of that guy. How do you put up with him Carrie?" asked Julie.

"He's really changed a lot since his parents were murdered."

"You are always making excuses for him. I don't like him much."

"I know you don't, Julie. You never have, but right now think about it. You lost your Mom and you know how to express your grief. Carter lost BOTH of his parents and maybe he just doesn't know how to show it. I do care for Carter and I am trying to be there for him."

"Whatever. He's your problem."

"Yes, he is. So let's drop it. We have enough to deal with. It has been such a rough time in our little community and everyone is feeling the loss. I don't think I will be able to attend another funeral or memorial service for a very long time. I know Carter's comments don't do anything to help you deal with what is going on in your life right now and I am so sorry."

"It's all right. It is not your fault. I just think you can do better than that creep. That's all," Julie said as she hugged her friend and walked back into the house.

Carrie frowned as her eyes followed her friend. There was definitely something going on with Carter she thought. He had always had a harsh side to him and most of the time she enjoyed his company, but not so much lately. She went back inside to help Julie clean up before leaving.

"Thank you for your thoughts and prayers. Dad and I will have enough food to last us for a while," Julie told the mourners as they left. "We appreciate everything."

Mack turned to Carrie. "You have been a gem, Carrie and I can't tell you how much I appreciate your being here for Julie and for me."

"No problem, Mr. Bradley. Julie has decided to stay with ya' tonight, but if ya' need anything let me know," Carrie said as she turned toward her car.

"Gosh. I am so glad everyone is gone and you are still here Goose," said Mack, handing Julie a cup of hot Chamomile tea. "Drink this. It will help you relax."

"Thanks Daddy." With hands trembling, Julie wrapped her fingers around the mug of hot tea, letting it's warmth seep through. "I really need this. You know, I was surprised Tori didn't come by. She was always so close to Mom."

"Well, maybe she's just had enough. After all, her Mom hasn't been gone that long and now she is dealing with Mimi's loss," Mack said. She did come to the funeral and probably she just couldn't handle anymore."

"That's true."

"It made me feel good to see that so many folks cared about Mimi. I have to say though, the constant stream of people that filled the house all day was exhausting. I'm glad it's finally quiet."

Julie sighed and said, "Yeah. I was hoping for a little peace but now, it is almost too peaceful."

"Drink your tea, Goose. It will help you unwind and then you should take a hot shower and go to bed."

"Daddy, I'm not six years old, you know and besides, I have a thousand things to do."

"You will always be my little girl, Goose."

The endearment brought the tears. She pressed them back, refusing to succumb. "My Father doesn't need a cry baby on his hands," she thought. Julie would save the waterworks for the shower, which she intended to take right away.

"Maybe you should take a little time off."

"Absolutely not, Daddy. I am going back to work tomorrow." She hopped up, hugged her Dad and asked, "What are you going to do?"

"Well, you know your Mom always took care of all the finances and other important paperwork. I need to go through the files and acquaint myself with everything. I guess I should have taken more of an interest in those kind of things, but I just never thought I would need to know about them so soon in our lives. Oh, Goose, what will I do without her?"

"You'll persevere, Daddy, and we'll hold all of our wonderful memories here," Julie said, as she tapped her heart. "That's what Mommy would have wanted."

Julie gave her Dad a hug and headed for the shower. Mack watched his only child stumble up the stairs and then he walked out onto the back porch and observed the night sky. He searched until he found the planet

Venus, twinkling brightly in the heavens. He thought about the many evenings he and Mimi had stood in this same spot, enjoying a glass of wine. Julie reminded him of Mimi with every passing day. Their daughter didn't physically resemble her Mother, but her mannerisms were so familiar to him. Mack knew his Mimi would live on in their child and every time he looked at Julie, he would see his beloved wife. Perhaps, if he was blessed, someday there would be a grandchild. Mimi had loved children and had really looked forward to grandbabies. He lifted his glass to Venus and said, "Good night, my darlin'. I miss you so much."

Upstairs, Julie stepped into the steamy shower and let the hot water flow down her face. She tried to ease the ache she felt deep within. Losing control she fell to the shower floor. Her tears came and blended with the water pelting over her body and as her heart broke, Julie realized it would take more than water to wash away this unbearable pain.

The exhausted girl toweled off and pulled on her underwear, sleep pants and a t-shirt as her thoughts drifted back to her Mother's funeral earlier that morning. She was reminded of the numerous tributes from those who loved her Mom. Mrs. Steelman gave the first eulogy.

"Mimi Bradley had a calling," Laronda Steelman had said. "She loved all children and her capacity for love was constant. I have never known a teacher, or an individual, who had such a natural born instinct when it came to children. They seemed to gravitate toward her and trust in her. They always knew they were safe with her, because she always went the extra mile. At one time Mimi and Mack actually took one of her student's into their home to keep him from being sent to a Shelter. I am proud to have known her." Laronda paused as her voice began to tremble. She cleared her throat, wiped her eyes with a tissue and continued with a clear voice. "I am so honored to have had her as a friend. She was a wonderful person." Mrs. Steelman returned to her seat as Cheryl Garza walked to the lectern.

"Mimi and Katie were my best friends," she had said. "We knew each other for over twenty years. I was their boss, but I never saw myself as such. It's for sure Mimi never had a problem letting me know if she disagreed with my policies," Cheryl smiled, as a few folks laughed. "Her children came first...always. And because they did, it was important to her to make her classroom into a safe and happy haven. Her students were always successful. Every year she drew a three legged stool on the whiteboard for her parents at Open House. She wrote the word Success on the seat of the stool and on one leg she wrote teacher...on another, parent...and on the third leg, student. She demonstrated for the parents that if a strong student, with a strong parent had a strong teacher, the stool would be solid and success would be achieved. She would continue by saying, if any one of those legs were removed, the stool would be weakened and become wobbly, but success could still be achieved. Obviously, if you took away two of any of the legs, the stool would collapse, as would Success. She also shared the lesson with her students. She wanted them to know they were just as accountable for their success as their parents and teachers were. Mimi was an artist when it came to visualizing information. That was another reason she was such a successful teacher. She was also a powerful leader on our campus and influenced many of the positive changes made in the entire District. She was a remarkable person, a loving Mother, and she was my good friend. My life was enriched by knowing her and there is an enormous void in it without her. I loved Mimi Bradley."

Cheryl returned to her seat as Zachary Marshall, Kolin's Father, took her place.

"This has been a devastating week," he had said softly. "I put my boy in the ground two days ago and have attended too many other services this week. Being here today is difficult for my wife and myself, but it was important to us both that I speak today. Mrs. Bradley was my Second Grade teacher twenty-three years ago. My wife Jenna and I had our daughter Kelly at a young age. I was only eighteen years old when she was born and my wife only seventeen. It was not an easy time. So many people judged us, but I remember visiting with Mrs. Bradley. She told me that I was a good person and that everything would be okay. We talked about a lot of things that day and I will carry our conversation forever in my heart. Jenna and I were good parents and we loved our little girl who had the privilege of being in Mrs. Bradley's class. God blessed us with a son seven years after Kelly's birth and we could not have been more happy and excited this year when our Kolin began Second Grade with Mrs. Bradley. She was a teacher who made you love learning and we couldn't wait for our son to benefit from her knowledge, compassion, and love. Kolin woke up every morning excited about school and anxious to share a knock-knock joke with his teacher." Mr. Marshall paused, swiped at his eyes and continued.

"I remember a lesson she gave the parents at Orientation the first week of school. She had placed index cards on each child's desk and she had instructed the parents to follow her directions. First, she told us to draw a circle on the card, then place a box under the circle and put four lines around the box. Next, she told us to position five dots on the large circle and to put a bow on the top of the circle. Then, following her own directions she drew on the board, ending up with a perfect little stick girl. Well, I'm not even going to try to tell you what my picture looked like." The mourners giggled, chuckled and some laughed, as Mr. Marshall continued. "Then this special lady informed us this activity was the best way for her to share her philosophy of teaching. She believed her directions were clear and even though everyone in the room did their best to follow the directions she had given, not everyone had ended up with the same result she had hoped they would. Years of teaching made her realize we all see and hear things differently and she needed to make sure students were able to clearly understand directions and never to assume they did. Her goal was for information to always be clear, concise and easy to follow. A lesson that we can all learn from. Mrs. Bradley cared for the entire child, because they were unique individuals. We loved you Mrs. Bradley and we know, we know. You will continue to take care of our children and please," he said with a sob. "Please, Mrs. Bradley. I know you are taking care of Kolin right now. Won't you give my boy a hug for me."

Tears fell from her eyes as she continued with her reflections. Julie picked up a photograph of her parents and lovingly touched her Mother's face. So many people assumed Mimi Bradley had had a perfect life and everything came to her easily.

"I remember when my Mother shared her history with me," thought Julie out loud. "Mom's parents had been poor and her Father was an alcoholic. He had beat his wife and daughter on a regular basis and Mom had also been molested by one of her Father's friends when she was only twelve years old. That was when she talked to me about Tori Roberts and shared a few of the things Tori had gone through."

I had asked my Mom, "How was it possible for you to become the person you are? How did you survive?"

"Everyone reaches a point in their lives where they make a choice Julie. You can choose to blame everyone and everything and expect to be pitied, or you can choose to take responsibility for yourself and make a life," her Mother had said. "I chose to make a life and I was fortunate enough to find and fall in love with your Dad."

"I think Mom's two favorites sayings came from life's adversity," Julie said to herself with a smile. I can hear her voice now saying, "A mistake is just an opportunity to learn" or "It's another day in paradise".

"Oh wow. The tea Daddy gave me earlier has definitely relaxed me, because I am having trouble keeping my eyes open," she said placing the picture on the nightstand.

"Oh, Mommy. I miss you so much," Julie sniffled and climbed into her bed, pulling the comforter up close. "I promise you. I will find out who did this...and why."

18
THE FRIENDS

"Let's raise a glass to our friends who have passed," toasted P.E. Coach James Bauer as he slouched on the barstool. The gentle, gregarious, giant of a man slapped his forehead and said, "Oh man. I didn't mean for it to come out like that."

"That's okay Jimmy. We know how much you loved Katie and Mimi. I still can't believe they are gone," Cheryl Garza whispered softly as she sat in the large enclosed booth at Smokies, a local barbecue place.

"They were just the best. Best friends, best teacher, best counselor, just the best," she said.

It had been an impromptu happy hour for the staff at Caradan Elementary. Everyone was still in shock over the shootings. The school had not yet been reopened after what was being referred to by the Media as the Caradan School Massacre. Cheryl was experiencing mixed emotions because on one hand, she needed something to keep her busy and on the other, she knew if she was back in the school everywhere she looked she would be reminded of Katie or Mimi…and those precious little ones she had known since Kinder. Currently, the school was locked, but she knew when they returned for the Summer Reading Program in a few weeks, she wouldn't be able to get the sight of those babies and all the blood out of her mind.

"Do you think the school can be cleaned good enough or will we still smell the blood?" asked the Coach.

"I'm afraid we will just smell blood that's been overwhelmed by bleach," she said. "You know. I didn't want our school to be reopened for summer school, but really had no choice. The School Board insisted they couldn't close the school permanently and everyone is expected to be here for the summer program and to return in the fall."

Do you think any of the kids will be back?" asked Janie Vargas.

"How about the staff?" asked Natalie Simon.

"I have heard some of the students won't be returning, but most of the personnel will," said Cheryl. "We are only losing two staff members."

"I guess that's a good thing," said the Coach.

"Yes," said Cheryl. Thinking to herself, she said, "I thought it would help my staff if we all got together, but who am I kidding? I wanted the companionship of others to fill the dreadful void left in my life."

She was still having trouble getting around all of the deaths that had surrounded their community. Cheryl was observing Tori Roberts, who was currently resting her head on the Coach's shoulder. What a lovely young woman she had turned out to be. Her marvelous mane of hair was filled with highlights and swept up into a mass of curls helping to draw attention to her long slender neck. She wore little make-up, but she really didn't need to because of her natural beauty; however, Cheryl frowned at Tori's choice of clothing. She wore an off the shoulder see through blouse, extremely short mini skirt and three inch stiletto heels. "Not terribly appropriate for a teacher," Cheryl thought to herself.

Tori had finally returned to her First Grade teaching position and Cheryl knew it must have been incredibly difficult for her. She had recently lost both parents. It had been such a scandal and then there was Mimi's loss. Cheryl was aware of how much time her friend had given Tori over the years and understood the overwhelming loss the young teacher was experiencing.

Her eyes gravitated toward Carrie James who had joined them for Happy Hour. The young lady was with her boyfriend, Carter Westin. Cheryl secretly smiled her approval as she observed the vivacious Carrie. The journalist was clad in a colorful western shirt and her slim blue jeans were tucked into decorated, hand-tooled, leather cowboy boots. Her blonde hair was tossed in a casual ponytail held in place by a pale ribbon. Her azure blue eyes were emphasized by gray eye shadow and a sweep of black mascara. A light dusting of powder enhanced her face and her lips were a translucent pink.

"She has to be just as devastated as me," Cheryl reflected as Carrie unexpectedly gave her a hug. Mimi had not only been a great friend to the girl, but was her second mother.

Carter Westin possessively placed his arm around Carrie's waist and pulled her to the other side of the booth. It appeared that he didn't like the fact that Carrie had hugged Cheryl.

"What's up with that? Is he jealous of me?" she wondered as she gave Carter her full attention. "I have never liked that boy, but what a good looking young man he is. Muscular biceps, curly blonde hair, and a stunning smile sure do make for quite the eye candy," she thought. "I have to admit I am a little turned off by the soul patch he's wearing on his chin. I can't believe he's allowed to wear it since he is a policeman and obviously, I think Carrie could do a whole lot better than him."

"A penny for your thoughts Cheryl," said Laronda, interrupting her silent meditation.

"What? Oh, just thinking that it is good to be here with you all," Cheryl said.

"I think we have all learned to appreciate our friends and to make the most of every day," said Laronda. "Haven't we?"

The delightful lady sat between Carla Evans and Mark Morrison. She and the teachers had given wonderful eulogies at Mimi's memorial.

Carla taught Fourth Grade at Caradan Elementary and she had shared that she wasn't aware of a teacher on their campus who had not requested that their own child be in Mimi's class when they started Second Grade.

Mark also taught at the school, but lived in a different town. He had applied for special dispensation so his son could attend Caradan Elementary and be in Mimi's class. Once, Mark had even taken a vacation day to observe Mimi in her classroom. He was constantly sharing what an awesome teacher she was and how much he learned from just observing her for that one day.

Laronda, dressed for the evening in her usual flamboyant outfit, had been present at both Katie and Mimi's services and had shared such wonderful comments about them. She articulated that over the years she had developed quite a relationship with the two ladies and felt they were outstanding professionals and caring individuals. Laronda had been retired for many years and she and her husband currently resided on their ranch outside Goldthwaite, Texas.

She had invited Cheryl to come spend some time with them over the summer. Laronda had said, "There is nothing more peaceful than sitting on the front porch enjoying a hot cup of coffee in the morning while listening to the birds sing; or drinking an ice cold glass of sweet tea in the afternoon and hearing the crickets chirping; or sipping some fine Merlot in the evening while observing the stars and constellations. During the day you can enjoy blue sky, green grass, and maybe catch sight of a wild turkey or a few deer heading down to the water tank. If you'd like you can even go for a hike or a horseback ride. It will do your soul good, Miss Cheryl."

"Maybe I will take her up on it," Cheryl said thoughtfully.

"How long had you known Mimi and Katie, Cheryl?" asked Kindergarten Teacher Guerry Koch, as she held her gin and tonic.

"We started working together the year Caradan Elementary opened. Let me see. That was in 1990. We became close during graduate school and applied to the new school at the same time. Believe it or not, we referred to ourselves as the Three Musketeers. I was hired as the new Vice-Principal, Katie the new Counselor, and of course Mimi as a Second Grade Teacher. I tried to get her to apply for the Reading Specialist position, but she declined. She wanted to stay in the classroom. Hopes and dreams. Dreams and hopes. It was so thrilling. We were going to change the world and you know…sometimes I think we did. Katie was so good with the kids and ya' all know how terrific Mimi was. I've never known a person who was such a fantastic role model, especially for new teachers and also such a wonderful advocate for kids."

"I will never forget Katie and her laughing green eyes," sniffed First Grade Teacher Annie Bettas, as she fumbled for a Kleenex. "She had the best programs."

"Yeah, remember the Pennies for Patients Program?" asked Connie Rubio. "Katie spent extra time passing out the little Pennies for Patient's cardboard boxes and had each class compete for the most donations. She had to count the money every day and keep track of how much each class had made. She put that big chart in the cafeteria and would graph it daily, so everyone could see how they were doing. The campus made so much money for cancer patients because of her hard work."

"The most special thing about Katie to me, was she didn't just help the kids, she helped parents and teachers too. You could always go to her for suggestions. I really miss her," said David Aldaco.

"Well, what about Mimi? She was so helpful and always willing to share her ideas," said Debbie Jones.

"Mimi. That Mimi," said Jennifer Parker. "She could be such a royal pain in the butt; however, when it came to the kids you definitely knew where her heart was and she did everything she could for them. I remember when Mrs. Bradley mentored me. The class was studying continents and we began with Europe. She had the children pretend to be tourists and started the trip in Rome, Italy."

"I remember that," said Cheryl. "Mimi used that lesson for several years."

"You know Mimi was so great at integrating everything," Jennifer continued. "She assigned seats with tape for the aisles, printed tickets for the trip and the kids even made their own passports. They were to bring their suitcases the next day and she told them not to forget their toothbrushes."

"It was hilarious," Cheryl said. "She made it so real that after school a parent called the office and wanted to know what time the plane left and how long they would be gone. His son was so adamant they were going on a trip, he had actually convinced his father that they would be leaving town the next day."

"It was pretty funny," said Jennifer. "But also so neat, because she could make learning such an adventure. She linked the trip to Italy with an author study about Tomie de Paola. They also researched Mt. Vesuvius and the kids made clay models of volcanoes. They created a hole in the center of their mini volcano, filled it with baking soda and poured vinegar mixed with red dye into the hole. The chemical reaction made the volcano erupt. The kids were amazed. She connected Science, Social Studies, Writing, and Reading all together in that one lesson. If I gained so much knowledge and fun from the experience, can you imagine what the kids got out of it? I absolutely loved working with her."

Debbie Reed said, "I remember when she mentored me. My favorite lesson was when we did the Oobleck thing. Everyone here remembers Oobleck, right? She used the book Dr. Seuss and the Oobleck for that tutorial. She read them the story and then had them fill out a Scientific Method chart, including their hypothesis. Then they measured water and poured it into their test tubes, adding green dye to the water. Next, they measured corn starch into containers and finally, poured the liquid over the corn starch. The children were so excited when they found they could pour the mixture into their hand and roll it around like a ball, but then when they held it in the palm of their hands they watched as it spread out and became a liquid again. Do you remember when children brought containers to different teachers to see if they would know if the material was solid or liquid?" giggled Audrey Rice. "Ha. Some of you didn't know the answer. Gosh, Mimi could put things together in an ingenious way and everyone had so much fun."

"It wasn't just the way she integrated curriculum," said Patti Douglas, the School Librarian. "It was how she taught life skills. The first week of school Mimi always checked out a book from the library that was so simple. It was the Pledge of Allegiance. I told her she was the only one in our school who had ever used it and I didn't get why you would need to read a book like that to Second Graders. Didn't they already know how to say the pledge?"

"Most children don't say the words correctly, but more importantly they don't understand what the words mean," Mimi had said. "I read it to them and explain what a pledge is and what words like allegiance, and nation, and liberty means. She also wanted them to know what the red and white stripes in the flag stood for, as well as the blue background for the stars. She said they needed to know why it is important for them to stand straight, proud, and with respect when they salute our flag and why we put our hand over our heart. Her words brought tears to my eyes, because she was right. I had never thought about the meaning behind the words when I said the pledge before. Even though I had been saying it for years, it sure changed how I said it after that."

"I know every year she checked out a book by Patricia Polacco the first week of school," said Cheryl. "The story described the author's inability to read as a child and how a caring teacher discovered she was dyslexic and helped her to overcome her learning disability."

"I know that book. It tells a great story, but why did she think it would be meaningful for Second Graders?" asked the Coach.

"She reminded me that about one fourth of her class had learning disabilities and had to leave her room for brief periods during the day to attend Special Education Resource Programs," said Cheryl. "She wanted her special ed. children, as well as her regular ed. children, to understand that just because they left the room to receive other assistance, it didn't mean those kids weren't smart. It just meant sometimes everyone needed extra help in different areas."

"I asked Mimi how she would use the Patricia Polacco book in her classroom," said Patti. "She said her lesson was that ALL her children need to know there was something special and unique about each and every one of them. For example, she would say. Sue is great in Art, but she needs some help with Math. Bobbie is a natural speller, but Tommy can study and study and still can't make a one hundred on the Spelling test. However, Tommy can run faster than anyone in the class. Everyone has something they are good at. That's the message she wanted them to learn."

"I am a perfect example of what that lesson could do for a kid. Her message came through loud and clear for me...that is why I am a reporter now. And a darn good one," said Carrie.

"I have a Mimi story to share," said Crickett Martin. "A few years ago, I was assigned to Mimi as her Teacher's Aide. I was responsible for a little girl named Michelle, who was in a wheelchair. My job was to assist Michelle in her learning. Every morning Mimi would have a brain game for the kids and my favorite was one she did with water and pencils. She would fill a baggie with water and had about twenty sharpened pencils. She asked the kids what would happen if she poked one of the pencils through the baggie. Of course they all said the baggie would pop and the water would run out. Mimi stuck a pencil through the baggie and nothing happened. She then asked them if they thought she could put another pencil through the bag of water without popping it. They all said no. She shoved the pencil through the bag without it bursting. She wanted to know how many more pencils they thought she could put in the bag before it burst or started leaking. They gave her all kinds of numbers and finally, she showed them she could push all twenty of the pencils in without the bag popping or leaking. The little guys couldn't believe it. Then she started withdrawing pencils and holes were left behind. When she tried to insert one of the pencils back into a hole it wouldn't fit. She asked them why and that led to a Science discussion. It took about fifteen minutes, but those kids learned something and had fun too. That's what Mimi was about. Learning had to be fun and she always had fun."

"Hey Dave. What's that on your shirt," Bobby Dodge said pointing to

Dave's chest.

"Where?" Dave asked as he looked down at the front of his shirt.

Bobby brought his finger to Dave's nose and bumped it.

"Gotcha. Made ya look. That was a Mimi trick," Bobby laughed, as he slapped Dave on the back.

"Ha. I remember that one." Carrie said. "She loved to play that joke on us even when I was in Second Grade. You know, Mimi was like a second Mother to me and I don't know what I would have done without her in my life. She was always there for us, wasn't she Carter?"

"Uh, yeah. Sure. She was."

"I wanted to be just like her," Tori murmured, slipping her purse onto her shoulder. "I wanted to be a teacher just like her."

"I know how proud she was of you Tori," Cheryl said. "She thought you were extraordinary and so proud of what a strong person you are."

"She always made me feel special. I was so tickled when I got to do my student teaching in her class. One of the most important things Mimi taught me was to make sure the kids knew they were valued. One day she was putting student work on the hallway wall. Another teacher, I won't mention any names said, "Mimi, why don't you give it a rest. You are always trying to make us look bad"."

Mrs. Bradley turned to me and quietly said, "In life Tori, the only person who can make you look bad is yourself. I can't make Miss so-and-so look bad. Only she can make herself look bad. I put my kids work on the wall because I want them to know I honor their work ethic. Why give kids work and then shove it in a folder, or backpack, or trashcan? I am so proud of how hard they work for me and I want them to always know how much I appreciate them and value them for doing their best work."

"Well, her scores showed how hard her kids worked for her. She made them love learning," said Cheryl.

"I hope to see some of Mimi's kids back in school," commented the Coach. "It will be a long time before any of the kids, especially those in Mimi's class, will be leading a normal life."

"If ever," said Mark as he tossed back his drink.

"I admired Mimi and Katie, but what breaks my heart is what happened to those little guys. I had Cameron in First Grade and I keep picturing his adorable face the morning he was killed. He was so proud. It had taken him forever, but he had finally lost a tooth. He came by my room before school to display the big gap in his wonderful smile. He was such a sweetheart," sniveled Anna Bettis, searching for the Kleenex again.

"You couldn't have asked for a more precious, compassionate, loveable tyke than Marguerite Hudson," said Leslie Owen. "I had her in First Grade and she was so helpful. She was one of those kids you hate to see move on at the end of the year."

"I need to leave. I can't handle any more of this," Tori cried mournfully as she stood up. "I'll see ya' all later."

"My heart goes out to her," Coach said, as he watched Tori walk away. "She's really been through a tough time. She hasn't talked about it, but I know losing her Mother has been hard for her."

All eyes moved to Carter.

"Uh. I know it has to be hard for you too Carter. Uh. I mean losing your folks so recently," stammered the Coach.

Carter shrugged, ignored the uncomfortable statement and instead said, "All these deaths so close together are unusual. I don't remember ever losing this many people in such a short time in Caradan."

Everyone agreed that it was very sad, scary and made them wonder who was behind it.

"It has to be a monster. A normal person couldn't do something like this," said Carrie.

"I just don't understand. Katie and Mimi tried so hard to help children. They both dedicated their lives to helping whenever and wherever they could. Who on Earth could think children deserved to die? I just don't believe I will ever understand," said Cheryl.

"I know what you mean," said Carrie.

"Well, I think I need to hit the hay. Are you ready to go Carrie?" Carter asked, checking his watch.

"I think I'll drive Cheryl home in her car. She probably shouldn't be driving herself tonight."

"Seriously? I thought you were coming over for a while."

"No. You told me you needed to get to bed early tonight. If you want I can call you later, but Cheryl needs me now," Carrie said with annoyance.

"Well, what about me? What about my needs?"

"Carter, please. You're making a scene. I will call you later when I get home."

"Oh, don't bother," he said.

"Carter, don't be that way," Carrie spoke with an exasperated tone as she tried to embrace him. He reluctantly allowed her to kiss him on the cheek. "I'll call later, okay?"

"Sure. Whatever," he said.

"Stay safe, Carter."

"Hmmf," he said as he stomped out of the restaurant.

"He hasn't changed much," Cheryl said.

"What do you mean?" asked Carrie.

"Well, I remember him as being a selfish, self-centered kid, who always had to get his own way and he doesn't appear to have changed much."

"I don't understand him lately. I practically walk on eggshells around him. One minute he is fun-loving Carter and the next minute he's an ogre."

"I hope I didn't run him off with that little slip about parents," said Coach.

"No. Don't worry about that. He works tomorrow and we were planning to leave early anyway. Besides, he really isn't that sensitive about his parents. It's kind of weird."

"He sure was sensitive about you staying to drive Cheryl home," said Coach.

"Sometimes he flies off the handle like that and I don't even recognize him," Carrie said.

"Has he told you anything about his parents' murder?" Cheryl asked.

"No, he won't talk about it and neither will Julie. It's kind of frustrating, but I understand their reasons. For one thing, sometimes I'm kind of the enemy because they're afraid they might find our conversations in the newspaper. I try to make sure they know when things are off the record, but I understand where they are coming from. Although I will say they are getting nowhere fast. Same with the school massacre."

"Poor Julie," a weepy Cheryl exclaimed. "She started working on the case, even before we planned Mimi's funeral. She is determined to find out who this sick, crazy killer is."

"And she will," cried Carrie, scooting out of the booth. "She won't give up. Listen. I need to use the Powder Room. I'll be right back."

Carrie was returning to her group and happened to notice Julie's partner, Devlin Ames, who was standing near a booth by the back door, observing her group. There was something familiar about his profile. Carrie stopped to study the young man.

Julie was incorrect, as the detective was fairly tall at six feet plus.

His extremely well built frame filled out his chambray shirt and blue jeans quite nicely. His jet black hair was a bit messy and reached the edge of his shirt collar. There was the beginning of a five o'clock shadow on his square jawline and his slightly bushy eyebrows were currently pulled together in a scowl as he watched her friends.

"Lord. It couldn't be," she thought to herself. However, the more she watched him, the more certain she was. Those mannerisms. That body movement. Suddenly, as if he could sense her stare, Dev slowly turned his dark eyes toward her then sat down in a recently vacated booth. Carrie leisurely moved in his direction, as if caught in a tractor beam, and slid into the bench opposite him.

"Why didn't you tell Julie?" she asked. "I can't believe you didn't at least let Mimi know you were back. After all this time, she still talked about you and besides, why didn't you tell me? We were supposed to be friends."

"I'm not surprised you were the one to out me, Carrie. I thought about calling you and the Bradley's, but when Julie didn't recognize me, I decided it would be easier not to say anything. I really wasn't sure how Mrs. Bradley felt about me. Honestly Carrie, I know the last time I saw any of the Bradley's, it wasn't good and besides, Julie never liked me. Still doesn't."

"It would have meant so much to Mimi. It still doesn't seem possible that she is gone. She kept up with you, you know. She said you were living with your Dad in Illinois and by the way, why are you using the name Devlin Ames and not Steven Barker?"

"My birth name is Steven Devlin Ames. My Mother changed it to her maiden name, which was Barker, when she took me. My Dad told me they always called me Dev when I was little, so when I went to live with his family I asked them to call me by that name. I wanted to forget those years with my Mom. I got to start a new life. I mean how lucky could I be?"

"Why did you come back to Caradan then?"

"Partly because of Mrs. Bradley," the detective said, lowering his voice. "I know it may sound weird, but the years spent with her instilled a confidence in me and made me believe I had value. If it had not been for her, I wouldn't have been reunited with my Dad and besides, I was tired of big city life and somehow I was drawn back to this little town. When I had the opportunity to transfer, I took it. Of course, I had no idea Julie was on the force and certainly never dreamt we'd be partnered."

"Well, you have to tell her who you are and it might help Mack if you go by and visit him. He and Mimi really loved you and felt so bad about the circumstances. I never knew exactly what happened, but I'm sure he would love to see the kind of person you have turned out to be."

"I think perhaps I will. I wanted to go see Mrs. Bradley, but obviously hesitating made me lose an opportunity. You know Carrie, I loved her too."

"You just reminded me of her favorite quote, "A mistake is just an opportunity to learn". So, Detective it'll be a mistake not to tell Julie. You do it or I will."

"I hear you."

"Well, I need to go, but Steven. I mean Devlin, or is it Dev?"

"Dev will do just fine."

"I want you to know that I am happy you are working with Julie on this. The fact that you knew Mimi gives you a vested interest in solving her murder and I'm counting on you."

"Thanks Carrie. I'm heading out too. You be careful on your way home."

"You too," Carrie said as she reached out and hugged him. "I've missed you, boy. We always had a connection, didn't we?"

"Yeah, we did. Still do," he mouthed as he turned and walked out the exit.

19

GUN REFORM

Carrie joined her friends and Annie asked about the good-looking hunk she was talking to.

"A very old friend," responded Carrie. "Did I miss anything while I was gone?"

"Only Jimmy giving us his opinion about gun reform," grunted Guerry Harden, dipping a piece of her hot wing into barbecue sauce and tucking it into her mouth.

"Okay. Scoff all you want, but I'll tell you one thing. If Melinda, or Katie, or Mimi, or well…if any one of us would of had a gun handy when that killer came a calling, Katie and Mimi would still be with us and so would those little guys."

"I think everything happened so fast I don't know if it would have made any difference or not. You know though, I wish Mimi would have had her gun," said Cheryl. "She had a concealed weapon license to carry and she kept a gun in a hidden compartment of her car. We had a conversation about it once because she had a recurring nightmare that was horrible. She described it as being on the playground and a man just walks onto the grounds. Although the school is locked entry to the playground is such an easy access. Anyway, she started toward him and he pulled out one of those assault rifles, started shooting and the bullets were taking out anything and everything in their path. She said she woke up in a cold sweat and wasn't able to breathe."

"I know, even if she had her gun she couldn't have saved everyone," said Jimmy. "But she might have protected a few."

"Do you know what she told me? She said you know the worst part Cheryl? The worst part was I felt totally helpless. I just had to stand there and let this insane person kill me. And my children."

Silence filled the room and everyone was thinking of Mimi and knowing that is probably precisely how she had died.

"I am just so sick of everyone blaming things for behaviors…it's videos, it's guns, it's bullying. We all know it, but we don't say it. I could name five kids in my room right now who are borderline sociopaths. We try to see they get the help they need through medications, but half of our parents don't believe they need the meds, or they are afraid of the side effects from the meds," said Anna.

"Well, I understand that, Anna, but it's easy for you to judge. You don't have any children. You might feel differently if you had a child that was learning disabled."

"Well, I'd sure be concerned if I had a normal kid in a classroom where teachers were forced to cater to everyone else's kid who had a problem and mine got lost in the shuffle," said the Coach.

"Stop it. The problem is we don't know what the answer is. We just keep on trucking and doing our best for all the kids," said Cheryl.

"Yes," said the Coach sadly. "All the kids."

They had tried to avoid discussing the deaths of the children in Mimi's class. They had cried so much at the funerals they didn't think they had any more tears left. The thought that Mimi may have been able to save those priceless treasures made everyone want to grab a gun. It was just too terrible to grasp and then suddenly, the sounds of sobbing filled the table.

"Oh, God. What are we going to do without them?" wailed Cheryl, as she searched through her purse for a hankie. "What am I going to do without them? They were my best friends in the whole wide world."

"Hey Boss. I think it's time for you to head home," Annie softly nudged Cheryl and handed her more Kleenex.

"Yeah, I guess we all need to head home," Cheryl said. "It's been a long day."

"Let me drive you home, or get a cab for you, Boss."

"Thanks. I'll take the cab and I will talk to ya' all later."

"No you won't," Carrie said. "Remember, I am driving you home in your car and bringing it back in the morning. I already told Carter to leave, so I don't have a way home myself, unless I use your car."

"Okay. I guess that will work," said Cheryl.

The evening was filled with a heavy fog and the air felt as dismal as their cheerless hearts. The clouds scudded over a colossal moon as Cheryl's colleagues waved goodbye and everyone headed off into the night….into the rest of their lives. A solo form watched them enter Cheryl's white Chevy Trailblazer and then hastily moved toward a waiting vehicle.

"What an enlightening evening it has been," the murderer thought. "So much misery and how sad it all was. They make it sound like sweet Katie and the wonderful Mimi lived their lives only for others. Always giving, caring, loving. HA. I knew better. I knew them for the selfish, egotistical, self-centered people they were. I couldn't wait to get out of Smokies before I said something that would give me away."

Carefully pulling away from the curb, the shadow followed the Trailblazer to Cheryl Garza's home.

20
JUNE 22, 2013

An incandescent full moon moved out from under the clouds and glowed with an intense energy, as black filled the skies around it. Carrie drove all the way to the end of Cheryl's darkened driveway.

"Uh, oh. Someone forgot to leave her porch light on," Carrie said. "Would you like me to walk you to the door?"

"No, that's all right. I always keep the light on, so I guess the bulb must need to be replaced. Anyway, as brilliant as that moon is, I won't have any trouble seeing and you've already done so much for me tonight. I really appreciate your driving me home, Carrie."

"No problem."

"Listen. I usually like to get up for a run first thing in the morning, so I should be back by 9:00 a.m. Give me a call before you bring the car back and when you get here I will treat you to breakfast at Murphy's. I can drop you off at your house afterward. Will that work for you?"

"Sounds, perfect. I'll call in the morning."

Carrie waited as Cheryl found her way to the front door. It had been a sad evening, but also one filled with good memories. She still couldn't get over Steven, or rather Devlin, coming back to Caradan. If only Mimi could have met him and talked to him again.

"Well, he'd better tell Mack and Julie," she said to herself. "They deserve to know who he is and if he doesn't' come clean, I'll tell them myself."

Cheryl unlocked and opened the front door, then waved good-bye to Carrie. As Carrie carefully backed down the driveway, Cheryl turned, entered and quickly closed and latched the door behind her. Fumbling around in the dark, she tossed her purse and house key on the small table near the doorway, turned on the entry light, slowly slipped out of her heels, and realized she didn't hear the beeping of her alarm system.

"Oh darn it," she said. "I must have forgotten to set the alarm when I left to go to Smokies. What is up with that?"

She pushed open the nearby swinging door, once again forgetting to engage the alarm's system. Walking into the kitchen, she flipped the switch and was blinded by the unexpected brightness. So many memories and as she looked around was reminded that when she purchased her little slice of heaven, Katie and Mimi were there to help her paint and decorate. Mimi had insisted the kitchen be yellow for sunshine and Katie helped her select the china with the cute little daisies on them.

"Oh, God," she said taking down a wine glass and uncorking a bottle of Merlot. "Why?"

She hadn't been honest with the others tonight. The truth was, when Chief Holden had talked to her, he said he was thinking Mimi's murder had been deliberate. Cheryl thought back to the conversations this evening. How everyone had something to say about Mimi. Katie was definitely well thought of, but Mimi had made such an impact on everyone's lives. The Chief thought the murderer apparently went directly to Mimi's room just to shoot her and he believed the only reason Katie was killed was because she got in the way. She was in the wrong place at the wrong time. The Chief thought the little ones were collateral damage as well.

"Collateral damage? What a horrible term," she said, carrying on a conversation with herself. "It has to be someone we know."

That is what she and the Chief had talked about. That and the fact that none of them would ever get over seeing those tiny caskets at the funeral services.

When she had asked the Chief how God could let something like this happen, he had told her he just didn't know.

Cheryl, along with many others in the community, found her faith had been shattered over the last few weeks. For some, their loss had brought them closer to God. Not for Cheryl. She was battling with finding understanding. Her Priest had visited her quite often lately and she knew he was concerned about her lack of faith. But hey, he hadn't seen those little bodies and he hadn't been able to give her satisfactory answers to her questions. All she really wanted to know was. Why?

Summer was here and the District wanted to hold a memorial for the victims of the massacre at the beginning of the school year. They had charged her to put something together and present it to them in July. She couldn't even bring herself to think about it. She was still reeling from all of the funeral services she had attended. Sometimes the Board members just didn't think.

Cheryl filled her glass and watched as the burgundy red wine flowed. She wandered into the living room, sat down, flipped out the foot rest and relaxed in her favorite recliner. She laid her head back, closed her eyes and let the memories come.

She always knew she was a better administrator than a teacher. She and Katie often commented on how the three of them had found their strengths and knew their weaknesses. When Cheryl became the new Principal, she had tried to get Mimi to accept the position of Reading Specialist, but she just couldn't convince her to leave the classroom.

"You are such a great teacher, but if you specialized Mimi, your talents would reach far more children," Cheryl had told her friend.

"Not going to happen, Cheryl. I love the classroom. I like being able to know my kids and that's what gives me a special relationship with them. If I only spent thirty minutes a day working with students, I couldn't get to know anything about who they were or what they needed."

Mimi had been obstinate and insisted her forte was being a classroom teacher and Cheryl really couldn't argue with that. She only wished all of her teachers could have been cloned from Mimi Bradley.

Her thoughts turned toward Katie. Cheryl had been close to Mimi, but Katie was like a sister to her. They were both single and their careers took precedent over everything. Neither had a love interest and they had spent many evenings debating how to make the school as safe, successful and happy as they could.

The last time they met the discussion had revolved around Tori Roberts. It had been a gorgeous Saturday and Katie had come by for lunch.

"I am so concerned," she had told Katie while preparing chicken salad sandwiches. "Yesterday one of Tori's parents said she had called them in for a conference and when they showed up, the teacher was acting really weird and was extremely rude to them."

"You know her rudeness has been happening a lot more since Tori's parents died," said Katie. "Do you think it's because she was so close to her Mom and that is how she has to handle it?"

"Could be," replied Cheryl as she placed the sandwiches on two plates, added a few pickles, as Katie grabbed a bag chips. "The problem is these parents actually want to remove their little boy from Tori's classroom and I don't know how to convince them to let the child remain."

"Well, I wouldn't want to be in your predicament, but you are the administrator and it goes with the territory, doesn't it?"

"Thanks so much for your enthusiastic support Miss Larson. Sometimes being the Principal sucks," Cheryl said sarcastically. "I am just not sure how to address this latest issue of Tori's insubordination, as well as her disrespect toward her students and parents."

"What do you mean by latest issue?"

Cheryl recalled how shocked Katie was when she told her about Tori's write-ups.

"This is the third write up Tori has received and I can understand the difficulties she has dealt with due to her parents' deaths. However, I can't and won't put up with her unprofessional conduct much longer."

"It's so strange, because some days Tori seems to be an outstanding educator and other days it's almost like she's an entirely different person," said Katie.

"True. But, this Dr. Jekyll and Mr. Hyde behavior needs to come to an end and soon," said Cheryl.

The two ladies had finished their lunch and decided to take in a movie. What a perfect afternoon it had been.

"If only Katie was here for me to talk to now," she said mournfully to herself. "I miss her happy chatter, good advice and most all her friendship."

"Time to head for bed," Cheryl thought as she pulled the lever on the recliner, sat up and took another sip of wine. "It will be hard enough to get up for my run in the morning, especially if I have a little headache. Oh well. I guess that's what aspirin is for."

She stood and carried her drink to the kitchen, topped off her glass with more wine, then headed for the bedroom.

She turned on the bedside lamp and placed her glass of wine on the nightstand. She grabbed a tank top, clean underwear and some boxer shorts from the dresser drawer and walked unsteadily into the bathroom. She turned on the shower, undressed and stepped into the hot, foggy enclosure.

"If only I could wash away the tears with a little hot water," Cheryl said, as she rinsed, turned off the faucet and reached for the nearby towel.

Thoughts ran through her mind. "It was so nice of Carrie to bring her home tonight, especially when that jerk she was with was so ugly to her. I never liked that Carter boy and I can't imagine what Carrie sees in him. I know Mimi never liked him much either. Oh well, to each his own, I guess."

After toweling off Cheryl slipped the tank on and pulled her underwear and boxers on. She took a minute to admire the writing on the tank top. It stated I "R" an Administrator. Mimi had given her the outfit for her birthday and really thought it was funny. Cheryl finished drinking her glass of wine, put lotion on her face, brushed her teeth, and wearily switched off the bathroom light. She walked back into the bedroom and realized she hadn't closed her bedroom door.

"I am so exhausted," she said as she walked over to close the door and returned to her bed and climbed in. She fluffed her pillow, pulled the sheet and light blanket to her chest. Deciding to read a bit, she grabbed her Kindle from the night stand. Before she knew it she had dozed off. Suddenly. She abruptly sat up.

"What was that?" she asked. "Did I hear something?"

Trying to decipher what the sound was, she tried to calm herself. The door to her bedroom was open and she always closed it when she went to bed.

"Perhaps," she thought groggily. "I forgot because I was so tired or it could have been too much of my favorite liquid beverage."

Sliding out from under the covers Cheryl walked to the door and firmly pushed it shut. As she turned around her heart nearly stopped. Standing by the foot of her bed was a figure clad totally in black and who was pointing a hand gun directly at her head.

"Hello Principal Garza. Did you have some sweet dreams? Were you dreaming about your friends and wishing they were here?"

"Where did you come from? How did you get in?" asked Cheryl. "Who are you? What do you want?"

"Why I am here to take the opportunity to correct a mistake. I am here to make sure you won't miss your friends anymore. It was such a lovely evening. Everyone had such nice things to share about Katie and Mimi and I just know they will have many good stories to tell about you also."

"I know who you are," Cheryl gasped. "Oh no. Why? Why? Why are you doing this?"

"Well," came the reply, as the gun was leveled. "It's an opportunity. Counselor Larson and you shouldn't have always taken her side. Now you have to pay for your mistake," and laughing bitterly the assassin fired, killing Cheryl Garza instantly.

The murderer stood over her body feeling the rush of power. One more down. Turning off the light, heading down the hall and closing and locking the back door, the villain carefully inserted the lock pick making sure the door was locked from the inside.

"Let's see them figure this one out. Ha. Ha."

Unexpectedly, Joe Zunker, Cheryl's neighbor, stepped out his back door and the predator slowly slinked behind a huge Elm Tree.

"I think it was a backfire from a car horn," he called to his wife. "I don't see or hear anything."

When the nosy fellow walked back inside, the killer pulled off the mask, tucked it into a pocket, along with the gun and began strolling two blocks to the parked car.

"No one can touch me," the killer thought. "No one can even see me."

The villain opened the car door, paused for a second to look around and then carefully slid into the vehicle, completely unaware of a jogger who was stretching in a nearby doorway. The observer checked his watch, making note of the time before beginning his late night run.

21

CHERYL

Carrie awoke with a start. She hadn't slept well, tossing and turning all night long. Dragging herself out of bed and into the kitchen she got the coffee brewing. She was doing a few toe touches to limber up when Julie walked in and startled her. Carrie did not expect her to be home.

"Darn. You scared the living daylights out of me. When did you come home?"

"Last night. I tried to be quiet and not disturb you. I just needed to get away from the memories for a while. You know I've spent my whole life in that house and I see Mom everywhere."

"Yeah, it's got to be hard. How's your Dad holding up?"

"He's doing better. I think having Pearl and Ruby there has been good for him. He acts like they annoy him, but I've caught him hugging my little girls when he thinks I'm not looking."

Ruby and Pearl were Julie's Blue Lacey puppies. They were only five months old and tiny balls of cuddly gray fur. She had purchased them from a friend a few months ago in an effort to get over the rejection she felt when she learned of her fiancé's illicit affair. Julie refused to admit to anyone that the guy had broken her heart, but she was certainly fortunate to learn about his lack of honesty and fidelity before they walked down the aisle. She remembered how hard it was for her Mom. Mimi had already purchased *Bride's Magazine* for her and was excited about planning a wedding. She took her Mom shopping for puppies instead of a wedding gown, to help them both come to terms with their disappointment.

"I think it was a good idea to take them to your Dad's, but I have to admit, I kind of miss having them around," Carrie said. "Do you want a cup of coffee?"

"Sure. Are you going to make breakfast, too?"

"Ha. In your dreams Miss Smarty-pants. As a matter of fact, Cheryl is

108

taking me to breakfast this morning. I drove her home last night and I'm returning her car in an hour. We are getting a bite to eat and then she'll bring me back home afterwards."

"Ah. I didn't recognize her car. I knew it wasn't Carter's, so I thought you might have found a new boyfriend. That's why I was so quiet last night."

"You are hilarious. I have to tell you though, the way Carter behaved last night, I may be rethinking him as my love interest."

"What do you mean?"

"Oh, he just made an absolute fool of himself. He acted like a teenager who wasn't getting the attention he deserved. First off, he told me before we even went for Happy Hour that he couldn't stay late 'cause he had the early shift. Cheryl had a little too much to drink and just wasn't up to driving, so I suggested I take her home in her car. I mean. I wasn't ready to go yet anyway, but Carter threw a fit in front of everyone."

"Really?"

"I don't know what's up with him. I try to be understanding because of his parents and him failing the detective's test, but you were right the other day. I'm tired of constantly making excuses for his childish behavior. One minute he is affectionate and the life of the party and the next he is a perfect stranger."

"I hate to say it, but I told you..."

"I know. I know. Anyway, it all worked out 'cause Carter drove me to Smokies and he left 'cause of his early morning duty and I was able to stay a little longer. When I dropped Cheryl off, she suggested we go to breakfast when I return her car this morning. I'm going to get dressed and give her a call. Hey. Would you like to join us?"

"You know what? I think I would."

"Well, she told me to call her at 9:00, so let's get ready."

Thirty minutes later Carrie was on the telephone. An hour later and after leaving several messages on Cheryl's answering machine, she and Julie decided to drive over.

"She probably overslept. She had a pretty good buzz on last night," said Carrie.

"Or, maybe her ringer was turned off," Julie said.

Carrie pulled into the driveway and the girls got out of the car. They knocked on the front door and when there was no answer, they went around to the back door. They tried peering into the house through the kitchen window, but were unable to see anything.

"Hey. What are you two up to this morning?" Cheryl's neighbor surprised them. "I might have to call the police, Julie."

"Very funny. You scared the crap out of me, Mr. Joe. Have you seen Cheryl around this morning?"

"Nope. Not a hide, nor a hair."

"Something just doesn't feel right to me," Julie whispered to Carrie. "Did you notice anything out of the ordinary going on in the neighborhood lately?"

"Well, we heard a car backfiring last night. Sounded like a gunshot. Woke Dawn and I up. I even got out of bed and checked around outside because it sounded so close."

"That worries me," said Carrie.

"Let me get my credit card and see if I can open the door," said Julie. "The worst thing that can happen is we wake her up. We just need to know she is okay."

"Here now. Hold on girls. I heard you whispering, but no need to use a credit card. Cheryl gave me a key to her house. Let me run and get it for you."

Joe moseyed leisurely back to his house while the girls waited impatiently. He returned a few minutes later with the key and after opening the front door, they knew something was definitely wrong. There was a metallic smell and the slight scent of gunpowder was in the air. Julie recognized it instantly.

"Carrie. Joe. Stay here, be quiet, and don't touch a thing."

She pulled her gun from her purse, assumed the correct stance and moved cautiously down the hall toward the bedroom, afraid of what she would find. There on the floor, near the open door, wearing her flowered boxers and a hole in the middle of her forehead, lay the last of the Three Musketeers. A stunned and troubled Julie said "My God. What is going on?"

She carefully backed out of the room, told Carrie and Joe to backtrack and reminded them not to touch a thing. They all walked outside and Julie used her cell phone to call in to dispatch.

"This is Homicide Detective Julie Bradley. There has been a murder at the home of Cheryl Garza, located at 1774 Forest Knoll. I am securing the scene and will wait for backup. Could you let Chief Holden and my partner Devlin Ames know I am here."

"Will do, Detective," responded the dispatcher.

"Thanks."

Hanging up her cell, Julie turned toward Joe and Carrie. "Look. I need both of you to stay here until the police arrive. Joe, I want you to be prepared to be interviewed about last night. You too, Carrie. What you saw, heard, anything you can share or that may have been out of the ordinary. Be sure to mention the time the backfire woke you up, Joe."

"Is Cheryl dead, Julie?" asked Joe.

"It looks like it Joe, but let's wait to talk until help gets here."

"Can't you tell us what happened. I mean did she fall or what?" Carrie asked.

"All I can say is she didn't meet with an accident."

"It wasn't a car backfiring, was it Julie?" asked Joe

"No."

"What is going on Julie?"

"My thoughts exactly, Carrie. My thoughts exactly."

22
SERIAL KILLER

"We have a serial killer on the loose," Chief Holden said to the four detectives standing in front of him. "I have no desire to bring in the FBI, but eventually we are going to have to. Right now however, we have very little to go on."

"Maybe Mrs. Bradley wasn't the target. It looks like the school itself might be the focus of the killer," said middle aged Detective Aaron Ross, hitching up his pants, as his protruding belly refused to cooperate.

"I agree that the Administrators were targets and obviously Mrs. Bradley and her students, but if it was the school, then why not hit other classes or teachers? According to the few witnesses we have the perp went straight to the teacher's room after shooting Miss Larson," added Detective Rosie Cortinas, rubbing her bloodshot eyes with the back of her hand. The trim, thirty year old detective had recently been assigned to the Homicide Division after taking a maternity leave of absence.

"Is that little girl sleeping through the night yet, Rosie?" asked Julie.

"No and her Father isn't much help."

"Ah," said her partner. "That's why you look like you've been out partying all night."

"I wish. This kid thing is about to do me in."

"Okay," said the Chief. "Let's get back on track Detectives."

"We have been assuming the Counselor was an accident, but what if she was on the hit list too?" asked Detective Ross.

"I think you have a point Detective, especially in light of the Garza murder," said the Chief.

"Have we got any information from IAFIS. The Integrated Automated Fingerprint Identification System?" asked Detective Ames.

"No, but the killer obviously wore gloves because we have not found any fingerprints or DNA that do not belong at the crime scenes," said

Cortinas.

"How about ACS?" asked the Chief.

"You mean the Ammunition Coding System? replied Julie. "Well, our perpetrator didn't bother policing his shell casings and the M.E. recovered bullets from all of our victims while performing their autopsies. That is how we know Miss Garza's death is related to the massacre. ACS matched the ammo used and the bullets came from a 9mm Smith and Wesson Glock."

"We need to be researching records to try to find out who bought the gun and where it is right now," said the Chief.

"We are already on it Sir," said Detective Cortinas.

"Okay. Now. We started out thinking the school massacre was the result of a spree killing, but obviously with Miss Garza's murder we know it has gone serial. Originally we assumed Mrs. Bradley was the target and the Counselor's death was unrelated. She was just in the wrong place at the wrong time and so were the kids. We assumed the murders were limited to the school with an emphasis on Mimi Bradley. Now. We need to completely rethink our investigation. Correct?" said Chief Holden.

"Look at the board. In the last two months, almost to the day, eight people have been murdered…three adults and five kids," quietly murmured Ames as he gazed at the Chief's whiteboard.

"Their connection has to be Caradan Elementary, Mimi Bradley, or both," Ross said.

"All of the murder victims were killed with precision, so we know the shooter is a crack shot. One interesting aspect was my Mom was shot in the chest, but the other victims were all perfect headshots," Julie intervened, as she reviewed her paperwork. "Our killer is an exceptional marksman and I think it's significant my Mom was the only one shot in the chest. I've given this some thought and the chest equates to the heart. I am pretty sure these murders revolve around my Mom and people who were important to her. I also believe there must be an emotional connection there."

"You have a point Julie. The headshots were cold and precise, but there must have been some emotion involved with your Mom's execution. Mrs. Bradley did not die instantly as the others did," responded Detective Ames as he continued to look at the dates on the whiteboard timeline.

"Well, it also may be related to her connection with the children. We have determined from the bullet wounds that the first five were exact headshots, but the remaining shots were erratic and not precise. It's almost like the killer became emotionally overwhelmed and was not as accurate. Fortunately although a few of the kids are still critical, five of them have been released," said Julie.

"Thank God for small blessings," said Detective Ross.

"Do you think the killer knew the five kids he shot in the head?" asked Cortinas.

"That is a possibility, of course," said Julie.

"Anyone who could shoot children has to be cold-blooded," said Ames.

"True. Okay, let's go over what we have so far," said the Chief. "The killer was slender, wore black, knew how to handle a gun, knew the school, the schedule, the location of Mimi's classroom, and it's possible Counselor Larson was also on his list and the kids weren't necessarily collateral damage. He knew where Cheryl Garza lived and we also know the type of weapon used. The school murders were carried out on May 22 and Cheryl was killed on June 22, exactly one month later."

"Is it possible the dates are relevant Chief?" Detective Ames asked cautiously. He was looking at the whiteboard again. "I was wondering about the dates of the other murders Julie and I have been investigating. The Roberts' were killed on April 22 and the case was closed as a murder/suicide."

"Oh, my gosh," Julie cried excitedly. "What about the Westin murders? They occurred on March 22. I remember the date because that was a few days after I got my notification for passing the Detective's Exam and it was my first case."

"Okay, folks," the Chief said. "Hold on a minute. It looks like we may have a connection on the dates, but I just don't know how in the heck these murders all tie together."

"There were no shell casings left at the Westin's murder scene, but the M.E. recovered bullets from the bodies," said Dev.

"Let's have ballistics check for a match on the bullets and see if they correspond to the ballistics from the Caradan massacre. What about the Roberts' case?" asked the Chief.

"IACIS didn't turn up any unusual fingerprints, but we do have bullets from the bodies," said Dev. "And we have the actual gun used in the Roberts murder/suicide. It is registered to Tori Roberts," said Ames.

"During the interview Tori said her Mom had asked to borrow the gun after the Mr. and Mrs. Westin were killed because Mrs. Roberts was worried about intruders," said Julie.

"I think we need to revisit the Roberts' murder book. I remember one point I found suspicious in the original investigation was the lack of fingerprints anywhere in the kitchen. Mrs. Roberts did have some gun powder residue on her hands and both she and her ex-husband were shot in the head at close range, but I was surprised to find the entire kitchen appeared to have been wiped down," said Detective Ames.

"Maybe Mrs. Roberts had just cleaned the kitchen," said Detective Cortinas. "If you're going to find a clean room, the kitchen makes sense."

"True. Just thought it was curious because Tori Roberts lived in her Mother's home and we didn't find her fingerprints in the kitchen. They were all over the remainder of the house, but not a one in the kitchen where the deaths occurred," said Dev.

"Did any of the neighbors see anything unusual going on?" asked Chief Holden.

"No," said Julie. "I tend to agree with Dev and we need to reopen the case."

"So do it. Did you find any fingerprints at the Westin home?" asked the Chief.

"We didn't find anything other than the obvious ones from Officer Carter Westin and his parents. We determined the perpetrator or perpetrators probably wore gloves," said Julie.

"You all need to interview everyone related to both cases again," said the Chief as he glanced at the whiteboard. "Now, our eye witnesses at the school told us that the killer was dressed in black and wore gloves. Have we got anything else?"

"Well Chief, we know a kid in Mrs. Bradley's class said the killer told the teacher he loved her and he needed to take care of mistakes. The other interesting fact is another of the kids mentioned the killer's shiny ring with a key," said Detective Cortinas.

"So he either had access to the school's master key or he was holding a set of lock-picks," said Detective Ames.

"I think the ring was holding a set of lock-picks. That's how he got into Cheryl's house as well. I noticed her alarm system was not armed when we went into the house. She must have forgotten to arm it and that probably gave the killer an opportunity to break in using a lock pick. Remember, the house was locked when we arrived so the killer must have let himself in and relocked the house when he left," said Julie.

"That's likely," said Dev. "We have no witnesses to any of the murders, but everything is pointing to the fact they are probably related. Man, this is so frustrating."

"It may seem exasperating," the Chief said as he twirled his droopy mustache. "But detectives you are doing an outstanding job. We are beginning to connect the dots, so get back to work. Keep putting your heads together. I know everything will fall into place. We are going to get this guy."

23
SECRETS UNLOCKED

"Julie, can I talk to you for a minute," Devlin spoke as everyone was leaving the Chief's office. "There is something I need to tell you."

"Sure, I guess so," Julie hesitated and bent to get her purse from her desk. "Let me stop at the Ladies Room first and then how about we go to Andy's for a cheeseburger and some fries. I feel like I could use some grease."

"Great idea. It shouldn't be too busy yet and that is as good a place as any to have this conversation. I need to speak to the Chief for a few minutes and then I'll meet you downstairs."

Julie turned and walked down the hallway as Detective Ames knocked on the Chief's office door.

"Come in," said Chief Holden.

"Do you have a second Sir?"

"Sure, Ames. What's up?"

Devlin closed the Chief's door and said, "Remember how I told you about the significance of the murders falling on the 22nd?"

"Yes?"

"Well, do you also remember when I told you about the dates of the Caradan murders?"

"Of course."

"You know my family was murdered before I came to Caradan, right?"

"Yes. I remember how difficult that time was for you."

"I really don't believe in coincidences Sir, and I have no idea how their deaths might fit into this situation. They weren't shot, but my family was killed on January 22. I have kept in touch with my former partner and he told me arson was involved in their deaths, but so far that is all they have."

"Yes. I know that, said the Chief."

"I wanted to mention the date to you, because I have a connection to

Mrs. Bradley. I lived in Caradan many years ago and went under the name of Steven Barker. I was in and out of boys' homes and the Bradley family actually took me in for a few months when I was nine. Mrs. Bradley showed a special interest in me when I was younger."

"I appreciate you sharing that bit of information with me Detective, but I have known the Bradley's for many years and I remember when they took you in. I also am aware of your story because the Department did a pretty thorough investigation when you went through our interview process and I really don't see a connection to the Caradan murders at all."

"Thank you for not making a big deal of it, Chief."

"No problem, but what I want to know is are you going to tell Mack and Julie who you are?"

"I plan to do that today, Sir. By the way, did your knowledge of my history with the Bradley's have anything to do with making Julie my partner?"

"No. I partnered you two because you are both talented individuals and I thought you would complement each other."

"Thank you, Chief. I appreciate your vote of confidence."

"No problem Detective, but I suggest you let the Bradley family know who you are and why you are in Caradan sooner, rather than later."

"Yes Sir. I am telling Julie at lunch and hopefully, I will let Mr. Bradley know soon too."

The Chief frowned as he watched Ames leave. It would be interesting to see how this scenario played out.

Julie was tapping her foot with annoyance by the time Devlin made it downstairs.

"I didn't think you would be so long," she said.

"Sorry."

"Well, I'm starving. Let's go."

The two detectives took the exit to the parking lot and Julie deferred to Devlin as he automatically slid behind the steering wheel. Neither of them spoke as they drove to Andy's Bar and Grill. Julie was not really thinking about what her partner was planning to share, although she was surprised at his sudden interest in collaborating. She was "mind reviewing" the cases, particularly her Mother's, when he pulled into a parking space in front of the eatery.

They entered the restaurant and Julie wondered for the hundredth time why on earth the place was called Andy's.

"Hey Raul," Julie called as she waved to the swarthy, slightly overweight Mexican. He loved to tell jokes and had entertained her for as long as she could remember.

"Why is this place called Andy's instead of Raul's?" asked Dev.

"You ask Raul why," said Julie.

"Hey, Raul. Why is this place called Andy's?" asked Dev.

"It jus always bin Andy's," said Raul with a big grin. "What you want to drink?"

"We'll have a couple of sweet teas, Raul," said Julie, as she slid into a booth facing her partner. Taking a minute to study him, Julie had to admit Carrie was right. Devlin Ames was a very fine looking man and if he wasn't so darn exasperating, she probably wouldn't mind getting to know him better.

"Hey, Ames," she said. "I just want to tell you how impressed I was when you put those dates together. No one had even thought about it until you brought it up. I think it may be the first break in these crazy cases. Maybe everyone is right about you."

"Right about me? What do you mean?"

"They think you are the best and brightest Chicago can offer and we were very lucky you decided to join our little police force. I have to admit you are pretty good at what you do and I guess my Dad was correct when he said I was fortunate to have you as a partner."

"Thanks, Julie, but you might change your mind after we finish our conversation. Do you remember a kid named Steven Barker?"

"Sure. Yeah. Vaguely, but that was a long time ago. He was a miscreant who broke my parent's hearts and nearly killed my dog. What has he got to do with anything?"

"I'm not sure of the best way to tell you this, so I'll just put it out there. When I was a young boy, I lived in Caradan with my Mother."

"So? I repeat, what does that have to do with Steven Barker?"

"Uh. Well, that is the name I went by then."

Devlin paused as the waitress served their drinks and took their orders. He watched as Julie assimilated the data and, as a scowl began to move across her forehead, he thought to himself. "Man, what a beauty she has grown into."

"Are you freaking kidding me? I mean you can't be serious. You're the jerk who hurt my Winston? What are you doing here? How? Why?"

"Settle down for God's sake. You're making a scene."

"Okay. Fine. Tell me how you ended up back in Caradan?"

"I had nowhere else to go."

"What do you mean?"

"My Dad, Step-Mom and little sister were killed in a house fire several months ago. My grandparents both passed away a few years before that, and I just felt at loose ends. I think some of my happiest times were with your Mom and your family, so when I saw an opportunity to transfer here, I jumped at it."

"Oh my God. Your entire family perished? That is terrible, Dev. I heard from the grapevine that you had lost a family member, but I had no idea it was your entire family. I am so sorry. I had no idea."

"I try not to wear my heart on my sleeve and I know my family would have wanted me to move forward with my life. I opted to come to Caradan when I had the chance and I try to stay busy with the job. It keeps me from feeling and thinking too much about what I have lost."

"I think I understand what you mean," Julie said. "How come you didn't let my parents know you were here?"

"I thought about it and I will never forgive myself for not visiting your Mom. I just couldn't get my nerve up and by the time I did, she was gone. I really would like to see your Dad though, if you think he would want to see me."

Julie narrowed her eyes. "Unfortunately, I'm sure he would love to see you. Personally, I am having a little trouble processing this information. Let me eat my food and then we can talk some more. Okay?"

"Sure thing. These cheeseburgers look great."

The two of them enjoyed the 100% all beef patties, topped with Raul's whole wheat buns, special chipotle sauce, with a mixture of onion rings and French fries on the side. During their meal Julie and Dev covertly eyed one another and when their repast was over decided to order some dessert. Julie convinced him to try the blueberry cobbler, assuring him it was one of Andy's most popular delicacies, especially when topped with creamy vanilla ice cream. After enjoying the treat and while drinking their coffee Dev leaned toward Julie and whispered, "I really did love your Mom. She was the most compassionate human being I have ever met and she did so many wonderful things Julie. Did you know about the Lunchbox Fairy?"

"Can't say as I did," she said, rolling her eyes.

"You know you are a beautiful woman, but the eye-rolling thing is a real turn-off."

"I guess it's a good thing I'm not interested in turning you on, then."

"Uh, yeah, I guess that's true. Okay, as I was saying. When I was in Second through Fourth Grade there was a Lunchbox Fairy who touched my box with her wand and left me the most wonderful nutritious and delectable stuff. I couldn't figure out how I could be so lucky."

"Okay?"

Shaking his head, Dev stared at his hands and sighed. "At your Mom's funeral I talked with the teacher I had in Third Grade at Caradan Elementary and she told me your Mom was the Lunchbox Fairy."

Julie just stared at him.

"Julie, your Mom made me aware of a world where people cared about one another and valued who and what you were. I know if it hadn't been for your parents, but especially your Mom, I think I would have ended up a very different person. She brought my Dad and I together and that changed my life. I intend to find this murderer, because I owe it to Mrs. Bradley."

Julie felt her eyes begin to tear up and she fought to keep them from trickling down her cheeks. She would not cry in front of this man.

"That story doesn't surprise me," she said. "It sounds just like something Mom would have done. You know, I could probably write a book documenting my remarkable mother's dedicated life."

Devlin Ames nodded his head in agreement.

"What about your family?" Julie asked softly as Dev handed the waitress his credit card. "It must have been hard for you."

"When I was two years old my Mom kidnapped me and changed my name. It was pretty rough for me those years I lived with my Mother. She was a drug addict and had a boyfriend who was pretty abusive. I'm sure my Mother loved me in her own way, but she loved the drugs more. To be honest I don't even like to think about that time in my life. Mrs. Bradley was instrumental in getting me back to my Father. My Dad and I had really gotten close and my Step-Mom tried to make me feel part of the family, even though it was hard for her. I think she kind of resented my relationship with my Father. I have to say though, my little sister…her name was Lyssy…she was a doll. She was four when I moved in with them. I still can't believe they are gone. Lyssy was going to begin grad school and was home for the summer when the fire…"

Lowering his head Dev tried to regain his composure and somehow, his tale tugged at Julie's heartstrings and she touched his arm gently.

"I guess I don't remember much about the time you came to live with us, but I know my Momma cried a lot after you left. My Dad was sad too and I remember hating you because you made them so unhappy. You and Carrie always hung together and wouldn't have anything to do with me at school.. I was so jealous of your friendship with her and resented your relationship with my Mom too, I guess. Have you talked to Carrie yet? Does she know you are back?"

"Well. I sort of ran into her the other night and she recognized me. She told me in no uncertain terms I was to tell you who I was or she would."

"That sounds like Carrie. Listen, I'm willing to forgive and forget. I'd like to think I've matured a little and I know my Mom always thought there was something worthwhile about you. How about we put the past behind us and I'll call my Dad and tell him I'm coming over with a surprise for him. He is working from home now, so he should be at the house."

"Are you sure he will want to see me, Julie?

"Why wouldn't he. He cared about you and I think if it hadn't been for me, he and Mom probably would have tried to keep you with them. I think it might help lift his spirits because he has had trouble bouncing back from Mom's death."

For some reason, as they made the drive to the Bradley house, Dev felt a sense of apprehension about seeing Mack, but was grateful Julie was finally on speaking terms with him. Devlin Ames.

24
THE REUNION

Mack was standing in the front yard, tossing a chew toy to Ruby and Pearl. Dev noticed the two little balls of fur cavorting after the toy and commented on how cute they were. Julie told him they belonged to her and she and the puppies had been staying with her Dad off and on since her Mom had been murdered. She was certain the pups had helped her Dad in dealing with his sorrow.

Mack shuffled slowly toward them. His gray hair was beginning to thin and peeked over his ears and he had a slight smile on his face when he saw Julie.

"He seems to be so much older that I remember," Dev thought to himself.

"My Dad has aged ten years since my Mother's death," Julie murmured, almost as if she could read Dev's mind.

Mack's wrinkled face broke into a happy grin and as he got closer, Devlin stepped forward. The older man paused, the grin fell open and he exclaimed, "I would recognize that face and those eyes anywhere. Steven."

"I go by Devlin now, Sir," he said.

"Is that right? Where did you find this young man, Julie?" Mack asked as he met them.

Dev reached his hand out and Mack grabbed it and pulled him forward into a huge hug. "How have you been boy?" he asked huskily, the tears glistening on his eyelashes.

It was more than he could bear and Dev hugged the older man back, as he blinked away his own tears.

"I've been good, Sir. I've been okay."

"I'm so glad to hear that," Mack said as he turned to give Julie her hug. "Let's all go inside for a glass of sweet tea. I just made some using Mimi's special recipe. Steven. Uh, I'm sorry, Devlin is it? Mimi will be so happy. I mean." He stopped and took a deep breath before saying, "Mimi would have been so happy to see you, Son."

The three of them headed into the sunny, gourmet designed kitchen. Dev paused for a moment and took in the room. His eyes roamed the lemon yellow walls, trimmed with white subway tiles and the recently purchased shiny stainless steel appliances. There was a wall filled with shelves adorned with colorful ceramic chickens. It was a lovely country kitchen, from the quaint oval hand-braided rug, to the crisp white, ruffled curtains at the windows. Mack invited them to make themselves comfortable and reaching into the cupboard, removed three large glasses, which he loaded with ice from the handy icemaker. He grabbed an antique pitcher filled with a dark, brown liquid and poured. After serving everyone their cold drinks, he joined them at the antique oak table which had been in Julie's family as long as she could remember. Devlin experienced a little tightness in his chest as he recalled being a part of this family, sitting around this very table for meals and doing homework, so many years ago. It was strange, but he somehow felt he had come home. Dev felt a dampness form behind his eyes and it hit him. She really was gone. He had lost so much in the last few months. Sometimes it just overwhelmed him.

Mack leaned over and patted him on the arm. He thought he knew and understood the emotions that were tumbling around within Dev's heart and mind.

"So how is it you are back in Caradan, Steven. Uh, Devlin?" he asked.

"Dev's Mother kidnapped him when he was just two years old Daddy. His Mom gave him the name of Steven Barker. When he went to live with his Father, they told him his name was Devlin and of course, his last name was Ames."

"It was because of Mrs. Bradley that the State was able to put everything together and connect me with my Father. I talked to Mrs. Steelman at Mrs. Bradley's funeral and she said Mrs. Bradley told her about the names I mentioned on several early morning drives to school. Anyway, to make a long story short, based on that information they located and reunited me with my Dad. I will always be grateful to Mrs. Bradley."

"Well, she truly loved you boy. It nearly broke her heart when we sent you back with Mrs. Steelman. It was not easy for either of us."

"I'm sure it wasn't easy, but I understand why you did it. Really, I do. I think I was a little messed up back then and who knows how I would have turned out if it hadn't been for you guys. I remember thinking when she put me in that car how bad I had ruined everything. I was so happy with your family and I thought about what I had done...a lot. It was the first time I could remember feeling sad. Feeling anything actually, so you know, it was probably a good thing everything happened the way it did."

"My Mimi always said everything happens for a reason Son, and I hang onto that belief. It is what gets me through most of my days now. Okay, now tell me how Julie found you."

"You are not going to believe this Daddy, but surprise, surprise. Dev is actually my new partner."

"Seriously?" Mack chuckled happily and Julie felt as if she had received a gift. It had been a month since her Dad had smiled or laughed so much.

"So this is the hot-shot from Chicago, huh?"

"Sir?"

Julie's face was a flush of red and she looked up under her lashes at Dev and then threw her Dad a scowl and said, "Hey Daddy. When was the last time you got a haircut? You have wings growing behind your ears."

"I guess I need to call Sam the Barber. I haven't worried too much about what I look like lately. Your Mother would not be happy about that. She was always after me to keep my hair trimmed up."

"Do you want me to make an appointment for you?"

"Sam doesn't make appointments. I just show up and either he takes care of me right away or I wait until he is ready. We old geezers sit around and shoot the breeze with each other. I kind of enjoy that."

"Don't wait too long. You are beginning to look like a homeless fellow and besides, it would be good for you to get out a little."

"I am listening to you Julie. Stop worrying so much about me, Goose," he said and then turned toward Dev. "Have you stayed in touch with anyone from town? Do you ever see or talk to your Mom?"

"No, Sir. I pretty much cut all ties to the town and my Mom when I left. My Dad did tell me my Mother died from an overdose ten years ago."

"Oh, I am sorry to hear that," said Mack. He paused for a moment and then asked, "Have you had a happy life so far, Steven-uh-Devlin?"

"Yes sir. I was able to spend a lot of great years with my grandparents. My Gram and Gramps had a little farm with a few head of cows, four horses, and even a couple of Bethlehem donkies named Henry and Leroy. I loved spending time with them. Did a lot of fishing and hiking with my Gramps and he taught me how to drive a tractor, repair fences, and brand cattle. My favorite thing to do was to search the rock beds for fossils." Wiggling his dark eyebrows he said, "You all must allow me to show you my fossil collection someday."

The comment brought a smile from Mack and a giggle from Julie.

"You should do that more often Julie," Dev said, as he flashed her a white smile. "You have a great giggle."

"Really," she said drily, as she again glanced at him from under her lashes.

"Yes, really," he said.

"So tell me about school. Did you play any ball. You sure have grown into a healthy young man," Mack said.

"Yes Sir," Dev smiled. "I played a little football and basketball, but baseball was something I didn't have a taste for, although I still have the bat and ball you and Mrs. Bradley gave me. I just never played the game. My Dad was always curious about the baseball mementos I had, but I just told him they represented good memories and bad memories."

Mack looked at him and nodded his head while Julie stood, collected their glasses, and took them to the counter to refill.

"You know I hated you. I really did," she said.

"Now Julie."

"It's all right Mr. Bradley. I understand how Julie felt and she probably had every right to hate me."

"We don't hate in this house. We dislike, but we do not hate and Julie knows that."

"Jeez Daddy, you sounded just like Mommy then. So let me restate that. I disliked you intensely, Dev. Not just because of my dog, but also because my parents never even asked me if it was okay for you to come and live with us. They just showed up with you and I was supposed to be okay with it. I felt like my life had been totally ruined."

"We were wrong for that, but we just didn't think and we have apologized Julie."

"I know Daddy. It's okay. I think I am ready to let that one go."

"Mimi and I always wanted a large family, Dev. Blessed as we were with Julie we would have liked for her to have a brother or sister to grow up with."

"One of my greatest joys was watching my little sister grow into a lovely young woman," said Dev.

"Wonderful. Wonderful," Mack said, then noticed the moisture in Dev's eyes. "It's all right Son. Mimi would have been so happy for you."

"I just wish I would have visited her. There was so much I wanted to tell Mrs. Bradley."

"Well, I know she would have loved that. Come on now. Tell us more about yourself. Where did you go to college, Dev?" asked Mack.

I attended Penn State on an academic scholarship. I loved everything about school and when I graduated, I applied to the Chicago Police Force. My family lived in Carrollton, which is a suburb of Chicago. I am pleased to say I moved up pretty quickly and joined the Homicide Division. I loved it."

"I'm sure you were very good at it. How about your family? You mentioned your sister?" said Mack.

"My sister Lyssy, was a beautiful human being. She was getting ready to attend graduate school at Colorado School of Mines and planned to major in Biomedical Engineering. She had a great career ahead of her. She was so pretty and really had a bright mind. I used to tease her that she got everything. It wasn't fair."

"What do you mean?" asked Julie.

"She got the beauty and the brains," Dev said. "I was so proud of her. We had a great relationship. Lyssy could be quite mischievous and loved to play practical jokes, particularly on me. She was the best and I miss her so much."

"You are referring to her in the past tense, Son. Why is that?"

Dev sadly explained how he came to be in Caradan and when he mentioned his family perishing in the fire, Julie noticed an unexpected reaction from Mack. Dev was also aware of the chilly response to his tale.

"Where were you when the fire started?" asked Mack.

"I was working Homicide in the Chicago area. By the time they located me, it was over and they were gone. The Carrollton Police Chief believed they were murdered, but so far don't have any real leads."

Suddenly, all the interest and enthusiasm for Devlin had gone out of Mack. The impression Dev got was Mr. Bradley was ready for him to leave and became irritated when he learned Julie was riding back to the office with him.

Mack followed them outside saying, "Julie, why don't you let me drive you into town."

"Don't be silly Daddy. I need to pick up some things and Dev and I still have to go over the cases we are working on. By the way, my partner made an interesting discovery today and we want to follow through on the information. I'll be home for dinner. Thought I would pick up some Chinese for us. Maybe we can invite Carrie over and Dev could join us too."

"No. I don't want to," Mack snapped and immediately turned toward the house. Glancing back he said, "You be careful, Julie. Watch your back." He threw Dev a dark expression just before he walked through the front door.

"Wow. What happened?" Devlin asked. "What did I do?"

"Oh, don't worry about it. He gets in some moods lately," Julie responded, but thought to herself, "Watch your back? What the heck was that about?"

The two of them shared snippets of information as they drove toward the Division Office and decided to start from the beginning and go over everything they had one more time.

Mack watched them drive away from the living room window and turning with a frown, picked up the telephone and called his friend the Chief of Police.

When he was put through to Chief Holden, he revealed his concerns about Devlin Ames and the Chief suggested he come in and talk about it, but he was sure Mack was worrying for nothing. Mack hurried out to his car and backing out of the garage all he could think about was the discussion he and Mimi had shared all those years ago. She had told him a story about Steven and a fire he started.

Mack wondered why Steven had really come back to Caradan after all these years. Trying to keep to the speed limit he rushed to meet his friend.

25
CLUES

"Hey," said the desk Sergeant as Dev and Julie walked into the Division. "There was a call earlier that you might be interested in. I put the number on your desk, Detective Ames. It's from a guy named James Sword who lives in Cheryl Garza's neighborhood. He might have some information about her murder."

"Thanks Jim," said Dev as he picked up the stack of pink message slips prominently displayed on his desk. He flipped through the slips looking for the one from Mr. Sword. He selected a paper, picked up the telephone, and punched in the phone number Jim had written.

"Sword residence."

"Hello, Mr. Sword. This is Detective Devlin Ames with the Caradan Police Department. How are you today, Sir?"

"I am fine Detective."

"I understand you might have some information regarding your neighbor, Cheryl Garza."

The caller stated that he was going for a jog around midnight on the night Cheryl was murdered and noticed a strange vehicle parked in front of his house. Mr. Sword was stretching prior to beginning his run and he observed a man, or could have been a woman, walking to the car from the direction of Cheryl's house. He said he didn't think the individual noticed him as he was standing on his portico, but due to the person's unusual behavior, Mr. Sword decided to hang back and just observe.

"Can you describe the person for me, Sir?"

"Certainly. The individual appeared to be young, slender, under 6 feet tall, with longish hair and dressed completely in black."

"Can you give me a description of the vehicle?" asked Dev.

"I'm not sure of the vehicle because it was a pretty dark night, but I got the impression it may have been new and it was dark and sporty looking."

"Was it an SUV?" asked Julie.

"No. It was a sports car coupe and was kind of small."

"How about a license number, Sir? Were you able to get a license number for us?"

"I'm sorry. I couldn't see the license plate, but you know, when I watched this person…it seemed like they didn't live in our area and he or she was acting kind of suspicious. I mean why would they park so far from their car. So when my neighbor told me about Cheryl Garza's death I thought the authorities should know what I'd seen. I'm just calling because the lady lived a few blocks from me and our Neighborhood Watch Captain tells us to notify the powers that be if we see something that is suspicious."

"We certainly appreciate your calling and following the advice of your watch captain and I assure you, any knowledge we gain is helpful," said Dev.

The information tied in with the time Cheryl's neighbor had heard what he thought was a car backfiring and it also matched the M.E.'s estimated time of death for Miss Garza.

"Hey, I just thought of something," Dev exclaimed. "We may be approaching this from the wrong direction. Why do we think the killer is a man? Do we have any information that suggests it couldn't be a woman? The caller just said it could have been a woman."

"Of course," Julie said. "The witnesses kept referring to the intruder as a he and I guess we assumed it was a man, but you are right. There is nothing to prove the killer is a male. I know lots of women, myself included, who are tall, have longish hair and are handy with a gun."

Their conversation was interrupted by the telephone.

"Detective Bradley," Julie said.

"Julie, it's Doc," the Medical Examiner said. "I wanted to let you know we have the ballistic results on the Westins. They are a perfect match with the bullets from the Caradan Massacre. The gunman who participated in that crime scene was also responsible for the Westin murders. I knew you wanted to know as soon as I got the results back."

"Thanks Doc," Julie said. "I appreciate the quick response."

Julie hung up the phone and turned toward her partner. "Looks like we have a match on the Westin murders so we know their killer is connected to the Caradan Massacre. My gut tells me it wasn't a robbery, but we still don't have any proof to dispute that it was anything else. Carter insisted a clock was missing from his parent's house. However, what we do know for a fact is the robber has a connection to the school murders."

"Hmmm. But what in the heck is it?" asked Dev. "Listen, I am going to take the murder books for Mimi, Katie, and Cheryl home to look over again. Why don't you work on the Westin and Roberts' books tonight."

"Okay. Sounds good. I am going to have a quick dinner and then I will come back here to work on the books."

The partners agreed to meet early the next morning to go over their results. Dev planned to stay at the office for a while, so Julie waved good bye and headed toward the elevators. She decided to work off the cheeseburger lunch she had enjoyed and took the stairs instead. Her cell phone began ringing telling her she had an incoming call from Carrie.

"Hey Girl. What are you up to?"

"I was trying to decide what to do for dinner tonight. Are you going to your Dad's, or will you be coming home?"

"I suggested Chinese to Dad, but he was not interested, so guess I will be home. Do you want me to pick up some Chinese?"

"Sure. That would be great. I was thinking of calling Carter and inviting him over and maybe taking in that new movie in town after dinner. He has been a real stinker and I've decided to give him one more chance to work some of his behavior out, or it will be adios amigo from me."

As Julie exited on the first floor she encountered Carter Westin, who was heading toward the lounge for a cup of coffee.

"Hey, Julie. Where are you going in such a hurry?"

Julie motioned to him to wait because she was on her cell.

"Carrie, I have Carter here. Do you want to talk to him?"

"Sure," said Carrie.

Julie handed Carter her cell phone and after making plans with Carrie, Carter hung up and returned the phone to Julie.

"I guess I'll be coming to dinner at your house tonight," said Carter. "Carrie and I kind of had a fight, so maybe I can talk to her and hopefully she'll be in a more reasonable mood."

"What was she being unreasonable about Carter?" Julie asked lightly.

"I just told her I had heard about her snuggling with Detective Ames after I left Smokies the other night. I didn't appreciate her hanging around him, especially since she refused to ride home with me."

"Oh come on Carter. Carrie just found out Devlin Ames was Steven Barker. You remember him? You guys were in a lot of the same classes when he lived in Caradan and all of you were in Mom's afterschool tutoring program, right?"

"Right."

"Carrie and Dev were pretty good friends then and besides, Carrie was just telling Dev he needed to tell me and my Dad who he really was. I can't believe you don't trust her any better than that."

"Yeah, she gave me that line, but Rodriguez was there and apparently they were getting real friendly. I don't know why a big shot like him left Chicago to come to this little berg."

"Well, Carrie and Dev were always friendly and Rodriguez should be ashamed of himself and you should be ashamed of yourself, too. I thought women were supposed to be the ones who liked to gossip. You are lucky Carrie is even speaking to you."

"Hmmm. I don't know about that, but I could use some Chinese food. Guess I'm still invited?"

"Carrie invited you, but I suggest you try to do a little listening tonight instead of a lot of talking."

"I am off duty in about an hour, so I can come straight from work."

"Catch you later, Carter," said Julie.

Julie began walking out the door, then made a decision. She turned around and sprinted up the stairs and burst into the squad room completely catching Devlin off guard.

"Good grief. What's going on, Julie?"

"Sorry partner. Didn't mean to startle you, but I was wondering if you would like to have dinner at my house tonight?"

Devlin looked up at her and hesitated. "Ummm. That sounds great, but uh…hmmm, I thought we were going to go over the murder books."

"We still can. Let's take the books to my house and we can work on them after we have a few cartons of MSG from the Fortune Cookie. I hope you don't mind, but Carter and Carrie will join us for dinner and then they are going to a movie."

"That sounds terrific," said Dev, who was pleasantly surprised. He told Julie he would bring the murder books to her house in about an hour. "How about I pick up a bottle of wine for us all to share?"

"That would be nice," Julie said. "See you in about an hour."

Julie left the building and walked to her car with an extra spring in her step. She pulled out her cell phone and sent Carrie a voice message before she climbed into her car.

"Hey Carrie. I am picking up the Chinese for dinner and have invited Devlin Ames over. I hope it's okay with you. I will be home in about thirty minutes."

Her telephone buzzed and Julie checked her text messages. Carrie had sent a text telling Julie it was fine and she was on her way home too.

Julie couldn't explain the euphoric feeling she was experiencing. It had really been a super day. Well, except for her Father's change in behavior. Still, she was looking forward to the evening.

Devlin went into the vault where they kept the Murder Books and filled out the appropriate paperwork to remove them. He found a container and began packing the books for transport to Julie's house.

Mack stepped out of the elevator just as Dev entered the vault, barely missing him. He went toward the Chief's office.

"Hey there Cindy," he said. "Is Matt in?"

"Sure Mr. Bradley. Go right on in."

The Chief was sprawled behind his desk. He stood to shake his friend's hand and give him a hearty hug.

"How are you doing Buddy?"

"Okay, but I have some concerns about Devlin Ames," Mack said and explained the reason for his anxiety.

Matt nodded his head then said, "I think you are making a mountain out of a mole hill, Mack."

"I guess I could be a little overly concerned Matt, but I just think it's odd that all of these murders started when he came to Caradan."

The Chief scowled and then reassured his friend. "Detective Ames comes highly recommended and if he had anything to do with his family's deaths, the Chicago Police would not have given him such a glowing recommendation."

"I don't know," Mack insisted. "I remember Mimi telling me a story about one of the times Steven, or Devlin, was taken from his Mom. She said he had tried to burn down the house. It seems like quite a coincidence is all I'm saying."

"Well, let me look into the fire and his family's deaths and in the meantime, don't you say a word to anyone. Dev has been up front with me and has been doing a great job for us. Unless there is a good reason, I won't have rumors getting started in this department. Caradan is a small community and something that isn't true can ruin a person just as easily as a truth can."

"I understand what you're saying, but it worries me that Julie is working so closely with him."

"Nonsense. They are partners and I believe you are worrying about nothing. If I had any doubts I would pull him, but I believe Detective Ames is a truthful and capable person. However, I will check into the matter. You need to go home and try to relax. Better yet, let's go to Andy's and see what's on the dinner menu. How does that sound?"

"Best offer I have had in the last hour, partner. But, I thought you were going to investigate Steven. Darn it, Devlin."

"I will handle that first thing in the morning. I want to get my thoughts and questions together before I make the call to the Chicago Police Chief."

"Well, the good thing is Julie left me a text telling me she was eating at home tonight with Carrie and Carter, so I guess she will be okay."

"Good. Now stop worrying," said the Chief.

"That is hard for me to do Matt, but I'll try. Are you planning to order Andy's Prime Rib?"

"You bet," the Chief said as the two men walked out of the Chief's office. "Let's take the stairs, Mack. I'll see you tomorrow Cindy," the Chief smiled at his secretary. "I'm having dinner with my friend tonight and I'll be at Andy's if you need me."

"Yes sir," said the secretary, as she watched the Chief and Mr. Bradley walk down the worn hallway and take the exit door into the stairwell.

"Hey Detective Ames. Do you need some help with that box?"

"No thanks, Cindy. I can handle it. You have a good evening."

"You to Sir. Enjoy your evening Sir."

"I plan to," said Devlin. He found himself grinning with anticipation.

"Dinner with Julie and Carrie," Dev thought to himself, stepping into the elevator. "I don't know how I can be so lucky?"

26
THE DINNER

"I didn't know he was coming for dinner too," said Carter, slamming a bottle of wine on the counter. "Julie didn't share that information with me."

"Julie can invite whoever she wants to dinner Carter and you had better start getting happy, or you can just leave," a frustrated Carrie said, as she began taking down wine glasses. "You better be nice."

Julie, who had been changing her clothes, ran to the front door to answer the doorbell's interesting ring. Her Mom had purchased the doorbell as a housewarming gift. It played the music from Louis Armstrong's "What a Wonderful World". The little tune had always made her smile and lifted her spirits a bit. More so now than ever."

"Hey there Dev," she said opening the door. "Let me help you with those books."

"Thanks Julie," he said as he admired her outfit. She was dressed in white cut-off jean shorts, coupled with a sleeveless pastel turquoise top that showed off her slender figure. Silver studded turquoise earrings swung from her ears. She looked dazzling. "I really appreciate the invitation for a meal," Dev said, trying to concentrate on why he was there.

"No problem. Like I told you, Carrie and Carter are still going to have dinner with us, but they will be going to a movie later. We can work on the cases then."

"Working with you sounds like a lot more fun that sitting home by myself eating cold pizza and maybe between us we can catch a clue as to what is going on with these murders."

He followed her into the kitchen and Carrie hurried over and gave him a big hug.

"I'm so happy you talked to Julie," she said and then teasing him added. "I told Carter the big secret, so your life is now an open book."

Julie and Devlin were both aware of an awkward silence as they entered the room and Carter was less than friendly.

"Hey Dev and Julie. I brought some wine," he said.

"Me too," Dev said as he lifted a bottle of wine from the box of books he was carrying and handed it to Julie.

"Hmmph," Carter said. "What's in the box?"

"Just some books Julie and I are going to go over this evening. I keep thinking we are overlooking something in the recent murders in Caradan."

Carter walked over to the box and began to take a book out. Julie reached out and grabbed his arm.

"Sorry Carter, but those are not for everyone's eyes."

"Just detectives, right?" he sneered and shot Julie a look that would have reduced her to tears if she had not been such a confident individual.

"That's right," she said. "Just detectives."

"You can never have too much wine," Carrie said loudly, as she angrily grabbed the glasses, picked up a corkscrew, opened the wine and began pouring. "Perhaps we'll save the movie for another time, Carter," she said, obviously annoyed with his resentful attitude.

"Carrie, I didn't mean anything by what I said. I'm sorry. I'm sorry Julie."

"Don't worry about it," Julie said as she started opening cartons of Chinese and placing them on a lazy-susan in the center of the large raised table. Carrie pulled a kitchen drawer open and took out some silverware and napkins, which she placed on the table. Four, high backed lattice bar stools surrounded the square table and the acquaintances selected their seats and began passing the containers to one another. They ate their meal in silence.

"I wish Dad had joined us," Julie said, breaking the tension. "I don't understand why he was so angry. One minute he was laughing and glad to see us and the next minute he wanted us to leave. He was almost rude. I hate it when he gets in moods like that."

"Oh, I am sure he's just short-tempered 'cause he can't change what's happened. I know how much he misses your Mom," Carrie said.

"He really weirded out on us this afternoon. One minute everything was wonderful and the next, boom. He wanted us gone."

"I beg to differ with you, Julie. His problem was apparently with me. He wanted me gone...without you," said Dev.

"I know how he feels," Carter mumbled under his breath.

"Excuse me," said Carrie. "Did you say something?"

"Uh, not really."

"That's what I thought," Carrie said. "You really aren't wanting to go to the movies tonight are you Carter?"

"No. I mean yes. I do," said Carter and then turned to Julie. "I meant I know how your Dad feels. He is just going through a lot right now and you need to give him some space."

"I guess you're right. I wish I could talk to him, but when I called him a little while ago, he didn't answer the house phone. I left him a text on his cell phone telling him I was having dinner with you all, but he hasn't responded to my message. I hope I'll hear from him soon."

"I'm sure he will call," Carrie said. "Everything will be fine tomorrow. Especially when he figures out he upset you."

The doorbell rang and Carrie leapt up to open the door. She was surprised to find Tori looking in through the beveled glass window.

When she turned the handle and began to open the door, Tori pushed through and rushed past her.

"Is Julie home?" she asked. "I have some things Mimi loaned me to use in my classroom and I don't know what to do with them."

"Yeah. She is in the kitchen."

Tori turned and headed for the kitchen, with Carrie close behind.

"Hey Tori," Julie welcomed her, as Tori rushed into the kitchen. "What's up?"

"I have several items your Mom let me use in my classroom and I wanted to find out who to give them to."

"Oh Tori. Anything my Mom loaned you belongs to you now. I don't have any use for classroom stuff and anyway, she would have wanted you to have them."

"Thanks Julie. I appreciate it," Tori said as she looked around the table. "I had no idea you were having a party. Sorry to interrupt the festivities, but isn't this just like old times? Of course, I wasn't invited, as usual."

"Give it a rest Tori," Carter said. "Dev and Julie are working on their cases and Carrie and I are going to the movies after we finish eating. It's not like we are having a birthday party and didn't invite you."

"Like that has never happened? Oh well, forget it. I've been in a bad mood all day."

"Maybe you and Julie's Dad should get together," Dev added sarcastically. "He's in a negative frame of mind as well."

Tori just gave him a long stare.

"Would you like some Chinese, Tori? We have plenty," said Carrie

"Yeah. I'll have some. I haven't eaten all day and I am actually starving."

Tori accepted the additional chair from Carrie and as she sat down she glanced toward a scowling Carter. Ignoring the scowl, she helped herself to Chow Mein from a carton. Julie pushed some of the sweet and sour pork at her and they finished up the meal in nervous awkwardness. Dev tried to break some of the strain by asking Tori about her folks.

"Hey Tori. Did your parents ever indicate their relationship was in trouble?"

"No, they were fine. I was the one having trouble accepting their relationship."

"What do you mean?" asked Julie.

"I just couldn't believe my Mom had been seeing that man behind my back, and then actually had the nerve to tell me he had changed. The only thing that changed was I grew up."

"When did you find out they were seeing one another, Tori?" asked Carrie.

"About three weeks before they died. I had gone home to loan Mom my gun, so I guess it was a week or so after Carter's folks died," Tori answered as she took another quick look at Carter. "Mom didn't know where I kept my gun and she was worried about intruders, because of the Westins My Dad had just been released from prison and he was at the house and she told me then."

"I thought you were living in your parent's house," said Dev.

"Let me correct you. I was living in my Mother's house. It had not been my parent's house for a long time. I was living there, but when I ran into him and found out Mom was seeing him again, I packed a bag and moved in with Anna Bettis. When they died, I moved back into Mom's house because I really couldn't afford a place of my own.

"Wasn't that difficult?" asked Carrie.

"Not really. After I had the place cleaned up it wasn't too bad."

"When did you find out your parents were planning to get remarried?" asked Julie.

"My Mom called me the day before they died. She asked me to come by the house the next day to talk about it, so I did and that is when I found them. I still can't believe my Mom killed him. Or that she killed herself. It just doesn't make any sense to me."

"Did they have any visitors or mention anyone being around before their deaths?" asked Julie.

"No, there was no one," said Tori.

"Why are you asking these questions?" asked Carter. "What's going on?"

"We are beginning to think the recent murders may have all been connected," said Julie.

"You're saying my parents and Carter's parents deaths are related to the school massacre and Miss Garza?" Tori asked with a frown.

"No. I'm not saying anything. Just asking a few questions," said Julie.

"That's ridiculous," laughed Carter, gulping down his wine.

"What about you Carter? Were your parents having problems with anyone?" asked Dev.

"So now you think I am involved in my parents' deaths?" asked Carter.

He immediately became agitated and responded by telling Devlin the only person he knew of that had been hanging around his parents' house was Tori. All eyes zeroed in on Tori.

"Oh, he's still upset because his folks decided to change their will and donate everything to a charity. They didn't leave poor little old Carter a single penny."

"Would you know the name of the charity or when the Westins may have changed their will?" asked Dev.

"How should I know? Everything I've heard about the charity and Carter's folks I read in Carrie's newspaper article. I do recall my Mom also donated to the charity, but that's all I know. Maybe you should ask Carrie if you want more information," Tori said angrily grabbing her purse. "I didn't keep up with Carter's parents and I don't have a charity, so I don't know what he is talking about. You all just need to stop asking me these stupid questions."

"My parents told me you came to the house and had them fill out paperwork leaving everything they owned to a charity called The K-9 Club. I don't know how you are associated with this organization Tori, but I know you are involved," said Carter.

"Nonsense. You don't know what you are talking about Carter," she said. "Anyway, I need to get going. I just happened to be in the area and decided to drop off the items Mimi had let me use, so I'm outta here guys. Thanks again for letting me keep the stuff, Julie."

"No problem," Julie said. "Like I said. My Mom would have wanted you to have them."

"Tori, if you know anything about that charity you need to let us know because the Chief has decided to investigate the organization," said Dev.

"I told you. The only thing I know about the organization is my Mom made a donation to it. I haven't a clue why Carter wants to make such unfounded accusations against me, other than he doesn't like me and that's okay, because I don't like him either. Well, thanks for the food and I guess I'll head out. Catch you later," Tori said as she hurried from the kitchen and out the front door.

"Boy, she sure vamoosed in a hurry. That girl has more information than she is sharing," said Carter. "I know I saw her leaving my folks house the day they were killed and they told me Tori was the one they gave the paperwork to."

Julie and Carrie glanced at one another.

"Hey Carter. When did you find out your folks had donated their money to a charity?" asked Dev.

"A few days before they died. I went to their house to tell them I hadn't made the cut…again…for the Detective's test and there was little Miss Goody Two Shoes leaving in her car. I was livid when I found out what they had done," said Carter.

Carter was incensed and the friends were shocked at the animosity he displayed toward Tori.

"My parents said she had come by to verify paperwork and had them sign some documents. My Dad thought the charity was for abused animals, or something. My parents didn't have a lot of money and it bothers me that Tori convinced them to give their money to a bunch of stupid creatures," said Carter.

"We need to leave if we want to make our movie," Carrie said, uneasily touching his arm.

He seemed to become aware of his surroundings.

"Let's go, Carrie," he said, telling Julie and Dev so long.

"Bye, ya' all. We'll talk later, Julie," said Carrie as she and Carter left.

"Wow. That was interesting."

"Yeah. Well, I never have understood Carter. In fact, I don't know what Carrie sees in him. I think she can do a whole lot better," said Dev.

"Oh. Ummm. By the way. Carter thinks you are interested in Carrie," Julie smiled, as she wondered why in the world she had mentioned that.

"No. I'm not. Carrie has always been a special friend, but I can't imagine seeing her in any other way. She reminds me a lot of my sister. I repeat. She can do a lot better than Carter Westin, but it's none of my business anyway," he said as he brusquely stood up. "How about we clean up and start working on the murder books? We need to find one thing that connects these cases and that will be all she wrote. I'll start with the Roberts' case and you look through the Westin's."

"Yes, Sir. Your wish is my command, Sir."

"Sorry, didn't mean to come off sounding like I was ordering you around."

"Don't worry, Dev. I'm just teasing you. You'll have to get used to my sense of humor."

She gently reached out and stroked his chin. For a moment, he was lost in those beautiful gray eyes, and then she casually trailed her fingers down his shirt. Oh, the thoughts that were running through his mind when Julie softly whispered, "Hey Dev. What's that on your shirt?"

When he looked down, Julie chucked him on his nose. "Gotcha," she giggled.

"Oh, you are your Mother's daughter," he laughed as he grabbed her and pulled her close. For a moment all they could see was each other, and Julie was drowning in those glistening chocolate brown eyes.

Dev brought his lips close to hers and barely kissed her. A whisper soft butterfly touch that left her weak in the knees.

"Ohhh," she murmured. "I think you could be dangerous."

"If you only knew," he muttered under his breath as he gradually moved her away. "Let's get to work."

An hour later found them carefully reading and showing signs of frustration. Neither one of them had developed any new clues.

"Dev," said Julie. "Didn't Carter say Tori had come by to verify the paperwork and have his parents sign some documents a few days before they died?"

"Yeah. Carter said he went by to tell them he didn't pass the detectives exam and found out they signed away his inheritance to a bunch of animals."

"Right. And he also said earlier today that he saw Tori at his parent's house on the day they died. Something doesn't compute here."

"Tori acted like she didn't even know what Carter was talking about, but he sounded pretty sure she was the one who sold his parents on the charity. She also mentioned her Mother had made a contribution to the K-9 Club. We need to follow that lead."

"Let's talk to Carrie about her article, too. I know she was doing some research into the charity," said Julie.

"Okay. I'm not getting anywhere on the Westin's case other than they were killed by the same individual responsible for the Caradan Massacre and Cheryl's murder. Now Carter has added that Tori was there the day they died. I wonder why he didn't share that information before?" asked Dev.

"Also interesting," said Julie, as she flipped a page in the Westin Murder Book, "Carter said he found his parents dead when he went to the house on the day they were killed. Why wasn't he honest with us?"

"He probably forgot his story and he was obviously upset with Tori today. His lie just slipped out."

"But why?"

"Good question and we will probably need to reinterview him."

"Yeah and we still need to canvas the Westin's neighborhood again to see if anyone else saw Tori in the vicinity that day. This just gets more and more confusing," Julie said.

"A lot of times that's what happens. I haven't been able to make any headway on the Roberts' case either. Let's have a look at the other books, but before we start, let's take a quick break. Do you have anything to drink?" asked Dev.

"I have coffee, sweet tea, or you could have another glass of wine."

"I think a cup of hot coffee would be perfect and will help compensate for the glass of wine I had earlier with dinner. Maybe that is why I can't concentrate," Dev said, all the while thinking to himself. "Truth is I can't concentrate because I am sitting here with you Miss Julie."

"Oh. Do you have trouble holding your liquor Detective," Julie teased as she placed a coffee cup in the holder, popped a container into the Keurig and pressed the button. The delicious aroma of coffee, enhanced with Hazelnut, filled the kitchen. She asked Dev if he needed any cream or sugar and he declined.

"No, Ma'am and I don't have a problem with drinking. I'm just trying to keep my mind razor sharp," he said.

Later, while sipping the hot coffee Dev was scrutinizing Mimi's murder book, and Julie was examining Cheryl's.

"Hey," Dev said. "I remember your Mom teaching us that, "A mistake is an opportunity to learn". If we make a mistake, it's okay. Everyone makes mistakes, but it's okay. She would say…remember boys and girls, "A mistake is just an opportunity to learn"."

"Yeah, I remember," Julie snorted, closing her book. "I grew up on that one."

"Look here," he pointed to a line. "Billy Jones told Detective Ross that the intruder said something about mistakes and opportunities. How did this get by us?"

"I don't know but, well. Now we just need to tie it to, well something, and we will have a great clue."

"Hey, smarty pants. It is a clue. I think the killer may have been one of your Mom's former students and he attended Caradan Elementary. And look here. Maddie Todd said the killer kept telling Mrs. Bradley he loved her and she hurt his heart. We need to start looking at people who are, or have been associated with your Mom, the Counselor and the Principal."

"You're kidding. Right? You're talking about thousands of students."

"Not really. Just the ones who were associated with Mrs. Bradley, Miss Larson, and Miss Garza. Come on. Let's go over everything again."

"Well what about the children? I still don't see the connection there."

"I think you may have been right earlier, when you said your Mom always went the extra mile for her kids. You know, a sick mind could resent the children and the importance they played in her life. Besides, we are dealing with a nutcase here. Aren't we?"

"Listen Dev. I have a friend who is an FBI profiler and I shared some of this information with her. I didn't tell the Chief because he said he wasn't ready to bring the FBI in yet. My friend says the individual is most likely a male, in the neighborhood of thirty years old and probably lost a family member recently. She also thinks that the family member's death may have triggered feelings of inadequacy and the killer has decided to eliminate the individual who is responsible for his misery. In his mind this person doesn't deserve to live nor do those who were supportive of him or her. She said we need to be looking at someone who spent time with the Counselor, the Principal and the Teacher, and anyone else who may have been closely associated with children at the school.

"Okay," said Dev. "And of course the date. The 22nd of the month, is in some way significant to the killer. That means we will probably be looking at another murder soon."

Julie found herself staring at him. "I keep thinking about Carter and

Tori. They both lost their parents tragically, spent a lot of time with my Mom, saw Katie for counseling and of course, attended Caradan Elementary. They are excellent marksmen and could both fit the profile. Tori and Carter lost their parents on the 22nd of the month, so based on the significance of the date and our profile, that makes them potential suspects.

"True," said Dev. "And you can add me to that list."

"What?"

"I fit the profile as well, Julie. My parents and sister died on January 22nd.

"That's true," said Julie and her thoughtful frown did not do much to encourage Devlin.

They spent most of the night reviewing the murder books, but didn't come up with anything else that pointed them in any clear direction. Dev did bring up the witness who described the unidentified individual on Cheryl's street as driving a dark sporty vehicle, being slender and having longish hair. He suggested that in spite of her friend's profile, he believed the killer was probably a woman.

"I disagree," said Julie. "Many men, including you and Carter, could be seen as having longish hair and besides, the killer was a skilled marksman."

"I guess you're right and we shouldn't stereotype. As you have said, you are a crack shot as well and drive a sporty vehicle.

"Well. That's true, but for your information Carrie and Tori are also crack shots and drive sport cars."

"Okay. Sounds to me like we have some evidence to follow. Let's begin with Tori, Carter, and me. The three of us have a connection to all of the victims."

"Not all. You never met Tori's parents or Carter's and I don't believe for a moment that you are responsible, so I say we start with them first. It is just so hard for me to comprehend that Tori or Carter could have killed all of these people. Especially my Mom," Julie said, swallowing her tears. "My Mom was always there for them. Always." She closed her eyes and held her head between her hands and then unexpectedly felt gentle arms cautiously moving around her waist and pulling her close.

"Oh Julie. You know when this is over it won't bring her back. Whoever took her from you. Whoever hurt you. All I can say is I hope I have a few minutes alone with the killer when we catch him or her. And we will. We will get them."

Julie bumped her forehead against his and their eyes met. He leaned in and kissed her tenderly and then pressed harder. She responded and was surprised when he abruptly withdrew from the embrace, turning to pick up one of the books they had been working on.

Julie tentatively placed her hand on his arm and asked, "What's wrong Dev?"

"I want you to know I am really attracted to you, Julie, but you are my partner and I don't want to mess that up, or the new friendship we have found. Besides, we have our jobs to consider. We can't ignore the rule about fraternizing within the Department. We both know it is not allowed and I just think we need to take it slow," Dev said.

"Okay. Okay," she said.

The two detectives had made a little progress. It could be a man or a woman they were looking for. It could be Tori or Carter. They decided to call it a night and as Julie walked him to his custom, 1976 black Dodge Charger, they paused to enjoy the evening.

"I love this time of year," Julie said. "The air feels like it's tinged with silk and it caresses your every sense. Mom loved it when the stars came out and you heard the crickets and those sad little whippoorwills. God, I love Texas."

He watched as she closed her eyes, laid her head back, stretched her slender neck and took in a deep breath of the fresh night air.

"She is exquisite," he thought, as he reached out and pulled her to him. She laid her head on his shoulder. They stayed motionless for an instant, both of them enjoying the tranquility of the moment and realizing the enormity of their feelings.

"You are a fine-looking woman Julie Bradley," he said, gazing into her eyes. He quickly gave her a short, firm kiss then, rotating, sprinted to his fancy car.

"See ya manana," he called as he hopped into his vehicle.

"Night," Julie said, smiling and went inside to another glass of wine, her comfy bed and delightful dreams of big brown eyes, yummy lips and strong arms.

27
JULY 22, 2013

"Jerry. Come on, let's go for that walk now. It's such a beautiful evening," Laronda Steelman said. "I want to watch the sun go down and we'll miss it if we wait much longer."

"Give me a minute, sweetie. I just want to finish this page of the newspaper that I didn't get to this morning and I'll be ready to go," Jerry Steelman said, as he sat at his kitchen table engrossed in the morning newspaper, his reading glasses slipping on his nose.

"Push those glasses up Jerry. You look like a little old man."

"I am a little old man," he chuckled as he returned to his page.

Laronda smiled as she relaxed in her rocking chair and joyfully surveyed their den. Her eyes traveled to the substantial bookcases built on either side of the massive rock fireplace filled with a collection of arrowheads and family photos. How they had enjoyed searching, cleaning, and mounting every one of those arrowheads and Laronda loved their comfortable home. She appreciated the cowhide rug located in front of the hearth and admired the unique fireside set placed near the fireplace. The poker, broom, and bellows were nestled in a stand that had been crafted entirely of horseshoes and stars. Her favorite detail in the room was the mounted longhorn centered just above the mantel. She had hated it when Jerry first brought it home, but it had become a part of the family, as had so many of their keepsakes and souvenirs.

Laronda couldn't wait for next Saturday to get here, because her grandkids were visiting for the week. She lived for those visits and this time she and Jerry would be entertaining all eight of their grandchildren without their parents tagging along. As a Mother she loved having her children visit, but there was something special about having the sole responsibility of caring for her grandchildren. Their adorable Hannah, who had turned three in April; her delightful brother, five year old Holden and tiny two-month old Hadley Grace, the newest member of the family; would be arriving on Saturday. Shortly after their arrival would come talented fourteen-year old grandsons, Walker and Taylor; sweet ten-year old Heidi Rose and precocious seven-year old Ryan. She also knew this would probably be the last time their clever granddaughter Madison would be coming for the week long summer visits with her grandparents. Maddie had recently graduated from High School with honors, and would be heading off to college in the fall.

"Where had the time gone?" Laronda wondered. She and Jerry had taken such pleasure in their children and grandchildren. God had been good to them and she was so grateful.

The recent loss of her friends made her realize how special each and every day was. She popped up from her chair, looked at Jerry, and smiled.

"Well, you go on and read and I'll meet you on the high pasture. I want to get there in time to see the sunset. When you come, be sure to bring your power flashlight, 'cause it will be getting dark by the time we head back."

"Okay, hon," Jerry responded absentmindedly. "I'll be right behind you."

"Sure you will," she laughed and called to Cassie, her faithful chocolate lab. "Come here girl," she said.

She grabbed a light sweater and her boots and stepped out onto the wide veranda. Jerry liked to call it a deck and she guessed that was okay since he had put every board and nail into its construction, but it would always be a veranda to her. She took a moment to gaze at the beautiful tank that currently held five happy ducks, floating and quacking as they searched for fish.

"I remember once when Mimi came to visit and I called it the tank. She had no clue what I was talking about. I had to explain that it was a ranch term and tank was synonymous with pond. We had a good laugh over that," thought Laronda.

Her eyes glanced again at the tank, and the dock, where a paddle boat and rowboat were tied up.

She pictured her grandchildren on their last visit. She and Jerry had purchased the paddle boat and those kids had used it nonstop.

"Yes," she thought. "Those children didn't stop unless it was to grab a fishing pole or jump in for a swim."

The paddleboat had definitely been a good investment. She and Jerry had even taken it out for a spin themselves, thinking they might lose a little weight. They found their old knees didn't allow them to continue paddling for very long, so decided it was for the grandkids to enjoy..

Her eyes continued to peruse their spread as ten Black Angus calves romped around their mommas. They were so cute, but not nearly as cute as the newest addition to the Steelman family. Their Bethlehem donkey Louise had recently produced a precious little girl donkey. Their granddaughter, Heidi, had named her Misty. Unfortunately, the little donkey's father…a jack…named Jack, didn't seem too interested in his offspring. Fortunately their Roan Gelding, Bob, had stood guard over the small foal. Laronda caught sight of their other horses racing across the low pasture. It was a beautiful sight. Their tails and manes were flying as they galloped amidst the lovely summer wildflowers which has just begun adorning the hillside.

She pulled her wrap and boots on and stepped off the porch, called to Cassie, and headed toward a well-traveled path to the high pasture. Her faithful pet followed closely behind, periodically nuzzling Laronda's thigh when she stopped to admire the evening.

"What a gorgeous day this has been," she said. "It is just so great to be alive."

Laronda stopped here and there to glance at the horizon, enjoying the colorful hues enhancing the countryside. The Live Oaks had finished dropping their pollen and hopefully allergy season was at an end. Redbuds, which were her favorites, exhibited their interesting shaped leaves. Here and there she saw a sprinkling of Crepe Myrtle trees with blooms of purple, red, pink and white. Jerry had not wanted to plant the trees, but she had fought for them. He said they were messy and she said they were pretty.

"I guess pretty won," Laronda whispered. "It is just another day in paradise. Oh Mimi. That was one of your favorite sayings. It's amazing how often you find your way into my thoughts my friend."

She and Mimi had started out as contemporaries, but they had ended up great friends. Oh, there had been so many kiddoes, teachers, and administrators they had worked with over the years. Laronda knew theirs had been a job well done. They had connected almost immediately and she really did miss her friend. Truly, she missed all of the Three Musketeers. Even though Laronda had been retired for the last seven years, she and the girls had found time for lunch every month or so. It was still hard to believe they were gone, but Laronda knew she had been lucky to have known them.

Poor Julie Bradley. The wedding Mimi had talked about and wished for would come someday, but without Mimi's presence. Julie's children, if and when she had them, would never know their Grandmother.

She and Jerry had been blessed with three outstanding children. Two girls and a boy. Of course, their children were busy with work and families, so they didn't see them as often as they would have liked.

"Our kids just don't like to be around us," Jerry had complained to her.

"No. That's not so," Laronda argued. "They just have their own lives and although we are loved, we aren't the center of their universe anymore and we shouldn't be."

"Well, I guess it is good we like each other as much as we do," Jerry had said. "I don't know what I would do without my best girl around to keep me in line."

"He probably would have to pay someone to keep up with his glasses," Laronda said to herself.

She had to admit, she missed seeing the children and grandkids more often, too. She and Jerry were just an extension of their lives now and the kids were so busy they didn't have time to think about their parents or grandparents being lonely for them.

"We have been so blessed," she thought. "Jerry and I have worked hard to fill our lives…and we have such full lives. We shouldn't complain."

Suddenly, her reflections were interrupted by Cassie's frantic barking, and Laronda shushed her saying, "Quiet Cassie. There's nothing there. I don't see anything girl."

She bent down to pat Cassie on the head and give her a scratch behind her ears.

"You are such a good girl. Oh, just look at that gorgeous Apple Blossom Sky. All those pinks and lavenders blending into the clouds. There is just nothing as wonderful as a Texas sunset."

Cassie began pushing against Laronda's leg, emitting a low pitched whine, that immediately moved into a vicious growl.

"What has gotten into you girl. You are being silly," she said, turning as she heard the footsteps behind her. "Well, it's about time you got here," she said as she again chastised her dog for whining. "Stop it Cassie, it is only Jer-r-."

"I'm sorry. Have you been waiting for me Mrs. Steelman?" the black clad figure startled her. "Have you been enjoying your last sunset?"

"Who are you? What do you want?" Laronda asked, holding the growling Cassie by the collar. "This is private property."

"Oh, questions, questions. It has been awhile since I last talked to you, at least as one of your cases, but surely you recognize me. Well, I want the last thing you see to be my face."

With a flourish, the killer whipped the mask off. "Do you remember me now?"

Laronda Steelman struggled for breath as her dog leapt toward the killer and was promptly shot in the head.

"God. Why did you do that?" Laronda cried as she knelt down and gently touched her pet.

"Opportunities, opportunities. You should have been on my side. Not hers."

"I don't understand. What are you talking about? Whose side?"

"Don't act so innocent. You were always on the wonderful Mrs. Bradley's side. Do you think I didn't hear all the lies you told at her funeral?"

"You are ridiculous. I was always on your side and so was she."

"Now, now. Arguing is a big mistake and a waste of time. Let's take advantage of this opportunity to learn, Mrs. Steelman."

The killer raised the pistol, pointed it at her head and pulled the trigger. Bam. Just like that, it was over.

"What a wonderful sunset and what a wonderful end to her life," the maniac said, as he ran down the path, darted over the fence and hurried back to the waiting vehicle. The killer could cross Mrs. Steelman off his list. She really hadn't been that important, but ending her life allowed the killer's life to begin anew. Parents, Counselor, Principal, Mrs. Steelman…all gone…and of course, Mrs. Bradley, who made sure no one was ever there for the child. It was all her fault."

The killer quickly slipped into the car and drove away, thoughts of Laronda Steelman and her pet had already been forgotten. The villain's mind returned to yesterday's activities.

"What fun it had been to pretend to participate in their conversations last night. We shared a meal and I acted like I was their friend. They don't have a clue to my identity. Jeez, they don't even know if I am a man or a woman. Interesting. They are beginning to make connections about the parents," the killer said, heading home. "…very interesting."

Jerry Steelman was running up the hill as fast as his legs could propel him. He had stepped out on the deck when he heard the gunshots and began running toward Laronda's favorite place to watch the sunset. He knew something was wrong because Cassie hadn't responded to his call. He kept calling, but in the twilight he couldn't make out his wife or pet. He turned on the flashlight just as he stumbled over Cassie's body and then Laronda's. He leaned over his wife and checked for a pulse, even though he could see the hole in the middle of her brow. Cassie was next to her with an identical hole in her forehead.

"Oh no. Please Lord. Who could have done this?" he moaned. "No. No."

Jerry took a few minutes, then gathering himself pulled the cell phone out of his pocket and dialed 911.

"What is your emergency, Sir?" asked the dispatcher.

Jerry Steelman tried to keep his instructions clear as he explained that his wife had been shot.

"I am sending an ambulance, Sir," she said. "And the police are on their way. Sir? Are you all right, Sir?"

"No. I am not all right," Jerry said, as he cradled his wife of forty five years in his arms. Just send the police. Please, just send someone," he said.

28

ANGER

"Why didn't you give me a chance to defend myself?" demanded an irate Devlin Ames. "Or why didn't Mack say something to me?"

"Look Dev. I don't know why Mack didn't talk to you. He may be my best friend, but he is also a concerned citizen. He brought his concerns to the Chief of Police and as the Chief of Police I have to respond when a citizen makes an allegation against one of my detectives."

"But I told you that the Carrolton Police are positive arson was involved. I keep in close contact with the Carrolton Police Chief, who keeps me informed of what is going on and I have kept you informed," said Dev.

"Yes, you have. It's just there are a lot of coincidences here, Son. You said yourself you didn't believe in coincidence. There is your relationship to the Caradan Elementary School, the Bradley family, Miss Larson, Miss Garza, and the fact that their murders happened after your arrival in Caradan. Also significant is the fact that your family perished on the 222nd of January, which is a date we've determined is meaningful to our killer."

"I understand what you're saying Chief, but what else can I do to assure you that I have been up front with you since the day I came to Caradan?" asked Dev.

"It's not me you need to reassure, Detective. I told you, but you need to work up a timeline and locate people who can vouch for you on the days of the murders. That way I can answer any questions about you and we'll get this handled as soon as possible. I want to repeat, Dev. I believe you and that is why I'm not sticking you behind a desk. It's nothing personal. You are a valuable asset to this department, but you have to understand my situation. I just need to perform due diligence. Okay?"

Dev did not reply, but stood up and turned to leave, then said, "It doesn't make me feel very valuable, but yeah, I guess I know where you are coming from. I'll get that information for you as quickly as I can, Sir."

"Is everything okay?" the Chief's secretary asked as Devlin strode by her desk.

"Oh yeah Cindy. Everything is just hunky-dorry," he said, making his way to his desk and picking up the telephone.

Meanwhile at the Bradley residence, an upset Julie was fussing at her Father.

"Oh for Pete's sake, Dad," Julie's voice quivered, as she sat on the porch next to her Father. She had joined him for breakfast in the hope she could figure out why he had been in such a bad mood the day before. As they glided back and forth on the cedar swing she had given her parents for their twentieth wedding anniversary, he explained his call and visit to the Chief.

"I can't believe you went to the Chief about this."

"Well, who should I have gone to? You Missy? It appears you are suddenly enamored with Detective Devlin Ames, but let me tell you. I know a few things you don't know young lady."

"I understand what you are saying Daddy. It's just I don't believe it. Dev is not a killer. It doesn't jive with the person I've come to know. I think he is a decent person and he insists Mom had a lot to do with him having a good life. I'm so confused right now and I need to talk to him. I'm going to go, but I will see you for dinner tonight, okay?"

"Sure thing Julie, but you need to be careful. We don't know what we're dealing with here." He hugged her as she headed toward her car and called out. "Love you Goose. Stay safe."

"Love you too, Daddy," Julie said as she jumped into her Mustang. She sat for a moment, trying to calm the overwhelming thoughts entering her mind and was reminded of the day her Mom died. She had been unable to get in touch with Dev. Julie had tried calling him for over an hour because she needed to discuss some specifics from the Westin murders. He never answered his cell and no one seemed to know where he was, but he showed up at the school even before she got there. What had he been doing and where had he been? She couldn't believe he had anything to do with her Mom's death. He just couldn't. Julie realized she had let Devlin Ames get too close to her heart.

She needed some time to think and decided to talk to Carrie. Julie had an hour before she reported to work, so she started her car and headed back home. Raindrops from an unexpected light Spring shower began to gently fall.

She pulled up to the home she shared with Carrie and quickly tumbled out of the car. She raced up the sidewalk to the steps, trying to keep from getting wet. Carrie pulled the door open just as Julie reached out to turn the knob.

"You are just the person I want to talk to," she told a startled and slightly damp Julie. "Come on inside and take a look at some of my notes."

Julie walked into the kitchen, grabbed a diet soda, pulled a chair up to the table and sat down. She noticed the kitchen table was covered with papers. Ignoring the litter, she told Carrie her Dad suspected Dev was responsible for his family's deaths and maybe even the recent murders in Caradan.

"My Dad actually took his allegations to the Chief, Carrie, but I refuse to believe any of it," Julie said.

"I think your Father needs to remember what Devlin went through as a child. He has grown up into a great guy and besides, there's a soft, kind, gentle person inside the man and I agree with you, Julie. Devlin Ames couldn't be responsible for what happened to his family, or to your Mom, or anybody else. Not possible."

"I know, but I'm still a little bothered by the fact I wasn't able to contact him the day my Mom died, Carrie. Where was he? What was he doing?"

"I think you need to ask Dev, Julie. I'm sure he will have an acceptable answer."

"Right. What is all this stuff on the table?" she asked.

"I have been trying to put together a timeline of sorts. Our dinner conversation with Carter the other night has really been bothering me."

"Oh, I think I know what you are talking about. His story seems to have changed since Dev and I interviewed him," said Julie. "Dev and I agreed we need to question his story again, because of the inconsistencies."

"I started questioning his story about his folks being murdered by a robber when I found something in his closet."

"What's that?"

"Well, you remember there was only one item stolen in the robbery?"

"Yes. It was his parent's antique clock," said Julie. "I remember thinking that was really odd."

"What's odd is, I found the supposedly stolen antique clock in a box in his closet," said Carrie.

"What? Are you kidding me? When did you find it?"

"Honestly. I found it last night. I decided to spend the night at his house after the movie. I knew you and Dev would be working late and didn't want to disturb you. Anyway, I went to the closet to get a blanket from the top shelf because I was cold. You know I am so short and I couldn't reach the blanket. I needed something to stand on, so I looked around and found a box. I pulled out the box and checked inside."

"Why did you check inside?"

"I didn't want to step on something breakable. Surprise, surprise. There it was…in the box…the clock."

"What did Carter say about it?"

"Are you kidding? I didn't ask Carter anything because his stories have been so ambiguous lately. I just closed the box, put it exactly where I had found it and went to bed. I didn't sleep all night worrying about it. I left his house before he woke up, came home and started working on this timeline. You were already gone."

"I had breakfast with Dad. I wanted to talk to him about yesterday. Look, I'm heading for work and I think you should come along and share this information with the Chief. It is important to the case."

"Okay," Carrie said as she began gathering her papers. "There's another reason I know Dev is innocent. I've been doing some researching and I overheard you all talking about coincidences. I've found a few unexplained coincidences myself."

"Shame on you, Carrie. Listening in on private conversations. What are you? A reporter for the Caradan Eagle?"

"Ha. Very funny, but I am serious. I found some things that don't add up. Let's wait until we have Devlin and the Chief together to discuss it."

"Okay, let's go."

"Can we take your car? Mine has been acting up lately."

"Sure."

Julie was intrigued by Carrie's announcement and as they drove down Caradan's Main Street, then past the Elementary School, she was reminded what a tremendous slice of her life this place had been. It was recess time at summer school and Julie observed children playing on the swings at the back of the school. Some were chasing one another in a game of tag and others were sliding down the curved yellow slide as their teachers monitored their play. She heard their laughter and knew their thrill at just being alive and suddenly, searching for her Mother on the field, the pain came out of nowhere.

"Are you okay Julie," asked Carrie glancing at her friend.

"I don't understand Carrie. Will it ever go away?" asked Julie. "Will I ever be reminded of my Mom and not experience this overpowering ache? It's just not fair. How can someone just steal a life in such a cruel and immediate way?"

"Because they're sick or just plain crazy," said Carrie.

"That reminds me of some comments my Mom made when that mentally-ill kid killed everyone at that Elementary School last year," said Julie.

"I remember the authorities and the media tried for weeks to figure out what had caused that unhinged kid to do what he had done," said Carrie.

"Yeah. My Mom believed there was no way to explain what had happened, because we can't control insanity or envision how an unhealthy and fanatical mind functions. She thought the massacre could have occurred due to something as ludicrous as a young man and his Mother having dinner in a restaurant. A First Grade teacher could have stopped by to share news of her recent engagement and in the young man's mind, both Mother and Teacher ignored him. Maybe the kid and his Mom went home and argued. He decided to kill her because she had discounted him earlier and in his sick mind he wanted to kill the other person who had also snubbed him."

"So he goes to the First Grade Teacher's classroom and of course after that in his unbalanced mind, everyone is fair game. Right?" asked Carrie.

"Yup. My Mom also made the comment the young man had the opportunity, ability and access to vicious video games and guns. From there, a crazy mind can craft whatever thing it chooses...to justify killing," said Julie and found herself shivering as she thought of the similarities between that massacre and the Caradan Massacre.

"Here we are," said Carrie.

Julie glanced up as her friend parked her car in front of the Caradan Police Department. They both got out and marched into the building, hiked up the stairs to the Homicide Division and headed straight for the Chief's office. Julie noticed Dev's desk was empty and wasn't surprised when they knocked on her boss's door, entered the office and saw the Detective sitting opposite the Chief.

"Good Morning, Chief," she began. "Carrie has something she wants to share."

Julie shot a furtive glance at Devlin and was astonished to see that he was sitting in a relaxed fashion. He didn't seem to be concerned about the accusations against him. The Chief nodded his head, encouraging Carrie to state her case.

"I'd like to start by maintaining my belief in and support of Devlin Ames. I don't believe there is a chance in Hell that Detective Ames is responsible for any of the recent murders. I realize it's hard to comprehend, but I will prove it."

Surprising her, the Chief calmly replied, "Well, Miss James. I also believe that Detective Ames is innocent of Mack Bradley's allegations. You will be happy to know we have documentation that Dev was nowhere near his family's home the night of the fire," the Chief informed them. "He was actually on duty in another part of the city. In addition, the Carrollton Police have found a connection to a hoodlum who was targeting a local family and he apparently got the wrong house. He is the one who set the fire and they are searching for the perpetrator as we speak and an arrest is eminent."

The Chief continued saying, "Detective Ames has also been able to account for his time on the day of the Caradan Elementary murders. He was at the bank investigating financial transactions for the Westin family. He has witnesses who saw him there."

"Why didn't you answer your cell?" Julie asked.

"What?"

"When I tried to reach you the day of the massacre, you didn't answer your cell and no one knew where you were."

"Actually, I found out my cell was dead when I offered to call and tell your Father to go to the hospital where they took your Mom. I'd forgotten to charge it the night before and I guess I didn't tell Cindy I was going to the bank."

"How did you hear about the shootings at the school if your cell phone didn't work?"

"Uh, duh Julie," he said sarcastically. "The dispatcher radioed the information to me and told me to go to the school. If you had really wanted to get me you could have had them radio me. Why didn't you?"

"Oh. I guess I wasn't thinking," Julie said.

"The date the Ames family perished seems to have been just a coincidence, so I guess we have accept that coincidences sometimes do occur. I have made sure the investigation into allegations against Detective Ames are without merit and satisfactorily concluded," said the Chief.

"I never believed you had anything to do with that," said Carrie.

Dev got up, slowly walked toward Carrie, and gave her a hug.

"Thanks," he said. "Thanks for standing by me."

Carrie shot Julie a glance and Dev just smiled.

"I'm so sorry, Dev," Julie said. "I had no idea Dad had called Matt, but he was just so worried and I really never doubted you. In my heart I knew you could never hurt anyone. Certainly not my Mom."

"It's okay Julie. I understand, but I don't want your Dad to think badly of me for a minute longer. Could you call Mack immediately and let him know the results of the so called investigation?"

As the Chief eyed the couple, Julie asked if the Chief minded if she called her Father and he nodded toward his telephone. After informing him of the details, Mack asked her to please apologize to Dev and bring him home for dinner that night. Carrie was pacing back and forth when Chief Holden turned toward her and suggested she tell them what the pacing was all about. She turned to the Chief's white board.

29
THE TIMELINE

Carrie stood in front of the Chief's white board and began writing. When she finished, they were viewing a timeline that covered the last few months. She summoned her courage and shared how hard this had been for her because of her feelings for Carter, but she kept coming back to her data and found she had to be right. Her facts were based on information she had gathered from conversations with Carter, as well as his unpredictable behavior.

"He's angry most of the time and he is constantly questioning my conduct and trustworthiness," Carrie said. "Originally Carter said he went by his house on the day his parents were killed to tell them about failing the detective's exam. He found them dead and said the place had been ransacked. He thought an intruder had robbed them and killed them in the process. Then, when we had dinner the other night, his story changed.

"That's right, Carrie," said Dev. "He told us he saw Tori Roberts leaving his house the day his parents were killed and that is when the Westin's told him they had signed the charity paperwork over to Tori."

"He didn't mention Tori at all when we interviewed him right after he found his parent's bodies," said Julie. "It was odd, because Carter seemed so detached. I thought he was in shock, but we've learned he wasn't very close to his folks. Carter came and went as he pleased...often going days without ever seeing them."

"Yes, but when the four of us had dinner and I asked him when he found out that his parents had donated their money to charity, Carter said it was a few days before they died. Remember he told us he went to the house to tell them he hadn't made the cut again for the Detective's exam?" said Dev.

"Uh huh. Then he said there was little Miss Goody Two Shoes leaving in her car," said Julie.

"His story is just not consistent. He said his folks were already dead when he went to tell them about the results of the Detective exam. Remember? He mentioned they said some unkind things to him, but how could that be if they were already dead? And if he did see Tori like he told us he had, then she must have seen the killer or she killed the Westins," declared Carrie as she paced back and forth.

"Tell them about the clock," said Julie.

"Okay. As you know the only item stolen from the robbery was a priceless antique clock. Last night I found the clock when I was looking for a blanket. It was in a box in Carter's closet. I don't stay over very often because I hate being in the same house his parents died in. I knew Dev and Julie would be working late last night, so I went home with Carter after the movie."

The Chief shot a look at Dev and Julie.

"We were working on the murder books, Sir. To see if we had missed something," said Dev.

"He lied about the clock being stolen, because he took it. I have to ask myself, when did he take it and why did he say a robber took it?"

"I'm still hung up on the fact that he lived with his parents. That is kind of weird," said the Chief.

"Carter is a little different," said Julie.

"Aren't you all listening to me?" asked Carrie. "Don't you hear what I'm saying? I can't believe it, but I think Carter killed his parents."

"Now, let's not get carried away here," said the Chief. "We still don't have any concrete proof that he is the killer."

"Sure we do. Go check his closet because the clock was the only thing missing from the robbery," said Carrie.

"I have to agree with Carrie," said Dev. "We would never had suspected it was a robbery if Carter hadn't said the clock was missing. That piece of information led us to believe a robbery gone bad had taken place.

"The house was messed up, but nothing else of value was stolen," said Julie.

"Carrie could be right," said Dev. "Carter didn't say anything about seeing Tori at his parent's house during our interview with him. Looks like his story keeps changing."

"Exactly," said Carrie. "I realized that the other evening and then, there is his peculiar behavior lately," Carrie continued. "Here is another bit of information for you. I was not able to contact Carter all morning on the day of the school murders. I needed to purchase tickets to a concert in Austin and they were kind of pricey, so I wanted to be sure he could go. I ended up calling dispatch and they said he had taken a couple of hours off because he didn't feel good. I drove by his house to see if he needed anything and he wasn't there. Later, after the murders I asked him where he was that morning, when he was supposed to be at home sick. He just got mad and said he didn't know what I was talking about. These details had slipped my mind until I started putting this whole thing together."

"I do remember when I got to the school he showed up in the middle of everything and he asked for directions on where we needed him. Officer Westin appeared to be fine," said the Chief.

"Right." Carrie said. "I don't think he was sick at all."

"Well, that doesn't prove anything. I mean look at my suspicions toward Dev, because I didn't know what he was doing, or where he was. I have noticed Carter just hasn't responded to all these deaths in a normal manner, though," said Julie.

"That brings me to another thing that has bothered me about Carter. He mentioned on more than one occasion he had terrible memories of Caradan Elementary School. He hated going there. You know, it's like the thing that makes you care isn't there for Carter anymore. I have to wonder if it ever was or if he has been putting on a performance for me all this time," said Carrie.

"My Mom was always there for Carter. Did he ever say anything about my Mom?" asked Julie

"Not directly, but he knew how much Mimi meant to me. He made the comment once that no one had ever been there for him when he was younger, even though they knew his parents did not treat him well. He never got into specifics, but I think the Westins must have abused him when he was a child and even as an adult I know they certainly talked ugly to him."

"I remember Mom commenting on what awful parents they were," Julie added. "But, like I said, my Mom was always there for Carter and I thought he loved her. I just find it hard to believe he could have killed her, or anyone else for that matter."

"He did tell me he was sad your Mom was gone Julie and that it wasn't right the little kids had been shot, but it didn't ring true. He just seems so shallow and his comments have really troubled me."

"Carrie, there is something you don't know. We have verified that the gun used to kill the Westins is the same gun used in the massacre...in all the recent murders."

"Oh no," said Carrie.

"You are quite the detective," Chief Holden said, as he observed the timeline.

"I appreciate the compliment Sir, but I need to get to work. I just don't know how I can face Carter now, knowing what we do."

"Maybe it would be better if you keep your distance from Carter for a while," said Julie.

"Okay. That shouldn't be too hard. I haven't particularly wanted to be around him lately and I think he's figured that out. Can you keep me posted?"

"Sure, we'll keep you informed, Carrie."

After the reporter left, Chief Holden turned toward his detectives. "Want to add anything?" he asked.

"I'm thinking of what the jogger told us the night Cheryl Garza was killed. The individual he observed appeared to be just under six feet, had longish hair, was slender, and drove a dark sports car. That description fits Carter to a tee," Dev said.

"That's right. He has been told to cut his hair on more than one occasion," Julie said. "You know Chief, I have a friend who is an FBI profiler and I talked to her after Mom was killed. She gave me what she called a loose profile and Carter matches the profile of the serial killer we are looking for."

"Copy that information to me Julie. I know we are going to have to call the FBI in pretty soon. I also want you to get started checking Carter's background. You need to question him and find out what he was up to, particularly on the day his parents were killed and the day of the Caradan Elementary murders," stated the Chief. "I find it hard to believe that one of our own could be responsible for these atrocities, but based on the information Carrie James just gave us, we need to check."

"We might also need to talk to Tori Roberts and see if there was any connection between her parents and Carter. He has been extremely angry at Tori and anytime we see her or bring her name up he gets hostile," said Dev.

"By the way Chief, I also have a little information about the charity Carrie was referring to. It is called the K-9 Club and the CEO is a woman named Kandi. Just Kandi. No last name and her secretary says Miss K is tall, slender and very sweet, but demands loyalty from her staff. She is hard to get a hold of, but the office assistant said she would try to get us an appointment."

"I will take care of setting up an appointment with the mysterious Miss K," said the Chief.

"It's almost lunchtime at the Elementary School so how about I call and arrange a conference with Tori. We can bring her lunch," said Julie.

"I'll meet you at the elevator in a few minutes," Dev told her as he headed for the restroom. Julie arranged the meeting with Tori, ordered a pan pizza Supreme and when she met Dev by the elevator, suggested they take the stairs.

"Why?" he asked.

"Because I ordered pizza for lunch, so we need to walk off those calories when we can."

"We haven't eaten the calories yet," Dev said.

"I know, but if we walk the stairs I can enjoy eating an extra slice of pizza."

"That doesn't make sense to me," said Dev and nearly ran into Carter as they were exiting the stairwell. Julie and Dev bobbed their heads in acknowledgement and told him they were going to have to re-interview him about his parents' deaths.

"Why?"

"We just need to go over a few inconsistencies in your story."

"My story? Are you accusing me of something?"

"No, Carter. We just need to ask you a few questions. In fact, let's go into the interview room right now. It will only take a few minutes."

"All right. Hey Julie," Carter said. "I've been calling and texting Carrie and she isn't responding. Have you seen or talked to her today?"

Julie looked over her right shoulder and mumbled she thought Carrie was okay and hurried into the nearest interview room. Dev and Carter followed her.

"What's up with these two?" Carter thought as he sat down.

The detectives heard a sound like a duck quacking and realized it was coming from Carter's cell phone. He had set up his ring tone to quack whenever Carrie called. She didn't appreciate the humor, but Carter thought it was pretty funny. He had told her when he heard quack, quack, quack, he knew it was a text from her. Carrie's message was brief, but to the point. She told him she needed some time to think over their relationship. That brought a frown to Carter's face and scowling he brought his fist down on the table.. This caused his colleagues to look up in alarm. His instant rage-filled fury startled them.

"Carter?" asked Julie.

"What? What do you want from me?"

"We'd like to know a little more about that antique clock of your parents," said Dev.

"I told you. It was missing from my house. The robber must have taken it when he killed my folks. Look," Carter said, jumping up. "I have work to do and I don't think I like getting the third degree from you two. I'm done.

Carter walked out of the room and Julie said, "We are going to need to get a warrant to check his house and find that clock.."

"Yes. We were stupid. We shouldn't have questioned him about it before we had the warrant. Hopefully, he won't try to get rid of it. I am going to put through the paperwork for a warrant right now."

"Then we can go to the school. Maybe we can get some info from Tori."

30
DIFFERENT

The light Texas rain had touched the day and in the midday sunshine, everything looked fresh and new, like a large aquarium that was shining after a much needed cleaning.

"It's another day in paradise," Julie said. "When you have a day like today, I can't believe the world is not always a beautiful place, in spite of what we learned this morning in the Chief's office."

Dev had to agree and after stopping off for the pizza and drinks, they headed to Caradan Elementary School.

Julie knew Tori Roberts was teaching summer school and had called ahead and found it was almost time for the First Grade lunch break. She had asked the Principal to inform Tori that the Detectives would be bringing her a pizza for lunch and they would need to talk to her for a while. The interim principal told them she would make arrangements for Tori to be available.

When they arrived, Tori was waiting for them and led them into the conference room. She thanked them for bringing her lunch and opened the box containing the pizza.

"Yummy. My favorite. Supreme. What else do you all have in those containers?" she asked.

"We brought sweet teas all around," said Dev.

"Thanks. This is quite a surprise. Why are you all here? What do you want?" asked Tori.

"We just have a few questions for you," Dev told her as he helped himself to a slice. "Do you have a connection to the K-9 Club, Tori?"

"Connection? No, I don't have a connection. Like I told you at dinner the other night, my Mom donated some money to it once. That's all I know."

"You can't give us any other information about it?" asked Julie

"Well, my Mom said the proceeds went toward animals at the local Caradan Animal Shelter. The Charity pays for neutering of pets and stuff like that."

"What was your relationship toward Carter's parents?" asked Dev.

"There was no relationship. I don't even know Carter's folks. I'm not even sure I've ever met them."

"Did your parents know Carter?" asked Julie.

"Why would they know Carter?" Tori said with great distain as she toyed nervously with a stapler. "My Father was in prison and my Mother wouldn't have any reason to know Carter."

"Carrie has brought up some interesting questions and we are just trying to sort through them," Julie said. "Carter has also made the accusation that he observed you visiting his parents on the day they died."

"I know what he said and he's such a liar," Tori spoke with contempt, her voice carrying an unusual tone and her body language began to change. "Let's talk about parents. Carter keeps saying he didn't know my parents, when in fact, it was Carter I saw driving away from the house on the day I found my parents dead."

"Interesting. That's the first time you have indicated he was at your parent's house," said Julie.

"Why didn't you say something sooner?" said Dev.

"Because you idiots didn't ask me," Tori said.

"Excuse me?"

"Well, I could have told you anything you wanted to know, but you didn't ask ME."

"Tori," said Julie. "Tori, are you all right?"

Suddenly, Tori held her head in her hands and massaged her temples with her fingertips. She was swaying back and forth.

"I have one of my headaches," she said

"Have a slice, Tori," Carrie said. "If you put something in your stomach it might help with your headache."

Tori took a sip of her drink and nibbled on her pizza. She kept shaking her head and Dev asked again, "Are you all right?"

"It's Carter. It's Carter I saw at my Mom's house."

"Why do you think he would have been there, Tori?" Julie questioned her as she began closing the pizza carton.

"That's just it," Tori said. "I don't know. I don't know anything," she wailed as her body shook and she stood up. "I have to go."

"It's all right. Take it easy, Tori," said Dev.

"I just don't get why these headaches come on so fast, and why I don't remember things."

"What do you mean?"

"I have been blacking out and lose track of time. Sometimes, it's like

I've been asleep and wake up and two or three hours have disappeared and I don't know where they went. It scares me."

"I'm sorry, Tori," said Julie. "Have you seen a doctor?"

"Not yet, but I do have an appointment next week."

"That's good. We do appreciate your candor though, and how about we talk to you later.

"Yes. I need a few minutes before I pick up my kids," said Tori as she left the conference room.

"Was it me or were things a little off with that conversation?" asked Dev. "I don't know what is going on with Tori, but she didn't seem quite right."

Julie agreed and as she watched Tori leave the room, she felt something pulling at her memory bank, but just couldn't tug it out."

Tori turned at the end of the hallway and stared intently at the two detectives as they stood outside the conference room. Her unexpected glare would have surprised her friends and she continued to glower as she walked to the cafeteria.

"It's time for me to pick up my rug rats," she said.

Dev and Julie turned to thank the Interim Principal, Margaret Owen and she asked if they had a minute to talk to her.

"Sure," said Julie as they followed her back into her office.

"I have been going over some of Miss Garza's notes and I am concerned about a few of the notations regarding Tori Roberts."

"What kind of notations," asked Julie.

"Well, for one, Miss Roberts has been missing a lot of school. She calls in sick and has already used up all of her sick days. My biggest concern is she doesn't always call in. When you need to hire subs for the day, it makes things pretty dicey when a teacher doesn't let you know she won't be in. There are currently three write-ups in her file. Miss Garza had cited her for conflicts with parents and negative interaction with her students. One of the parents complained that during a conference, Miss Roberts was rude and made some off color comments. He said it was almost like the teacher was another person. Miss Roberts' colleagues told Miss Garza she was yelling at her students in a very unprofessional manner, again, almost like it was another person. Finally, the last write-up was for insubordination. Miss Garza stated that Tori had not sent in her lesson plans when she took leave for her parents deaths and when Cheryl asked about it, Tori was disrespectful and totally unconcerned."

"Have you noticed or heard anything about Miss Roberts' behavior since she began working for you?" asked Dev.

"Well, I haven't had much to do with her or any of the staff, what with Miss Garza's murder, and just trying to get everyone back on track. We waited a whole month to start summer school. She has taken off early a few times and we have had to scamper to cover her class. After reading her file, I did call her in to ask if everything was okay and she said she had been getting severe headaches and thought she had even blacked-out a few times. She has an appointment with her doctor next week."

"She mentioned headaches to us as well," said Julie.

"Thank you for the information, Mrs. Owen. You never know when a small clue can open a door," said Dev.

"You're welcome, Detective. I don't expect you to find out why Miss Roberts behavior is so erratic. That is my problem and hers. It's just that with everything that has happened lately, I have become hyper-alert because in my experience, when ordinary behavior becomes extraordinary there is a cause for concern. Since you were here to talk to Miss Roberts today, I decided to pass the information on to you. I am not sure why you came, but I want you to know Miss Garza did make another notation in the teacher's file. It stated she was extremely concerned about Miss Roberts, because her behavior was just so out of character for the person she had known for several years. Miss Roberts had always appeared to be very professional and her career was important to her."

"Thanks again, Mrs. Owen and if you don't mind we would like to do a walk-through of the school," said Dev.

"Of course I don't mind, Detective. Let's just get you some visitor's tags."

Boy, it hasn't changed much, has it?" commented Dev as he and Julie walked by the Counselor's office and headed toward the Second grade hallway.

"No," Julie said. "I still find it difficult to accept my Mom isn't here. It's hard to envision Caradan Elementary without her."

"Yeah, and I can't believe we have absolutely no real witnesses, considering how many people saw the perpetrator."

The two detectives left the school and returned to the Division office.

"I do think Carter is a viable suspect," said Julie as she poured over the Westin Murder Book.

"Yes, but I am thinking we need to consider Tori too," said Dev as he worked at the desk opposite of hers.

"My profiler friend said the killer was a man, Dev."

"Well, maybe she is wrong. I don't think we should eliminate anyone right now. It isn't like we have a long list of suspects."

Julie stood up and stretched.

"Man, I am tired. These cases just seem to be going nowhere and fast."

"Yeah. How about if we go to Andy's for some dinner?"

"Sounds good."

The couple drove to the cafe and ordered the special.

Suddenly, Dev and Julie's radios started going off at the same time.

"You're kidding," Julie cried, after calling in.

"We're on our way," said Dev turning off his radio.

They hurried out of the cafe and Dev slid behind the wheel as Julie hopped into the rider side of their unmarked car. Julie slammed the cherry on the roof of the car as they exited the parking lot and Dev quickly accelerated. They had been instructed to hasten to the Steelman Ranch immediately. There had been another murder.

31
ANOTHER VICTIM

Dev and Julie pulled up in front of the Steelman's home and parked amidst the multitude of official vehicles. They were met by a patrolman as they exited their car.

"The victim is up that trail, Sir. Ma'am," the young, mustached officer told them as he tipped his hat.

"Do we know who it is, Officer?" asked Julie.

"It was the lady who lives here, Ma'am. She was shot and the killer also got her dog."

"Good Lord," said Julie.

"Her dog?" asked Dev.

"Yes, Sir. The lady had her dog with her. It was a chocolate lab. A pretty animal. The dog is dead too."

"Just follow the lights, oh and detectives, here is a flashlight."

"Thanks, Officer."

The two detectives began hiking along the bushy trail, picking their way through the foot tall grass, a result of the recent rains.

"That kid couldn't be but five years younger than me," said Julie. "I don't know how I feel about him calling me Ma'am."

"Know what you mean. It makes you feel old somehow," said Dev.

They entered a clearing at the top of the hill and ducking a few low hanging tree branches followed a group of spot lights illuminating a large pasture. A sorrowful Jerry Steelman, Chief Holden, the Medical Examiner, Forensics Specialist and several police officers, were standing around the yellow caution tape that was tied to the trees that surrounded Mrs. Steelman's body and that of her pet. The Detectives overheard the Chief consulting with the M.E. as they approached.

"I would be willing to bet the bullets we recover from the victim and her dog will match the ballistics from our other victims," she was telling the

Chief.

"You are probably right, Doc. I think this lady's murder is most likely related to our Serial Killer. She was a friend to Mimi Bradley."

"What happened Chief?" asked Julie.

"The victim and her dog were coming up to this pasture to watch the sunset. According to her husband she makes the trip most evenings. When he heard the shots he ran up the trail and found them. Apparently, the killer had parked on the roadway, climbed the fence and came up behind her. It appears the victim and dog were shot immediately. The killer had already disappeared and Mr. Steelman said he didn't see anyone. It's all kind of preliminary right now, but that looks like what happened."

"Shouldn't he have heard a car leaving?" asked Dev.

"He says he didn't hear anything. I think he was so shook up he wouldn't have heard a tank if it pulled up next to him. I am pretty sure he's in shock right now," said the Chief.

"I can't believe this. Why would anyone want to kill Mrs. Steelman. I just talked with her the other day and she told me she's been retired for several years. So, I mean, she hasn't even worked around kids in a long time. What the heck is going on?" said Dev angrily.

"It looks more and more like our killer knew all of his victims and they were people from his or her past," said Julie.

"Except for the children," the Chief added. "They may have been shot because they represented something to the killer."

"What do you mean, Sir?" asked Julie.

"It's just an idea I'm forming. I think it is time to include the FBI in this. Julie, can you get me the name of your friend, the profiler? Perhaps we can bring her in since she is already familiar with the case," Chief Holden said. "I'd appreciate it if you get me her name and number and I will take it from there."

"Sure Chief."

"Detectives," said George Kwan, the Forensics Specialist, interrupting their conversation. "I haven't found much, but I did get the imprint off a running shoe. Looks like about a size eleven, so I think your perp is a man."

"Thanks for the information, but you know what? We still don't know if our killer is a man or a woman. I've known a lot of women who had big feet," said Dev.

He received scowls from the ladies in the group.

"I'll try to find out the style based on the sole as soon as I can and will let you know," said Dr. Kwan.

"The removal team is here Chief. It's time to take the deceased," said the Doc.

"Where? Where are you taking my wife?" asked Jerry, who had been standing off to the side and trying to ignore the commotion going on around his wife's body.

"To my lab, Sir."

"The Doc has to perform an autopsy, Mr. Steelman. We would also like to do one on your dog. We need to know what kind of bullets the killer used," said the Chief.

"Oh. Okay," Jerry whispered, appearing a little disoriented. "I guess I need to call my kids."

"Let us know if you need anything, or if we can do anything for you Mr. Steelman," Julie said.

"Thanks hon. I appreciate it, but there isn't much anyone can do for me right now, unless you can bring my Ronda back."

Dev, Julie, and the Chief watched Jerry Steelman stumble back down the path and suddenly Julie, grabbed her cell phone.

"What are you doing?" asked Dev.

"I am calling my Dad. Someone needs to be with Mr. Steelman right now and my Dad can come over and stay with him until his family gets here. Besides, Mom and Dad were friends with the Steelman's and my Father would want to be here.."

"That's a good idea Julie. It will help both of them," said the Chief as the trio turned and carefully made their way back down the path.

"Take the dog with you, Doc," said the Chief over his shoulder. "Let us know your findings as soon as possible."

"Yes Sir."

"One thing I don't understand, Chief," said Dev.

"What's that Detective?"

"How did the killer know when and where to find Mrs. Steelman?"

"Good question. We can add that to the long list of questions we have about this killer," said the Chief. "Let's get back to the office."

"It looks like Caradan will be having another funeral soon," said one of the officers as he observed the Detectives and the Chief walk down the path as a rumbling was heard overhead.

"Looks like a thunderstorm is blowing in. It is crazy what is going on. I don't get it and it's kind of scary. You don't know who will be next," said his partner.

"Yeah. It's unbelievable that a small city like Caradan can actually have a serial killer on the loose."

"That's why the Chief is taking such a special interest in these cases."

"Guess so. Well, those detectives have another month to try to catch the guy. The talk is the killer likes the 22nd to do his work. Hopefully they will be able to get him before there is another murder. Let's get those slickers out. We are going to need them tonight."

32

SUPER SLEUTHS

Driving home, the killer wondered irritably, "What is going on? It appears the super sleuths are onto something and it looks like perfect little Miss Carrie is at the bottom of it. I may have to change up my plan a bit. Good old Julie, everybody's buddy and of course, the daughter of my nemesis, was going to be my next target. I hadn't decided whether Carrie would make it to my list or not, but the way she's behaving, I am putting her at the top. It is clear she really doesn't care about me and was just pretending. Going through the motions just like all the others. I guess Carrie will be next, or perhaps I can take her and Julie out at the same time. After all, they do share a house."

"Yes," the destroyer said chuckling with delight. "I will begin putting my plan together immediately."

The sky had filled with murky clouds the color of dark steel, as the killer pulled into the driveway. It had been a gorgeous Texas day, but the nasty weather moving into the town somehow seemed a fitting end to the day.

While sitting in front of the large picture window, the assassin thought out loud, "My parent's home. It was never a home to me. It was just a house." Lifting a glass of red wine, slowly sipping and observing the gathering thunderstorm, lightning flashed on the horizon. The killer said, "This is what living in Texas is all about. A person can experience tremendous heat and three hours later, the temperature will drop by thirty degrees. The weather is much like me, a shape shifter. Indeed, I am the slayer, the exterminator, the eradicator. I am invincible."

All of a sudden the killer thought about Carrie.

"Too bad, as I had grown to like the girl," said the destroyer, getting up from the chair. "She had always treated me fairly and sometimes she really did seem to care about me. But, from what I have learned, she is getting too close to the truth."

The killer smiled a secret smile. Carrie appeared to be a better detective than those other imbeciles. The murderer slowly walked down the hall and into the bedroom. The bedroom that was filled with horrible memories and yet, the maniac had been unable to move into another room. Glancing from the bed to the closet…the closet that had been such a safe haven so many times long ago.

"Do it. I won't love you if you don't," the Father had said.

So the child did it, hating the Father. Quickly thrusting the memories aside and bending down to pull the uncomfortable boots off and slide into slippers, the killer walked to the closet and pulled out the black outfit and began stroking it.

"Come on. Try to do it right just once," the Father said.

So the child tried to make the Father happy, feeling frustrated and angry. Why couldn't he love me for who I was. I tried to be good. I tried to make him happy, but it was never enough. The killer remembered when it had gotten so bad. When it didn't seem right or fair. The closet was there for refuge. A sanctuary.

Pushing the daydreams aside, the killer recalled the information gained at last night's dinner with friends and thought briefly of the recently committed murder.

"How fortuitous I overheard Mrs. Steelman giving Cheryl Garza directions to her ranch when we were at Smokies. The lady shouldn't have shared so much information about where and when she liked to spend her evenings. It took me awhile to get there and locate her favorite spot. Thank goodness it was so close to the road. I spent hours trying to figure out her routine, but then it seemed too easy. I didn't get the charge I needed out of killing Mrs. Steelman. Perhaps tomorrow night is a good night for another new opportunity to kill. I won't wait to take care of my mistakes any longer. I would love to take both Carrie and Julie out at the same time, but I guess a little caution is wise. I will make a few calls and decide on my plan of attack."

33
ENEMIES

It had been a long day. There had not been any other leads on Mrs. Steelman's murder, but the Doc had informed them earlier that morning she would let them know as soon as she could about the bullets she had taken from both Mrs. Steelman and her pet. They wanted to know right away if the bullets were matches to their serial killer's gun. At least the Detectives knew there wouldn't be another murder for a few weeks. Of course, that would depend on the killer's time-table of the 22nd of the month staying the same.

That evening, Carrie, Julie and Dev found themselves at the Bradley home. Mack had invited everyone for dinner. It had been a welcome diversion and they looked forward to the opportunity to get away from it all. The anxiety of the investigation was beginning to take its toll on everyone.

"Carrie, I know Carter has been calling you. Wouldn't it be better to just talk to him?" asked Julie. "You don't have to see him, but maybe just make it clear you need some space."

"I don't know," Carrie murmured in her West Texas drawl. "My emotions are so jumbled. Hey, I am grateful to you and your Dad for inviting me to dinner tonight. It helps take my mind off everything."

"No problem and I appreciate your driving me to Dad's this evening. I was planning to ride with Dev, but he had some errands to run."

"What's wrong with your car?"

"I'm not sure, but it has been acting up lately. I guess I'll take it into the garage tomorrow," said Julie.

"Well, I hope it's nothing major," said Carrie who was dressed casually in blue denim cut-off jeans, a red Texas Tech t-shirt and red toe sandals. Her blonde ponytail was pulled back with a red tie.

The young women were standing in the Bradley living room enjoying a glass of sweet tea, while Mack and Dev were reclining in rocking chairs on the front porch, sharing memories and getting reacquainted.

"I am sorry about the misunderstanding Dev," said Mack, his green eyes squinting at the young man. "It's just I remembered Mimi telling me about a time when you were younger and your Mom had you sent away because she said you had tried to set the house on fire."

"I remember that time Mr. Bradley, but the truth is my Mom used to accuse me of lots of things if she got tired of me or if her friend did," said Dev, who had changed into some comfortable khaki shorts and a bright yellow polo before making the drive to the Bradley house. The yellow complimented his gleaming black hair and showed off his dark tan. His appearance had caught Julie's attention, as had the subtle musky scent of his aftershave when he hugged her and handed her the six-pack of beer he had brought.

"I feel real bad about going to Matt. I regret I didn't talk to you first," said Mack.

"Of course, I would have liked for you to have given me the benefit of the doubt and talked to me, but I guess we haven't had enough time to develop that kind of trust. I understand and actually, it turned out to be a good thing because I was able to put everyone's mind to rest. Especially hers," said Dev as he pointed his thumb over his shoulder toward the living room.

"Uh, yeah. Julie was awfully upset with me," Mack smiled as he observed the Texas thunderstorm sweeping across the horizon. "We sure have been getting a lot of rain this month and that is kind of unusual for this time of year."

"Well, at least the rain has kept it from getting so hot and we won't have to worry about having a fire ban like we did for the Fourth of July celebration a few weeks ago," said Dev.

"I can't believe July is almost over already. My Mimi loved the fireworks and I am kind of glad the town eliminated the celebrations. It would have been hard to celebrate anything this year. We always fired up the grill, brought out the hot dogs, hamburgers, watermelon, and homemade ice cream. We would sit here on the porch after pigging out and watch the fireworks in town. It was a perfect view and Julie used to get so excited. That girl still loves sparklers."

"I know what you mean. Fourth of July was special to my family too. My folks had a small cabin on a lake and they owned a catamaran. I remember Lyssy and I would take the sailboat out while my parents unpacked a picnic lunch. After a few turns around the lake we would bring it in, eat dinner and then we would make sure the boat was tied down to the dock. There was enough room for all four of us to stretch out and recline on the tarps of the boat. My folks on one side and my sister and I on the other. It was so special when we watched the fireworks explode over the water as the boat swayed gently. It was awesome and sometimes, when Lyssy was smaller, the soothing motion of the boat would rock her to sleep. What I remember most was when the show was over my Step-Mom and I would follow my Dad as he carried Lyssy up the path to the cabin. I felt like we were a family."

The men sat quietly, each briefly transported back in time to that place in the heart where happiness and heartache lived.

Julie looked relaxed and content in her navy blue knee pants and plaid sleeveless top, which she had tied at her slender waist with just a little bit of skin peeking out. She glanced out the living room window, viewed her Father and Dev's friendly demeanor and gave a tiny smile.

"I am so happy everything has turned out so well, Julie. You seem to have developed your own special soft spot for Detective Ames," Carrie said as she hugged her friend.

"Yeah," Julie said as she grinned and returned to the kitchen to complete the tossed salad that would go with the delicious Frito Casserole her Dad had prepared for dinner.

"What do you think Mommy would say?" she asked, turning her head as her friend walked into the kitchen.

"She'd say he is a good man and she would be thrilled," Carrie said.

"I miss her so much," Julie said as she began placing tostados, guacamole and salsa on a platter.

"Me too," said Carrie taking the platter from Julie and carrying it out to the porch.

Julie followed with four ice cold bottles of Lone Star beer. She and Carrie placed their treasures on the table of the outdoor lawn set and invited the men to have a seat and enjoy some appetizers while the casserole was heating. Devlin and Mack joined the women and after clicking their bottles in a salute, they all chowed down on the snacks.

"We had better eat fast," said Mack as he dipped a tortilla chip in the guacamole. "That storm is almost here."

"I can't believe how quickly it blew in." said Dev.

"That's Texas for you," said Mack.

"Whoops. You spoke too soon. I feel the raindrops," said Julie as they gathered up their food and raced into the house, slightly wet and laughing.

The men relaxed in the living room and Julie went to check on the casserole. Carrie followed her into the kitchen with the empty platter.

"I think it's ready Carrie. Would you call the men?"

"Sure," Carrie said as she yelled, "Come and git it boys."

"Well, I could have done that," Julie said.

The laughing men washed up then they all sat down to enjoy their meal in Mimi's comfortable country kitchen and as the storm began to rage outside, the quartet reminisced about Mimi.

Julie reminded her Dad of the time her Mother had walked in from grocery shopping, said hello to Julie and Mack, and then got upset when they started laughing at her.

"What?" Mimi had asked. "What are you laughing at?"

Mack had pointed to her sunglasses and asked if she had been to the grocery store looking like that. When Mimi examined the glasses she noted one of the lenses had fallen out. She put them back on and gave them a one eyed ogle, giggled and told them she had thought something was amiss.

"Daddy, there must be thousands of them," Julie said. She and Mack's riotous laughter made Carrie and Dev realize this was an inside joke.

"We were going snow skiing one winter and while driving across New Mexico, Mom didn't have her contacts in. She looked out at the desert and said, "Look at all the deer. There must be thousands of them," said Julie.

"The joke was she was looking at tumbleweeds. We had a lot of laughs at her expense, but she was such a good sport. I think she loved making us laugh," said Mack.

"Oh gosh," Carrie said. "Do you remember the time I spent the night and the bat got into the house?"

"A bat?" asked Dev in the midst of Julie and Mack's howling.

"Yeah, a bat had gotten into the house through the attic vent and somehow ended up in Julie's room. Mack had gone to get a net to catch it and Julie and I hid in her bathroom. I peeked out and there was Mimi covering her eyes with Julie's night mask," said Carrie.

She leered at us and said, "Do you see the bat?"

"Julie and I screamed just as Mack stepped in and snagged the bat with a net while it was sitting on her back," said Carrie.

"I thought Mimi was going to have a heart attack," said Mack, wiping his eyes.

They continued to share anecdotes from their Mimi memories and Dev was filled with such content. How great it would have been to be a part of this family, he thought.

Dev shared his story about the lunchbox fairy and Carrie told how Mimi was responsible for her being a journalist.

"I loved writing in spite of my dyslexia. She constantly encouraged me and always made me feel so special," Carrie said.

"You *were* special to her," said Julie.

"I think we all were. All the kids. I just can't comprehend why someone would want to take her life, or the lives of the people she loved," said Dev.

They continued to talk about the day's findings and suddenly, Julie considered her Dad for a moment.

"Daddy, do you remember Carter Westin when he was a little boy?" she asked.

"Yes. Sadly I do," Mack said. He sat back and thought for a few minutes and began telling them Carter's story.

"Your Mother believed Carter's Dad abused him physically, but she could never prove it. He was emotionally abused too, but there were no laws against that. Mimi thought there should be, because she always believed emotional abuse was worse than physical. She said we could see a person's physical wounds, knew how to treat the resulting damage and we could watch the injuries heal, but emotional abuse hurt the heart and you were never sure how deep the damage went. Carter was a small and frail kid, who was very quiet when he was little and no one could ever figure out what was going on in his head. He used to come stay with Mimi after school, but was still terribly aloof. She was never able to connect with him and Katie was always a little scared of him."

"That doesn't really sound like the Carter I know," said Carrie. "Well, unless you count the last few weeks."

"Mimi said as Carter grew older, he became kind of a bully. He had a small group that pretty much did whatever he told them to do. Sorry Carrie, but she didn't like him much."

"That's okay, Mack," Carrie said. "I'm not sure I like him much anymore either."

"We were all surprised when he went into law enforcement, but Mimi thought it was because he liked guns. It made her nervous, but then, same could be said for Julie," Mack said, trying to lighten the mood.

Everyone laughed, even though a bit uncomfortably and unexpectedly, the Bradley telephone rang.

"Hello, Bradley residence," Julie answered with the response she had used since she was a small child and was greeted with the dial tone.

"Who was it Goose?" Mack asked.

"Just a hang up. Guess it was a wrong number."

They were interrupted by Dev's radio going off. He checked the number and called the Division office.

"Hello, Detective Ames returning your call."

"Ames, this is the Doc. I wanted to let you know we got the ballistics back on the bullets used in the Steelman murder and you made a good call. They match the ballistics from our Serial Killer."

"Wow," Dev said. "Thanks, I'll let Julie know."

"Let me know what?" asked Julie.

Dev shared that the M.E. had confirmed that the ballistics from the Serial Killer's gun matched the ballistics from the gun that had killed Mrs. Steelman.

"Oh my gosh," said Julie. "I can't believe Carter could be the Serial Killer or that he could have killed his own parents."

"Are you saying he may have killed his parents?" said Mack.

"We haven't made it public yet Daddy, but the ballistics in the Westin murder matched the serial killer's weapon."

"It's hard enough to believe he would kill Mimi, but his folks? That is just plain crazy."

"It's all crazy," said Carrie. "I think the hardest thing for me to understand isn't just killing adults, but the kids. The killer had to be willing to murder those innocent little kids. That makes no sense at all. They never did anything to anyone."

"Well, the weather is letting up a bit," Julie pronounced quietly. Carrie's cell phone chirped with an incoming text. She took a moment to check the caller and saw it was Carter.

"Where are you, Carrie? I want to see you tonight," he had texted.

She decided to take Julie's advice and sent him a response, texting she was at the Bradley's house and was getting ready to go home and that Julie would be spending the night with her Father. She was tired and wanted to be alone. She would talk to him later.

Carrie's cell phone buzzed again and she looked at a message from Tori, who wanted to know if Carrie would like to go to a movie with her. Carrie texted her back and said she was going home and was planning to spend the evening alone. Maybe they could take in a movie another time.

The Bradley telephone rang and Julie answered, again saying, "Bradley residence."

"Hey Julie, this is Tori. I am kind of lonely tonight and was wondering if you wanted to go to a movie with me," she said.

"Oh, Tori. I appreciate the invitation, but I am at my Dad's house and I don't think I could make it there in time. Besides, I am probably going to take it easy tonight. We can talk for a while if you like," said Julie.

"No, that's okay. Don't worry about it. I guess I'll call the Coach and see what he is doing. I'm sorry I bothered you," said Tori.

"You didn't bother me and I want you to call me back if you want to talk. Okay?"

"Sure." Tori said.

"Wow. I haven't ever heard so many telephones ringing and buzzing," said Mack.

"I agree," said Julie. "Tori must really be down in the dumps, because she doesn't usually want to spend time with me. I know she and Carrie are good friends, but we have never really clicked."

"Maybe it's because she lost her Mom and you lost your Mom," said Carrie. "Tori really isn't a bad person, just a little different."

"Well, has everyone got their plans made for the rest of the evening?" asked Mack.

"Yes Sir, Mr. Bradley. I plan to help you clean up and then I need to be heading home. You're staying here tonight, right Julie?" said Carrie.

"No. I think I'm coming home. I have some laundry I need to get done tonight and besides, I need to take my car into the shop tomorrow."

"We have a washer and dryer here, Goose."

"I know Daddy," Julie said as she pulled Mack aside. "If it's okay with you I think I'll go home. I feel like Carrie needs me right now. You understand, don't you?"

"Sure hon. I know how hard this is for Carrie. Your Mom thought Carrie and Carter might get together one day, permanently. Can't say it pleased her too much," he said turning to Carrie. "You girls go on ahead and I can clean up. Besides, Dev and I are going to do a little more catching up."

"I thought I'd take you up on that offer to stay the night Mack, if it is still open," said Dev.

"You bet," Mack said and hugging both girls, told them how much he had enjoyed the evening and reminded Carrie how much she was loved by both he and Mimi and how she was always welcome. Telling them to stay safe he went into the kitchen to clean up.

Dev walked them to Carrie's car and after giving her a hug good night, he turned to Julie and pulled her close, kissing her lightly on the forehead, then her nose and finally, her lips.

She felt it all the way to her toes. He helped her into the car and told them good night as he headed back to the house. Julie turned sparkling eyes toward Carrie and her heart dropped. There were tears in her best friend's eyes.

"Oh Carrie? I am so sorry."

"It's okay, but I think my relationship with Carter is over and I think you may need to start worrying about being a detective," Carrie said.

"What are you talking about?" asked Julie.

"Doesn't the police force have some kind of rule about fraternizing with co-workers?"

"Oh," Julie frowned as Carrie started the car and began the drive home.

34
NEXT VICTIM

The intruder was once again dressed in the all black outfit and used the lock-pick to gain entrance into Julie and Carrie's house. Quickly turning off the alarm and sauntering into the kitchen the killer said, "Thank you Miss Carrie, for sharing your alarm pass code with me."

After making a few phone calls, the perpetrator had found out Julie was at her parent's home and that Carrie would be alone tonight. As much as the assassin would like to eliminate them both at the same time, this would probably work better. No mistakes, just opportunities.

The killer had spent a few hours at home that evening carefully planning Carrie's demise. Suddenly, the intruder became aware of muddy footprints on the kitchen tile. Looking in a drawer, pulling out a kitchen towel and rubbing the mud off black Reebok soles, the perpetrator retraced steps back into the living room. The intruder cleaned up, tossed the towel into the laundry area, and then began searching for the telephone junction box, which was fortunately located just inside the back door. After unplugging the telephone line, the intruder walked to the window that overlooked the kitchen sink, took out the 9mm Glock, checked the cartridge and observed the night sky.

The rainstorm had moved through town much quicker than the villain had anticipated and fortunately caught sight of Carrie's car as it was driving up the hill to her house. Immediately dousing the lights and scrambling for a hiding place, the killer barely had time to move to the area behind the kitchen door before hearing the garage door going up.

"Crap! I forgot to turn the alarm system back on. Ah, it's too late," the intruder said. "She is too early. It's too soon. She's ruining everything. I am not ready for her surprise," the killer said angrily.

Carrie pulled the car into the garage and parked next to Julie's Mustang. and pushed the button to close the garage door. The girls rolled out of the sports car and walked into the house.

"I'll disarm the alarm," said Julie laughingly as they walked into the entry way.

"You are such a comedian," said Carrie as she made her way into the kitchen while Julie expressed surprise that the alarm wasn't engaged.

"Hey Carrie. How come you didn't set the alarm?" she asked.

Carrie didn't respond to Julie's call, so she called out again. "Carrie, did you hear me?"

When Julie still didn't get a response from Carrie, she felt the hair on the nape of her neck begin to tingle. She carefully moved to her purse which was located on the entry table and slowly pulled her service revolver out. She thought she had heard something, but all was quiet now. Julie called out to Carrie once more and then once again. Still. No reply. Her heart was beating a staccato pattern in her breast and she hesitated by the kitchen.

"Where would Carrie have gone when we first came in?" she asked herself.

She tried to sense her roommate's routine. Okay, she thought, she usually goes straight to the kitchen. Julie continued to wait soundlessly by the kitchen entrance. She decided she couldn't wait any longer and realized the kitchen light hadn't been turned on. Julie cautiously reached around the corner and flipped it on. A black shadow stood over Carrie's supine body, pointing a gun toward her friend's head.

"Freeze. Police. Drop the weapon," yelled Julie as the intruder swung the gun up and leveled it in her direction.

The shadow fired as Julie ducked, missing her by a hair.

She returned fire and the intruder spun around and raced for the back door. The shooter was gone before she could fire again. She ran to Carrie and took her pulse. After checking the gash on the back of her friend's head, she tried to call 911. The phone line had been unplugged, so she searched her pocket for her cell phone to call for backup and an ambulance.

The intruder ran the two blocks to a parked vehicle, cradling a slightly wounded right arm.

"No, No, No. She was supposed to be alone. Liar. Liar. Liar. I didn't expect both of them and they came too soon. I thought I had another hour to prepare. She was supposed to be alone. No, No, No. It wasn't supposed to happen this way."

The killer was pounding away at the steering wheel and rocking back and forth. After a few minutes, the rocking slowed and the figure took a cleansing breath, creating a calming effect.

"All right. It's okay. No harm done. I'll just have to plan better next time. I'm still the one in charge."

Starting the ignition and moving the car forward, the shadow watched as police cars and an ambulance raced by and then smirked.

"It's okay. I'm good, but they weren't supposed to be together. If I had known, I could have taken them both out tonight. They are all against me. They are liars. Julie was supposed to be at her Dad's tonight and they ruined everything. They can't be trusted and that's why it's my job to kill them," the nutcase said furiously and began the drive home.

Dev had received the call about the intruder and Carrie's injury, so he and Mack headed to the hospital. In the meantime, Julie rode in the ambulance with Carrie and used her cell phone to call and talk briefly with the Chief, who was also on his way to meet them at the hospital. Detectives Ross and Cortinas had been assigned to the case and stayed with the Forensics Specialist at the girls' house to gather evidence.

"What is going on, Julie?" asked Mack as he and Dev walked into the hospital room.

"The killer was inside our house when we got home," said Julie.

"My God," said Mack.

"How is Carrie?" asked Dev.

"I don't know. They just came and took her to x-ray," said Julie. "She has been unconscious since the attack and I guess the doctor will determine the extent of the damage."

"Is she going to be okay?" asked the Chief as he joined the group.

"She has to be," said Julie.

"I can't believe I am so stupid," said Dev. "We have a serial killer knocking off people Mrs. Bradley loved and we didn't even think about her connection to Carrie."

"Or to Julie," Mack said. "We need to think about Julie, too."

The friends spent the next hour waiting for the doctor and finally he met them in the waiting area and told them Carrie was being moved to ICU because she had not yet regained consciousness. She had received several stitches and had sustained a severe concussion. The x-ray showed she had been hit with a heavy object, possibly the butt of a gun, that caused a blunt force trauma. The doctor had scheduled their friend for an MRI first thing in the morning in order to determine the severity of the injury.

"You may visit her briefly, two at a time and you can stay in the family waiting room," said the Doctor. "However, right now she is unconscious and cannot tell you anything and she really needs to rest."

Mack and Dev went in first to check on her.

"I can't imagine losing her too," said Mack.

"Me either," said Dev. "I just found my friend again."

Dev and Mack returned to the waiting room and Julie took her turn.

"Oh Carrie. You have to be okay," she sobbed as she held her hand. "I don't think my heart can take losing you too."

After a few minutes, a nurse told Julie she needed to leave and so she went back to the family waiting room. Mack, the Chief, Dev and Julie spent the next several hours drinking bad coffee from the vending machine and worrying.

Detectives Ross and Cortinas came by to let them know they found blood in the backyard and there were footprints in the mud. They shared that the Dr. Kwan said they were size elevens and matched the print found near Laronda Steelman's body.

"I'm sure I shot him in the upper body," said Julie. "It could be his shoulder or his arm."

"You're right, we did find blood. The perp is starting to make mistakes," said Rosie Cortinas. "It's just a matter of time before we catch him."

"If it is a him," said Detective Ross.

The next morning, just as the sun began rising, the Doctor talked to them saying Carrie had awakened for a short time and had been moved to a regular hospital room. Her Doctor believed the fact that she woke up and said a few words meant she should have a full recovery, in addition to a splitting headache.

Once Carrie had been moved to a new room, her visitors were all allowed to join her. She had been sedated and was asleep, but Julie was able to hold her hand.

Suddenly, there was a hullabaloo in the hallway and the hospital door burst open, allowing a disheveled Carter Westin into the room. A small, compact nurse with a whip thin body, angrily followed closely behind.

"I'm sorry. I told this young man this was off limits, but he says he knows the young lady," said the nurse, apologizing for the intrusion.

"It's okay, Ma'am," said the Chief as he turned to Carter and the compassion was automatic. The young man's eyes were bloodshot red and his hair stood on end. His sallow skin featured blue tinged pads under his eyes. He had obviously been drinking and he wildly lurched toward Julie.

"Why didn't any of you call me? I had to hear about this from Rodriguez," he yelled. "Carrie. Oh. My God, Carrie. Honey. Come on. Look at me. Oh, Babe. Oh, Babe. What happened?" he bellowed. "Who did this to her?"

All eyes were glued to Carter and Julie finally walked over and put her arms around him. She explained what had happened and said she thought they had surprised an intruder in the process of prepping the house for their arrival. Julie informed him she had taken a shot at the killer and was certain he had been hit. They found blood in the backyard and though the intruder got away, they got enough blood to test for DNA to see if he was in the system. Unfortunately, it would take a while to get the results, but the shooter had also discharged his weapon at her and although he missed, he did leave a bullet and shell casing behind. Detective Ross had begun the process of running it through AEFIS. She kept hugging him and telling him how sorry she was and he just limply stood there.

Finally, Carter slowly pulled away from her and said, "Rodriguez told me every was saying I was the murderer. I tried to get Carrie to meet with me, but she wouldn't, so I started drinking. Then Rodriguez called me to say Carrie had been hurt and was in the hospital, so I came right away."

"She's going to be okay, son. She just got a bump on the head and as soon as she wakes up, you'll be here for her," the Chief told Carter and then looked to his detectives and nodded toward the hallway.

They stepped into the outside hallway and Julie whispered intensely, "It can't be Carter. The person that stood in my kitchen was totally put together and in control. Carter could not have messed himself up so much in such a short time, unless he is one heck of an actor and besides, I pressed his arms and chest hard when I hugged him and I don't think he was wounded."

Mack joined them in the hallway saying he was going to head home. It looked like Carrie had plenty of people hanging around and he asked them to call him if she woke up.

"Good night everyone," said Mack.

"Good night Daddy," said Julie.

"See you later," said the Chief as Mack waved his good bye.

The Chief then regarded them and quietly spoke. "I have a thought," he said.

35
THE MISTAKE

The two detectives and the Chief quickly exited the patrol car and hurried to the Division. They entered the Chief's office and he walked to the whiteboard that still contained Carrie's timeline. Pointing to the board he said, "I know you thought I didn't put much credence in Carrie's detective work, but stay with me for a minute. Look at these notes. Who, besides Carter would fit this profile?" He was directing his gaze toward Dev and Julie.

Julie shook her head for a moment and then murmured, "Tori Roberts."

"Exactly," said the Chief. "She knew Carter's parents and there was money involved."

"She wasn't happy with her parent's decision to remarry," said Dev. "And she had a history with Mimi and the other murdered victims."

"She is 5'10" tall, has longish hair, is slender and drives a dark blue sports car," said Julie. "So she matches the murderer's profile."

"You all may have freaked her out when you went to the school and started questioning her," said the Chief.

"That's right," said Dev. "We told Tori that Carrie had brought up some interesting questions and we were just trying to sort through them."

Julie said, "Oh my gosh. Tori was so nervous and hey Dev, remember the interim principal telling us how inconsistent Tori's behavior has become lately? She said Tori had practically developed into a different personality."

"I'm afraid by mentioning Carrie's questions we may have pushed her to move up her killing timeline and she didn't wait for the 22nd," said Dev.

"I don't want to believe it, but that is definitely a possibility," said Julie.

The Chief suggested they pay Miss Roberts a visit and see how she was feeling. Dev and Julie headed for their unmarked vehicle. He hopped behind the wheel and they began the journey to Tori's house.

It was early morning, the sun was just peeking over the rise and the streets were quiet. They passed under a colorful banner that was stretched across the street. It advertised to the public that the local Goat Cook-Off would be taking place at Caradan's Public Park.

Once, these things had been important to Julie, but they had lost all meaning since her Mother's death. The 4th of July was over. There was a time when she used to get excited about the fireworks and picnics, because the holiday had been her Momma's favorite. It had passed unnoticed this year.

Julie felt the tears gathering behind her eyes as they passed the park. She had so many memories. "Swing me higher Momma. I'm going to the moon. Look at me Momma, I'm a monkey. Can you catch me Momma?" Pictures of the woman and child tumbling in the leaves and then a flash to the woman and adult child on their last visit to the park. It had been Christmas and Julie had observed the wonder of the lights, hot chocolate, and her Mother's beautiful laughter, as they moved through a tunnel of shimmering, glittering lights.

"Oh, Momma."

Julie hadn't realized she had voiced her thoughts. Dev stopped the car and placed his hand around the back of her neck.

"Julie?" he questioned.

She burst into tears and kept wailing, "Why? Why? Why?"

Dev took her into his arms and held her gently.

"Oh, Baby," he squeezed her. "Oh, Babe."

Julie took a few gulps of air and then carefully pushed him back. "I'm okay. I'm sorry."

"No, You're not okay. You needed to let it out a long time ago. I know how hard this is for you and you may not see my tears, but Sugar, I'm crying right along with you."

Julie wiped her eyes and borrowed Dev's hanky and after a few sniffles, she told him to head for Tori's place. He slowly turned the key in the ignition and judiciously pulled onto the road, pointing the car toward the Roberts' home.

Mimi had shared with Julie that she could never understand why Tori's Mom would continue to stay in the same house all this time, considering the unhappy memories connected with Tori's early years. Of course, she was extremely surprised when Tori decided to stay in her family home after her parents' deaths. It did seem strange to Julie, but then, Tori had always seemed a little strange.

"I am so angry, Dev. I can't believe we are going to talk to the woman who may have killed my mother. The woman my Momma spent her whole life trying to help. It's not right."

"I know, Julie. Can you handle this?" he asked.

"Of course," she said. "I know everyone was surprised the Chief let me stay on this case because of my Mom, but I am okay. I am a detective. A darn good detective."

"Yes. You are."

Dev pulled into Tori's driveway and they stepped out of the vehicle, both unhooking the snaps on their holsters.

"This is so surreal," Julie said. "I've known Tori most of my life. I just can't believe she could be responsible for these killings. I thought she loved my Mom."

"Take is easy, Julie. Let's see if she will talk to us, but let's be prepared, just in case. Tell me again you are okay?"

"I'm okay. I'm okay."

Dev rang the doorbell and they heard the chimes from deep within the house. He rang it again and the sounds of shuffling and grumbling came to them.

"Okay. Okay. Hold on," Tori yelled and suddenly the door was thrown open. "What do you want at this hour?" She was dressed in her pajamas and had quickly pulled a robe on. Rubbing at her eyes, she stood back from the door and told them to come in.

Julie and Dev motioned for her to go ahead and they followed her into the living room. Tori reclined on an overstuffed chair and stared at them. Devlin and Julie took seats on the sofa opposite her.

"Why do you have your hands on your guns?" she asked casually. "Are you afraid of me?"

Julie was looking her over and quickly stood up and asked Tori to stand and take her robe off. The woman huffed a little, but then complied. She didn't have a mark on her arms. Dev asked her if she was willing to go into the other room to let Julie check her out without her clothing on.

"I don't think she likes me like that, Devlin," she cackled. "What is going on? This sounds kind of kinky."

"They obviously hadn't thought this through," Julie said to herself. "It was better not to be in a room alone with Tori and Tori's behavior seemed a little odd."

"Tori," Julie said smoothly. "I need to see if you have any injuries on you. How about if I just frisk you? Will you to let me frisk you?"

"Whatever floats your boat," Tori said and put her arms over her head and beckoned to Julie. "You know, it might be more pleasant for Devlin to do the deed."

"Why are you acting so strange, Tori?"

"Tori? Tori?" she shook her head and said, "I'm sorry. I have another of my headaches. What do you want. I'm tired."

Julie glanced at Dev as she began a quick pat down of Tori's body. She didn't appear to have any injuries and other than her unusual behavior, physically seemed to be fine. Julie casually asked Tori what she had done earlier that evening. She gazed at them, her body shuddered a bit and shaking her head, Tori focused on Julie.

"What did I do?" she asked. "I had dinner with Coach at Andy's and then we went over to the Caradan Theater and caught a movie. He bought me popcorn and brought me home around eleven o'clock. Why?"

"What was showing at the theater Tori?" asked Dev.

"Ummm…Zero Dark Thirty or Forty, or something like that," she said. "I didn't particularly like it."

Julie and Dev once again exchanged looks and Devlin stood up and joined Julie. They apologized for bothering Tori and they hurried out the door, hopped into their car and raced back to the hospital.

"There is definitely something going on with Tori, but she is not our killer," Dev said. "We should have checked Carter out more carefully."

"Right, right," Julie agreed as she slid the cherry onto the top of their car as Dev took the corner on two wheels.

"We screwed up. Do you think he'll hurt Carrie?"

"I don't know, Julie. I don't know. Call and see if the Chief is back at the hospital and if not, see if he went ahead and posted someone to protect Carrie."

Julie listened as the Chief's cell continued to ring and finally went to voice mail. She quickly left information about their visit with Tori and their suspicions about Carter and requested that he call her as soon as possible. A few minutes later, the Chief returned her call and told her he had left Carter with Carrie. Carter said he would stay in her room and so the Chief didn't think he needed to post anyone. He was on his way back to the hospital and had already called for patrol back up in case they needed it. The detectives blasted into the hospital entrance, jumped out of the car, sprinted through the lobby and hustled into the waiting elevator praying their urgency was not necessary.

36

OVER?

The killer sat in the silence, the darkened room enveloping him. What had happened? How could he have messed up so badly?

"You couldn't find your head if it was screwed on boy. Are you surprised you can't accomplish anything? You are a loser. A fool. You do it or I'll blow your head off."

"Shut up! Shut up! Why can't you just be quiet? I took care of you didn't I? Why can't you leave me alone?"

"You think that girl lying there, that Carrie, cares about you? Forget it. None of them care about you, you worthless piece…"

"Stop it. Stop," Carter said as he held his head in his hands and cried.

"Carter?" asked Carrie timidly peering at him from her bed. "Who are you talking to?"

"No one Carrie. You need to go back to sleep."

"I don't want to sleep. I want to know what is going on. What happened to me?"

"Well, Carrie. I'll tell you what is going on. I thought you cared about me. I thought we had a future together, but I don't matter to you. I don't mean a thing to you. You were trying to out me to the Chief, Julie, and Dev. Good ole Dev. You always had a thing for him didn't you?"

"Carter," said Carrie. "I do care about you and Dev is just a friend. That is all he has ever been. In fact, I think he and Julie are developing a relationship. You are scaring me. I just don't understand why you have been so strange lately."

"Could be it began with me killing my parents, Carrie. Maybe that did it," Carter laughed as he moved his head back and forth. "Or it could have begun with me killing Tori's folks. Who knows, Carrie. Or it probably began a long time ago with Mrs. Bradley and her bunch. The "we don't care about Carter" group. I tried so hard to get people to like me and no one

186

cared. My Dad used to beat the living daylights out of me. Do you know one time, Carrie, he actually put a shotgun to my head and told me he was going to blow my head off if I didn't stop sniveling. I was only nine years old."

"Oh God, Carter," said Carrie.

"Yeah, you act like you care, but I know better. No one cares. No one cares."

Carter pushed the button on her bed table and when the nurse came in he told the nurse that Carrie needed a sedative.

"No," Carrie told the nurse.

"He's right dear," the nurse said. "The doctor said you need your rest," and before Carrie could stop her, the nurse injected medication into her IV to help her sleep.

"No. Noooo," Carrie cried as her words began to slur.

"You are going to be all right dear. You just need some rest," said the nurse, as she looked sadly toward Carrie . Turning to Carter she asked, "Do you need anything Sir? I could bring you some coffee."

"No thanks," Carter said. "I don't drink coffee." And the nurse left them alone.

He looked at Carrie, who had fallen asleep and was resting comfortably.

"Good," he thought. "I need some time to think."

He knew she would figure everything out, so he decided to tell her what was what. It didn't matter anymore. Nothing mattered. God, he was in a lot of pain. Julie's bullet was still lodged in his shoulder and he felt like he was losing sensation in his hand. It's a good thing it was his right hand. Must have damaged some nerves, he thought to himself.

That was a close call earlier and he was surprised they bought his act. It wasn't easy to let Julie grope him. He wanted to scream or hit her.

Maybe his Father was right. He was a failure. His mind wandered back to the day he went by the house to tell his parents about the test results. Why couldn't they have given him some support, just once. But no, his Dad always making fun of him. "Damn Boy, you are such a loser. You never will amount to a hill of beans." My Mother just sitting there with her head down. Then when I asked what Tori had been doing there, his Dad said, "That lady from the K-9 Club? We just signed over any inheritance you might ever have, Boy. Just filled out the paperwork."

He was laughing at me. "Hell, Boy. A dog is worth more than you."

I was so angry and it was just too much. I hated them. No, I loved them. I loved her. No, I hated her. I'd had enough. I went to my room, got my back-up Glock, returned to the kitchen just in time to hear my Father telling my Mom how useless I was and it was probably about time to kick me out. Boom. The Glock was in my hand and my Mother was screaming and then it was so, so quiet. So peaceful. I felt so...powerful. It was magnificent. Such energy. I showed them. I went to the mantle and took the clock down. The antique clock my Dad told me I would never get. I hid it in the box in my bedroom closet.

Carter remembered how he had gone all through the house, tearing up the place, trying to find any paperwork related to the K-9 Club. He didn't find anything, so he called 911 and made up the robbery bit.

As Carter sat in the darkened hospital room, he recalled going to Tori's house to get the paperwork she had taken from his parents. He hadn't planned real well for that one. When he got to her house, she wasn't there. Her Mom said she was staying with a friend and then her Dad commented on how upset Carter looked. Carter said he just needed to talk to Tori and Mr. Roberts said he'd let her know.

"It's all a mess now," Carter said as the pain in his shoulder became unbearable. He remembered coming home, worrying about not being able to get the K-9 Club papers back. He needed that money. He checked the calendar and realized it was the 22nd, exactly a month after he had killed his parents. He wasn't sure how, but he ended up back at Tori's house. She still hadn't returned home and when he asked her parents to let him look through her room to see if he could find the paperwork, her Mother had said no. He went into her room anyway and the old bag followed him with a gun and told Mr. Roberts to call the cops. Carter took the gun away from Tori's Mom. She didn't have a clue how to handle it and he grabbed it and shot Tori's old man as he sat at the kitchen table. Then, when Mrs. Roberts had tried to run, he caught her and put the gun in her hand and forced her to shoot herself in the head. He had quickly wiped down the kitchen, just in case he had touched something. It was so easy. Killing was so easy and he had become a force to be reckoned with.

Carter slumped in the chair of the darkened hospital room. It was hard for him to remember, but he understood that was the beginning. That was when he realized he needed to rid the town of the pretenders. The ones who wanted everyone to think they helped. The ones who believed they were good. He realized everything had been predestined. He had eliminated his parents and now he must eradicate Mrs. Bradley and all those people who had supported her. The ones who had not been there for him. The ones who had always taken her side.

He was transported back in time a few weeks after the Roberts murders. He had been at the grocery store and ran into both Tori and Mrs. Bradley.

Mrs. Bradley had always thought Tori was so great, so perfect. Tori this and Tori that. He had asked Tori about the K-9 Club paperwork and she pretended she didn't know anything about it and she had laughed at him. Called him a loser.

Bringing himself back to the present, he shouted. "No. I am not a loser. Everyone is wrong. I am in charge. I have the power with me. I will take care of Carrie, then Julie and Tori, and finally Steven...uh, no Devlin. That will be the end to them all."

The delirious Carter stumbled from the chair and moved unsteadily toward the now sleeping Carrie's bedside.

She had been a disappointment. He had thought she was different, but he should have known better. She was like the others. She didn't care about him now and never had. He drew his gun from his pocket and trained it on the center of Carrie's forehead. Dev gently pushed the door open.

"Step away," he ordered, as he aimed his weapon at Carter. "It's over."

Carter spun around, pointed his gun and fired. Dev grabbed at his left temple and pulled the trigger. Carter collapsed as Julie rushed into the room and dropped to Carter's prone figure. She checked for a pulse as she pushed his gun to the side. Feeling no pulse she quickly moved to Carrie's side. Her friend wasn't moving and at first, Julie thought she had been injured. She patted her on the face and Carrie moaned and rolled over.

Assured she was okay, Julie turned and went to Dev. The bullet had grazed his temple and he insisted he would be fine. The Chief and two patrolmen cautiously and with guns drawn entered the room, with a doctor following closely behind. After examining Carter, the doctor looked at them and shook his head. Just like that, it was over. Carter Westin was dead.

The Doctor moved to Dev and told him to follow him downstairs to the E. R. so he could stitch up his head. Later, while Dev was being treated and Carrie was settled in for her stay. Julie rode to the Division office with the Chief and began filling out the report of the evening's events.

"Hey Julie, are you still here?" the Chief asked as he came out of his office an hour later.

"Yes Sir. I'm trying to get the report done."

"Why don't you go on home. You and your partner can come in tomorrow and finish that report," said the Chief. "You need to get some rest."

"Thanks Chief. I will. I also need to let my Dad know what has happened."

"Good idea. And Detective...I am so sorry."

A dispirited and exhausted Julie shrugged her shoulders and told the Chief good-bye. She called a cab to take her to her parent's house. She had decided to spend what was left of the morning at her Dad's.

37
FUTURE

Mack awakened as he heard the taxi cab drove slowly up the winding driveway. He was just at the bottom of the staircase when the door opened and Julie walked in and fell into his arms, sobbing.

"Honey. What is it?" he asked, as he held her close. "What has happened? Is Carrie okay?"

"It's over," she wept. "It's over Daddy. It was Carter. Carter killed Mommy."

Father and daughter held onto each other for a long moment and then Mack stepped back from his daughter and examined the dark circles under her red eyes and her sheer and utter exhaustion.

"Goose," he said. "Why don't you wash up, get comfortable and come back down to a cup of hot tea. Then we'll talk."

"Okay, Daddy," she said. Julie turned and sluggishly climbed the stairs, walked down the hallway and opened the door to the bedroom where she had spent her entire life. Everywhere she looked she was reminded of her Mother. So many milestones had been achieved in this room. She picked up the Raggedy Ann doll her Mom had lovingly made and given to her when she was two years old and which had slept in this same bed every night since. Julie envisioned an eight year old walking into a lime green room accessorized by a lime green gingham canopy bed with ruffled curtains to match. Her Mom had worked so hard sewing and painting and then surprising her after school one day. Just because she was special. She also recalled herself as a preteen who had outgrown the canopied room and requested white wicker furniture. She and her Mother had shopped for the furniture and then purchased store-bought accessories, because Julie didn't want homemade things in her room.

"What a brat I was," she said to herself.

She remembered when she turned sixteen and decided she wanted designer furniture, so she and her Mother had spent an entire weekend spray painting the white wicker furniture black and painting the bedroom walls a pale lavender and then had allowed Julie to put her own touch on the room with a black enamel chevron design on the white closet doors. Her room looked awesome, but Julie was reminded that when she left home for college a few years later, her Mom had used three coats of paint and lots of elbow grease to repaint the closet doors. It took her another two weeks to repaint the wicker furniture white.

Her Mom had always gone above and beyond for her and never complained. She always made Julie feel like she was special. She deserved the best and she gave the same consideration to her students. To Carter.

Julie gathered underwear, a pair of Texas Tech sleep pants and a lightweight tank from the wicker dresser drawer she had used since she was a teenager. She walked into her bathroom and was reminded of how fortunate she had always been. Not everyone grew up with their own bedroom en suite or a Mom who made you feel like you were a princess.

As Julie stood under a steaming hot shower, she soaped her hair and body, and tried to clear all thoughts from her mind. Suddenly, the tears began slipping down her cheeks and she was howling as she slowly banged her head against the shower stall and finally, fisting her hands she used them to lever herself to the floor.

"Why, Carter? Why?" she cried and the agony of the actions of a person she had grown up with…a person she had worked with…a person who was her best friend's boyfriend…a person who she thought she knew…a friend…it punched her in the gut. "Why, Carter?"

For a moment she couldn't breathe as the water streamed over her head. Settling herself she stood, turned off the faucet, stepped out of the shower, toweled off and pulled on her panties, sleep pants and tank top.

Staring into the bathroom mirror she observed the dark smudges under her eyes and felt such a sense of hopelessness. She massaged moisturizer into her cheeks, pulled her hair up into a ponytail, brushed her teeth and walked downstairs and into the kitchen.

She paused when she saw her Father sitting at the kitchen table with his head in his hands and he was crying. Whimpering like a baby.

"He looks so old," Julie thought, as she studied the graying hair, the wrinkled face. "When did my Daddy get so old?"

Julie walked over, placed her arms on his shoulders and laid her face against her Father's. Time stood still for Father and Daughter as the sense of despair and loss permeated the room. Finally, Mack reached up and patted Julie's hand. Suddenly, the sun reflected off a vehicle as it moved up the driveway.

"What on Earth. Who could that be?" asked Mack.

Julie and Mack walked to the entryway together and as the doorbell rang, Mack looked out the peephole and said, "It's Dev."

He opened the door to Dev, who had a bandage wrapped around his head.

"What happened?" asked Mack. "Are you all right?"

"I'm fine, Sir. It's a long story. Is Julie okay?" asked Devlin.

"A little overwhelmed with the goings on, but I think she will be all right. Come on in and join us. You guys can fill me in on what has been happening over a cup of hot tea."

"You should be resting, Dev. How did you know I would be here?" Julie asked.

"I'm okay. I was worried about you after you left so I called the Chief. He told me you were coming home and I took a chance that home meant here."

Mack took the tea kettle off the stove and poured the hot water into three mugs filled with English Chamomile teabags, each picked up their mug and pulled out their chairs around the kitchen table. Once they were seated, there was a pause as they were quiet and then Julie verbalized the question they were all thinking.

"Why? Why did Carter do it?"

"Mimi was always there for her kids. She tried so hard with Carter and I know she fretted all the time that she had not been able to get through to him, but she tried," murmured Mack as he shook his head back and forth. "She tried."

"I just don't understand why he did this," said Julie.

"You know, your Mother and I often talked about the circumstances that could possibly create a killer," said Mack. "She didn't believe they were naturally born to kill but as children, were cultivated and developed from that little seed that makes them different. She thought it began with the kid whose eyes never reached yours and who is alone in a room full of people. The girl who pulled the wings off a grasshopper, used a stick to poke a snake on the playground, or took the same stick and ran it through another child's arm. She thought it could be the one who is abused emotionally or physically."

"It seems like you should be able to tell," said Julie.

"According to your Mom it's impossible to know for sure, Goose, but we always suspect there is something "off" about them. They are always a little odd…they rarely fit in…are never remorseful and one day, when we hear about their crimes, we say, "I'm not surprised… there was always something not quite right about him or her.""

"I remember when the Columbine Massacre occurred and everyone put the blame on bullying for the killers' behavior," said Dev.

"Right after that, Mimi said the schools immediately implemented instructional videos and lesson plans to assist the system in developing more caring and compassionate individuals and everyone thought they had created a safer and more secure environment for children. Of course, then Sandy Hook occurred when that twenty-year-old in Newtown, Connecticut shot his mother, drove to the Elementary School and shot his way into a supposedly LOCKED school," said Mack.

"Yeah, and the media and our government immediately jumped on a bandwagon of blame for that horrible act. They blamed video games and guns, even though the killer was autistic and had a history of being socially different," said Dev.

"Your Mom sometimes felt her classroom was filled with potential Sociopaths, because of parents who physically, emotionally, or medically abused their children. Mimi felt some parents could either add to an illness or actually create one by refusing to accept that their child was different and needed help."

"I remember Mom saying once that human beings found it easier to blame society for our problems instead of taking responsibility for our troubles and figuring out what to do," said Julie.

"Your Mom always believed Carter was emotionally and physically abused and it must have been pretty bad for him to have ended up the way he did," said Mack.

"I have to admit I sometimes wonder if I might have turned out to be like Carter if it hadn't been for Mrs. Bradley. That is what I don't get. She was always there for us."

"I think he was sick or maybe he was just plain evil," Julie said.

"Sick people do evil things. There is no understanding, or even explaining his actions. I do believe it all started with him killing his parents and perhaps, that created the trigger for the other murders, but I guess the truth is we will never understand why he killed," said Dev.

"Are you sure he killed his folks?" asked Mack.

"I am pretty certain when we check the weapon he used on me in the hospital, it will match up against the bullets recovered from his parents, as well as Mimi and the other victims. I think he has to be our killer. Why else would he try to eliminate Carrie?" said Dev.

"What about the Roberts' murders? Do you think he had anything to do with them?" asked Julie.

"I don't know," Dev said. "But who knows? If we believe what Tori said. Well. I still believe there is something suspicious going on with Tori and remember, her gun was used in the Roberts' apparent murder/suicide."

"I have always wondered about her Mom shooting her Dad and then turning the gun on herself. I feel like there should have been a suicide note. Obviously, the house was wiped down to remove any fingerprints and you know Tori was really strange earlier. Put that with all the other stuff we are hearing and it makes me wonder if she is a little unbalanced."

"All that stuff about "K" or Kandi," said Dev. "Remember at the school, she told us "K" was the person in charge of the funds for the Charity."

Mack scrunched up his forehead and said, "You know, when Tori was in Mimi's Second Grade class there were some bad things going on with her Dad and that was why he was put in jail. I vaguely recall Mimi talking about Tori seeming to have a dual personality. Tori had gone through therapy and they hadn't heard any more about it, so Mimi had assumed there wasn't anything to it. Your Mother had been so proud of Tori. She appeared to have overcome her past and had a bright future as a teacher."

"We will follow up on Tori tomorrow," an emotionally drained Julie sighed. "I need to go to bed. I began the preliminary report, but we have a lot of additional paperwork to deal with and I guess we can check on the K-9 Club then."

"Dev," Mack said. "The offer of your old room is still there, if you'd like to stay. You all must be operating on fumes and I am not sure it is safe for you to be driving home."

"I'd like that, Mack," Dev said. "I guess that was kind of my plan when I came to check on Julie. I appreciate it."

"You can also give me a ride to work tomorrow."

"Well. Sleep well you two and I'll see you later."

Mack gave his daughter a hug and shook his head as he said, "I'll never understand. I guess we cannot influence or control the choices others make, but maybe we can begin to heal now."

He turned to head upstairs and as Julie put the cups in the sink, Dev put his arms around her waist and she relaxed. Resting against his chest, then turning around, she found herself nestled in his strong arms. He kissed her lightly on the forehead and held her close. Julie drew strength from his embrace and then sighing again, pulled away from him, reached up and kissed the tip of his nose. She gently touched the bandage around his head.

"Does it hurt?" she asked.

"A little. They wanted me to stay in the hospital for observation, but it was important that I be with you and Mack. I'm okay."

"Oh Dev," Julie said as she took his hand and held it to her cheek. She looked into his eyes and saw a promise.

"You need to get to bed," he said as he pulled her up the stairs. Stopping at the door of his old bedroom he looked at her and Julie slowly placed her arms around his neck and kissed him. A kiss so meaningful and filled with such potential. She felt it all the way to her toes. When they parted, he quietly stepped into his old room, told her to sleep well and closed the door.

Julie floated to her room and looking out the window, focused on a couple of doves cooing in her Mom's rose garden.

"Oh Momma," she crooned, as she slipped under her down comforter. "Guess what? I think I am in love with your Steven."

38
A GREAT DAY

It was a beautiful day and regardless of recent events, the members and guests in the Bradley household awoke late to a day filled with promise. Mack was singing as he scrambled eggs, flipped pancakes, and fried bacon. He had already set the table for breakfast, with orange and cranberry juices, butter, and maple syrup at the ready. The coffee was perking and the fresh aroma drew Julie down the stairs and straight to the coffee pot.

"Mornin' Daddy," said Julie. "I can't believe I slept round the clock."

"You all really needed the rest. I tried to be quiet so I wouldn't disturb your sleep."

"Well. It obviously worked, because Dev is still sleeping."

Julie reached into the cupboard, selected a mug and poured herself a cup of coffee and there was Dev right behind her nudging her to move over so he could get at the mugs.

"Who's still sleeping?" asked Dev.

"Mornin', Dev."

"Good Morning, Julie."

"You are sure in a happy mood Daddy," Julie said. "I guess you got a few good hours of sleep too."

"Yup. I feel totally refreshed and ready to go and of course, I'm just happy to have my kids home is all," Mack said as he placed a jar of picante sauce on the table.

Julie shot Dev a look and he just smirked at her. He looked as goofy as her Dad was acting, as he carefully filled his mug with hot coffee.

"Daddy, breakfast looks so good."

"This is great," said Dev.

"It needs to be quick because Dev and I have a lot of work to do," Julie said.

"Everything is ready to eat. You all just need to sit and chow down."

Julie and Dev pulled their chairs out and sat down. Mack handed both of them napkins before he took his seat.

"Could you pass me the eggs, hon?" asked Mack.

"Sure Daddy. Would you like the bacon, Dev?" asked Julie.

"Thanks," said Dev clearing his throat. "This feels so comfortable. Like we are a family."

"Mimi would be so happy," said Mack. "She always wanted us to be a family."

They continued eating their food in silence and when finished, Julie hopped up to carry dishes to the kitchen sink.

"Don't worry about that, Goose. I can handle the cleanup. You two get on your way."

"Okay Daddy. Thanks," Julie said as she bussed Mack on the cheek and Dev shook his hand and thanked him for everything.

"I appreciate your letting me sleep over, Mack. The toothbrush and razor was also appreciated this morning. I actually feel pretty good considering I look like a partial mummy."

"You look superb," Julie said and ignored her Dad's knowing look.

"Love you Daddy," Julie said.

"Back at you, Goose."

"Breakfast was wonderful as always."

"Thanks, hon."

"See you later Mack," said Dev as he walked out the door.

"Have a safe day you two," said Mack.

Dev slid behind the wheel and Julie joined him and off they went into the freshly washed day, heading toward Caradan.

When they arrived back at the Division office the two completed their paperwork. When they handed it in to the Chief for his evaluation, he invited Detectives Bradley and Ames to have a seat, and complimented them on a job well done.

"Have you decided to close the Roberts' case?" the Chief asked.

"We aren't ready to do that yet, Sir," said Julie.

"We believe Carter Westin killed the Roberts and are still working out the details of the case," said Julie.

"Have you found any new information on the K-9 Club Charity?" Devlin asked the Chief.

"Actually, I have made an appointment for you two with Miss K this afternoon at 1:30," the Chief said. "It looks like this person has managed to get half the town to contribute a one-time donation or write the Charity into their wills. It's unbelievable. This lady is making some big bucks out of this. She is the CEO, but there is no board. She is the board. The money and decisions begin and end with her."

"Is that legal?" asked Dev.

"Apparently," said the Chief. "Just keep me informed. Oh and by the way guys, we do have some rules around here."

"Sir?" asked Dev.

"I'm just saying," the Chief responded with a huge smile.

"Well, Chief," Julie said, flushing slightly. "We are going to go by the hospital to check up on Carrie."

"Tell her I said hello. And Detectives?"

"Yes Sir."

"You did an awesome job."

"Thank you Sir," said Dev. "Just wish we could have figured Carter out earlier."

"Or understood the why," said Julie.

Julie and Dev walked into Carrie's hospital room and found her staring out the window. She looked so small and sad. Julie walked over and put her arm around her.

"How ya doing, Buddy?" she asked.

"How could I have cared for someone like that," she said. "Why didn't I see what he was? I keep thinking of all the lives he took and changed, but why. Why?"

She turned toward them, her face full of anguish.

"Oh Carrie," Julie hugged her and held her close. "Carter fooled us all."

"Don't you see Julie," Carrie said with a voice overflowing with agony. "Don't you see. I think I loved him. What does that say about me? What kind of person does that make me?"

"It says you are human, just like everyone else. It makes you the person my Mom found value in and loved with her whole heart. It makes you my sister. I love you, girl."

"Oh Julie," said Carrie.

"Carrie, you are one of the best people I know. Believe that, because I love you too," said Devlin Ames.

Carrie and Julie both reached their arms to Dev.

"You need to get back in bed Carrie," he said as he hugged them both.

"I want you to stay with my Dad for a few days when you are released, Carrie," Julie said.

"I can go home. I'll be fine," Carrie said.

"No. Your folks aren't back from vacation yet and I don't want you to be alone right now, so you are going to keep Dad and the pups company for a few days."

"That's not necessary."

"No, but that's what's happening, Carrie. You get to make dinner at least one night, okay? Besides, Dad needs a little company too."

"Well, if you insist."

She appeared to be scowling, but Julie caught the grin that touched her friend's face as Julie turned toward the door. Carrie's folks were vacationing in Europe and would be home in a week. In the meantime, Mack could take care of her.

Julie knew it would be good for everyone concerned. Mack could use the company, Carrie could use the fussing and Julie could use the peace of mind.

"We will check on you this afternoon," said Dev.

"We are going to meet the infamous Miss K this afternoon," said Julie.

"Good luck," said Carrie. "You all be careful."

Julie and Dev decided to grab a cool drink before they kept their appointment with the CEO of the K-9 Club.

"Why don't we go to my house. I can offer you a sweet tea or soda," Julie said.

"I could use a Diet-Coke if you have one."

When they drove by Carrie and Julie's house, they realized it was still being processed and they were unable to get into the house.

"Let's go to my place and I can offer you that drink and a sandwich, too," said Dev.

He drove to his apartment and held the door for Julie as they walked in. Julie took in the clean, but sparse surroundings. It was a typical single guy's home and it was obvious Dev was a neat freak. Everything was in its place and the floors shone.

"Would you like a Diet Coke? Is ham and cheese okay?"

"Sounds great. Man, I'm not used to being waited on like this," said Julie.

"Well, don't get too used to it. The way I figure it, Detective Bradley, you owe me a home cooked meal."

"Right you are. You and my Dad. Maybe we can do that this weekend. How about a barbecue?"

"I think that sounds so normal. So good," said Dev as he placed Julie's sandwich, pickle, and a few chips in front of her. "Eat up," he said. "We have an appointment in an hour."

39
MISS K

"Good afternoon," the perky blonde with the see-through blouse and tight spandex skirt said. "May I help you?"

"Yes," Julie said, feeling pretty plain in her khaki trousers and navy blue blazer. "We have a one o'clock appointment with Miss K."

"Oh, that's right. Chief Holden from the Caradan Police Force set it up. Correct?" she asked as she checked Dev out.

"Correct," Julie said placing her hand on Dev's arm. "Is she in?"

"Who? Oh…umm. Just a second, please," said the distracted young lady, as she shot a suggestive look towards Dev.

"I said, is she in?" Julie asked, stepping in front of Dev, placing her hands on the desk of the curvaceous creature and observing the desk name plate. "We need to see her now, uh, Tootsie?"

"Hmmm, of course," the young lady named Tootsie said, picking up the telephone, punching a number and speaking softly into the receiver.

She stood up and asked them to follow her down the hallway. Julie watched Dev as his eyes gravitated toward the luscious lady and her sashaying body. He just looked at her and shrugged.

"Right," she snorted. "Tootsie? Seriously?"

"What are you going to do?" said Dev.

"Excuse me?" the blonde asked turning to Dev. "Did you say something?"

"When did Miss K come into the office?"

"Oh, she arrived about thirty minutes ago. She doesn't have to keep regular hours you know. She is a very busy person. She has to spend much of her time locating donors, you know."

"Yes," Julie said sarcastically and rolled her eyes. "We know."

"The blonde stopped before a door that had "K-9 Club" and "K-President" smartly engraved on the door.

"Wow," Julie said. "I'm impressed."

"Me, too." said Dev as he watched the blonde move her hips and stroll back down the hallway.

Julie rolled her eyes again and knocked on the door.

"Please enter," answered a melodious voice from within.

Devlin opened the door and followed Julie into the room. The navy carpet was complimented by the white leather furniture and the luxurious gold window dressings. Sitting behind a massive solid cherry desk, was Miss K.

She stood and gracefully reached her hand out to Devlin. Julie was taken aback for a moment. The lovely woman was dressed in a gorgeous blue silk dress that must have cost a fortune. Her beautifully coiffed hair was swept to the top of her head and in her three-inch stiletto heels she stood eye to eye with Devlin as he shook her hand.

"How are you doing today, Tori?" he asked.

"Excuse me," Miss K said.

Julie just stood, mouth open and stared.

"What is going on Tori?" asked Dev.

"I'm sure I don't understand the question, but won't you please have a seat," Miss K said lightly. "Can I offer you a drink?"

"Water," said Julie. "I need some water."

"I guess I could do with a drink," said Dev. "Maybe you have some tequila," he muttered under his breath.

"I'm sorry, Detective, but I don't imbibe in alcoholic beverages. I can offer you a soft drink, coffee, or water, Sir."

"Thanks. I'll take some water," Dev said.

"Of course," Miss K said, as she pushed a button on her phone and requested some water for her guests.

"Now, what can I do for you?" she asked.

"You can tell us why you are pretending to be Miss K, Tori," said Dev.

Tori, or Miss K, just pursed her lips and stared at both of the detectives, with an indignant look on her face.

Julie was still stunned and seemed unable to form words. Tootsie, brought them a couple of bottles of water. She handed Julie hers and leaned forward as she gave Dev his, along with a nice view of her very ample chest.

"Thank you Tootsie," Dev said as he smiled at the lovely girl, while trying to avert his eyes, but not having much success.

Julie snorted and quickly screwed the lid off her drink and took a gulp.

Dismissing Tootsie, Dev asked, "Tori. What is the deal?"

"Stop referring to me as Tori. Tori is not here," Miss K said icily. "If you continue to be so rude, I will ask you to leave. I do not have to meet with you. I agreed to do so as a favor to the Chief of Police.

Julie continued staring at Tori or Miss K. She really favored Tori, but there were some distinct differences. It was more like Miss K could be Tori's twin.

"How long has your organization been involved in Caradan?" asked Dev as he looked at Julie.

"I opened my organization one year ago. I found there was a need for financial support of the local animal shelter."

"Did your organization exist prior to that time, or were you located in another city?" asked Dev.

"No-o-o," Miss K stuttered. "I don't think so."

"What do you mean, you don't think so?" asked Julie.

"I don't know," said Miss K as she shook her head. Suddenly, the lovely young lady put her head in her hands and then looked up at them and said, "What is going on? What do you want?"

"Tori?" Julie asked softly. "Are you all right?"

"I don't know what you are talking about," Miss K said.

"I know, sweetie. I know. It's going to be okay."

Tori put her head in her hands again and then, looking at them through her fingers said, "I think you need to leave. You are not welcome here."

"Of course, Miss K. We are going to leave now and we appreciate all of your help." Julie said, as she stood and motioned for Dev to follow her out.

Once outside in the corridor, Dev asked, "What's the deal, Julie? Why did you tell her we appreciated her help? She didn't do anything to help us. And what is up with this? One minute Tori is Miss K and the next she's Tori and then here comes Miss K again.

Julie said, "Dev, I think we just witnessed two personalities in there and a battle going on between them. I don't know what to do."

"Ah Ha. That is pretty strange."

"Yes. It is strange, but also scary. I wish my Mom or Katie were here. They could tell us how to help Tori."

"Well Babe, I don't know what to tell you."

"Dev. Like I said, a war is going on and we need to get Tori some help. I want her to win this war."

Later that afternoon, the two detectives were filling the Chief in on what had transpired at the K-9 Club offices earlier.

"I think we need to ask Tori, or Miss K, if she saw Carter Westin at his parent's home the day of their murder. I am thinking she was Miss K at the time and that is why Tori has no recollection.. It makes sense now. So do the frequent school absences and the fact that several people actually thought Tori was like another person, and the blackouts too. We need to talk to her and get her some help."

"Call her and see if you can get her to come in. Julie, she knows and trusts you. Why don't you try to arrange a meeting for us."

"Sure, Chief," said Julie as she flipped out her phone and called Tori.

"Hey, Tori. It's Julie," she said when Tori answered her phone.

"What's up?"

"Do you think you could come into the Division offices tomorrow and meet with Dev and me?"

"How come? What's going on?"

"We just have a few more follow-up questions to ask you. I hope you don't mind."

"No problem, but it will have to be after 2:00 because I am still teaching summer school," Tori said.

"That will be fine, Tori. We really appreciate it."

Shortly after 2:00 p.m. the next afternoon, a nervous Tori was sitting in an interview room at the Division office.

"Tori, it's all right," said Dev when he and Julie walked into the room. "We just wanted to ask you a few questions."

"Okay. I am not sure what else I can help you with, but I'll try."

"Do you remember meeting with us yesterday afternoon, Tori?" asked Julie.

"Noooo. The last time I saw or talked to you was when you came to my house early the other morning and woke me up," said Tori.

"Okay," said Julie. "Do you remember anything at all about talking to Dev and I at the K-9 Club office yesterday?"

"I told you no. I was teaching and got sick, so I went home yesterday. That's what I remember."

"I understand," said Julie. "Is there anything you can tell us about the K-9 Club?"

"That's the charity my Mom donated to and the one Carter made a big deal about me taking money from his folks for. I have already answered that question several times. Why do you keep asking me about it over and over?" asked an agitated Tori.

"We don't mean to upset you. Tori, you mentioned you were sick yesterday. Have you seen a doctor yet?" asked Dev.

"Not yet. I plan to," she said as she began rubbing her forehead.

"When do you think you will be making your appointment?"

"That is not any of your business," Tori said. Her voice had changed dramatically and it was obvious the detectives were no longer talking to a first grade teacher. "Who do you people think you are?" a haughty Miss K asked.

"We are Tori's friends," said Julie. "We want to help her and you too Miss K."

"I don't need any help from you, Miss Bradley. I plan to take care of Tori all by myself."

"Tori? Tori? Can you hear me?" asked Julie.

"That's it. I'm finished with you people." Miss K jumped up and began stalking out of the room.

"I think you need to see your doctor right away," said Julie.

"And why is that Miss Detective?" asked Miss K, whirling around.

The change in her voice was fascinating. It was like talking to a completely different individual.

"Hey there Miss K," said Dev. "Why don't you sit down and let's talk about you and Tori."

"I don't know why you invited that silly girl here," sniffed Miss K. "She doesn't know anything."

"I'm sure you are right," said Julie. "But, I'll bet you can answer some questions for us, Miss K."

"Just ask."

"Were you at Carter Westin's house on the day his parents were murdered?"

"Yes, I was. In fact, I saw Carter pull up as I was leaving. I could have told you a long time ago that he was the one who was responsible for his parents murder."

"Why didn't you?"

"Because she fights me tooth and nail. I think I am getting stronger, but it has not been easy to break through. Not like I did when we were little."

"Why do you think it was easier to get through lately?"

"Because of what they did. Her Mom taking that jerk back after what he did to Tori."

"Miss K, did you kill Tori's parents?"

"Are you serious? I would not have minded putting the creep away. But Tori's Mom? Well as much as I hate her, Tori would never let me do it. You still haven't figured it out have you?"

"What's that Miss K?"

"Carter killed Tori's parents. I saw him just as I was coming back to the house. Walked in and there they were. Tori made it easier for me after that."

"Can we talk to Tori?" asked Julie.

"That's not how it works," Miss K said. She stood up, turned and walked out the door.

"We need to get her some help, Dev."

"Yes, but we will have to wait until we can catch her being Tori. That woman won't lift a finger to help us or Tori, with anything."

There was a knock at the door and Devlin opened it. A confused Tori stood there, as she pinched the area located above her nose."

"Is this where we are meeting?" she asked.

"Yes Tori," said Dev. "Come on in and thank you for meeting with us."

"It's okay Sweetie. Do you have another headache?"

"Kind of."

"I'm so sorry. I think we need to get you to a Doctor." Julie took her hand and lead her into the room. "It's going to be all right Tori."

40

EPILOGUE

Julie, Carrie, Dev and Mack sat on the front porch watching two little fur balls rolling around on the front lawn.

The sky was an azure blue, there was a gentle breeze blowing and you could hear a few doves cooing nearby.

"What a wonderful morning," said Carrie.

"Are you feeling better?" asked Julie.

"Much. I can't tell you how much I appreciate you all letting me stay here."

"You know this is your home whenever you need it to be," said Mack.

"I feel so blessed to have you all."

"You are family," said Julie.

Carrie smiled and then stood and walked to the end of the porch.

"My heart hurts for her right now," Julie said softly.

"Yeah," said Dev. "Carter really put one over on her."

"He put one over on all of us," said Mack with a huff.

They turned to go into the house as a familiar blue Honda pulled up the drive.

"Tori," shouted Julie, as she ran to meet the young woman. "How are you?"

"Fine," Tori said. "I'm fine. I just wanted to tell you I have an appointment with my psychiatrist tomorrow. He told me he could hypnotize me if I needed him to and I think I will let him. I want to know why I keep having these headaches, or blackouts. They seem to last longer and are more frequent."

"I'm glad. We have all been worried about you," said Julie. "Would you like to come in for a minute?"

"No thanks. I just wanted to let you know I made the appointment."

Tori noticed Carrie standing on the porch. "Do you think I can to talk to Carrie for a moment?"

"I think she would like that," said Julie.

Tori stepped out of her car and strode briskly up the sidewalk to join Carrie on the porch. The girls hugged and Tori said, "You know Carter and I never cared for one another, but I feel bad for you."

"I think everyone was upset when they found out he was the killer. I sure am having a hard time dealing with it. I can't believe I didn't figure it out. How could I have been so blind, Tori?"

"Don't be so hard on yourself. You are a good person."

"So are you. How are you really doing, Tori? I know the loss of your parents was hard for you and then Mimi's death. She meant so much to both of us."

"Yeah," said Tori as she touched her right temple.

"You mean the loss of her Mother?" angrily asked Miss K. "That jerk didn't matter to her."

Carrie was startled at the sudden change in Tori's attitude and voice.

"Tori, are you okay?"

"There is no Tori," Miss K said.

Carrie watched as her friend whirled around, danced down the steps and headed toward her car. She hopped into her vehicle and glanced at the group standing on the porch. Julie waved as their friend drove away and turned toward a puzzled Carrie.

"Oh my gosh. I think I just met Miss K," Carrie said. "That's what you were talking about. It's like she instantly became a totally different person."

"That girl really needs some help," said Mack.

"Tori said she had an appointment with her psychiatrist tomorrow."

"Maybe we can be there when the doctor hypnotizes her and we can record her telling us if she saw Carter at the Roberts or Westin houses," said Dev.

"Oh, my Gosh," said Carrie. "I just remembered. When Carter was in my hospital room the night he attacked me, he told me he killed his folks and the Roberts. I forgot all about it. The nurse gave me some drugs right after he told me and I guess I just forgot."

"Tell us exactly what you remember," said Dev.

"He said he got mad at his parents for making fun of him and he snapped and killed them. Later, he decided he needed the paperwork they gave Tori. I don't know why. So, anyway, he went to their house looking for Tori, but she wasn't there. I guess Mr. and Mrs. Roberts made him uncomfortable and later, Carter began to worry about them. I don't know. It didn't make much sense to me, but he said he went back and Mrs. Roberts had a gun and threatened him or wanted him to leave. He said he grabbed her gun, shot Mr. Roberts and then made Mrs. Roberts shoot herself. Oh, I can't believe I forgot that."

"It's understandable sweetheart," said Mack. "You have had a rough time of it. How about you go lay down for a rest?"

"Not yet, Carrie. What else did he tell you about his parents?"

"Just that he killed them. He said they abused him and made his life hell. He blamed Mimi and everyone for not helping him. That's really all I remember."

"All right, Carrie. You go on and rest now."

"I think I will. I think I will."

Carrie went into the house and headed up the stairs. Mack sat down on a porch recliner and Dev and Julie chose the porch swing.

"Well, that clears that mystery up. Perhaps now we can close out all the cases," said Dev.

"Yes," said Julie. "Wow. Can you believe Carter?"

"It is unbelievable, that is for sure." said Mack.

"I hope Tori gets some help with her problems," said Julie.

"She is headed in the right direction," said Dev, as he placed his arm around Julie's shoulders.

"I think I will go inside and get some lunch started for us," said Mack, patting his knees with his hands, getting up and walking slowly inside.

"Your Dad is a good guy."

"Yes, he is," said Julie. "And so are you."

Devlin turned her in his arms and was immediately lost in the depths of gorgeous gray eyes.

"Julie," he said.

"Yes, Dev?"

"What is that on your blouse?"

"Where?" Julie asked, as she looked down.

"There," Dev said as he brought his finger up to touch her nose. "Gotcha."

"Oh Dev," Julie giggled, putting her arms around him, pulling him close and touching her forehead to his forehead.

"What are you thinking?" he asked.

"I'm thinking…it's just another day in paradise." Julie smiled radiantly and placed her head on his shoulder.

ANOTHER DAY IN PARADISE
The Caradan Series – Book Two

PROLOGUE

It was dank, dark and cold. She awoke with a moan. When she tried to sit up the pain was excruciating. What had happened? Where was she? The questions were following one after the other, slamming into her brain so fast she couldn't slow them down enough to figure out the answers. Oh God. What was going on? The sobs came uncontrollably, as she tried to comprehend her situation and vaguely began to assimilate her circumstances. Struggling to remember, scraps of memory began to slip in. She had been in the kitchen mixing cookie dough.

"I think it was chocolate chip, or was it peanut butter?" she asked herself.

"That doesn't matter," she screamed in frustration.

"Yes, it does matter. I need to figure out what is going on," she yelled, her cry echoing in the prison that confined her.

"Okay," she said, trying to calm herself. I was baking cookies. They were chocolate chip. I remember the knock on the back door. There was a man. Yes, there was a man. I remember looking through the screen door at him and he smiled. He had a nice smile…such a nice smile."

"I was wondering if you could help me find 304 Sycamore?" he had asked pleasantly. "I am supposed to meet my realtor and my GPS is on the blink. I thought it was in this area. I have been driving in circles looking for it, but with no luck."

"Oh," she had laughed. "I know what you mean. We have so many roundabouts in this subdivision and if you get off on one, well, it is easy to get lost."

"Do you know this street? Can you help me?"

"Sure," she said. "Believe it or not, you just need to go two blocks and turn left from the roundabout. Before you enter the loop, make a quick right and go one block. The street will intersect with Sycamore."

"Wow. Those are great directions. I am impressed."

"Actually, you are in luck. My brother lives on Sycamore," she said.

"Thanks for the information. I appreciate your help," he said and began walking toward his black SUV.

"No problem."

He had stopped, turned back toward her and said, "Looks like I picked the right house."

"What a nice man," she remembered.

"Who was that man, Mommy?"

And then it came back to her. Crashing into her brain…just like the hammer he had clobbered her with…and she remembered. Oh God. She remembered. Her last memory, before succumbing once again to the dark, was of two terrified little faces.

1

MAY 31, 2014

"Oh my gosh. You look absolutely gorgeous," Carrie James cried as her best friend Julie Bradley walked into the bedroom. "I had forgotten how fabulous that dress was when we picked it out."

"It is lovely, isn't it?" said Julie with a quiet smile, twirling around in the ivory white wedding gown, her eyes glistening with moisture.

"You look spectacular and yes," Carrie said, reading her friend's mind. "She would have been so proud and happy."

"I still have to remind myself that she is gone."

"I know what you mean, but she will always be a part of all of us Julie.

Carrie found herself recalling the beautiful Texas morning her boss had sent her to Caradan Elementary School to investigate a shooting. She was not allowed access to the school because the police had locked down the campus. Carter Westin, Carrie's boyfriend at the time, was on duty and informed her that the school counselor was dead, Julie's mom Mimi Bradley was critically injured, and the teacher's second graders had been shot, some fatally.

"What are you thinking about Carrie?" Julie asked.

"Nothing important," Carrie said as she picked up the sleeveless black silk sheath lying on the bed.

"It brings back the memories, doesn't it? You are thinking about Mom, Carter and Tori, aren't you?"

"It is hard for me to think of your Mother without thinking about them and what happened."

"I know, but even though I was the Detective, you are the one who helped solve the case."

At first, the school shooting had appeared to be an open-and-shut spree killing by a lunatic dressed in black and wielding a gun. Later, when Mimi Bradley died and the killer began eliminating those close to her, Julie realized the murderer was someone who knew her Mom. She zeroed in on former students whom Mimi had loved, trusted, and nurtured and Julie had grown up with…her friends. The list included her best friend Carrie James, police officer Carter Westin, and teacher Tori Roberts. The fourth prospect on the list was a neglected boy named Steven, who had actually found shelter with the Bradley's until he maliciously injured the family pet. He was sent away to a Children's Home and hadn't been heard from again.

"You know, we would not have caught the killer without your investigative reporting Carrie. The timeline you prepared helped put us on the right track."

"Yeah, it is still hard to believe that the death of Carter's parents was the trigger for all the murders. I don't understand how that kind of illness can become so convoluted. I get that abusive parents can traumatize children and the trauma can be triggered even when the kid becomes an adult. What I don't get is that someone can transfer that kind of hate onto people who have done nothing, but try to be there for you."

"I know what you mean. My Mom was the best person and such a terrific teacher. Carrie, I have decided there are some things you cannot explain. Otherwise, you would go out of your mind. I've let the past go and will only remember the good things. You need to let it go too."

"Yeah, you're right and I'm sorry. This should be a happy time for you and here I am being a "Debbie Downer". Come on…turn around for me."

Julie slowly whirled gracefully in the gown as it billowed elegantly about her ankles, a vision of loveliness as she stopped in front of the full-length mirror. Tall, lanky Julie Bradley was a coffee-black brunette with eyes that shifted from shades of black to gray. The gown's off-the-shoulder beaded bodice was accented by a tiny waist which was emphasized in the back by several rosettes gracing an extremely low-cut back.

"Carrie, can you help me attach the train?"

"No problem," Carrie said as she stepped behind Julie and fastened the train just below the rosettes. "Oh, my, Julie. It's so lovely. Let's get that veil on you too."

"You know," Julie said as Carrie placed the veil on her head. "I wasn't sure I wanted a train, but it does add a finishing touch, doesn't it?"

"Oh yeah and your veil is gorgeous."

"It was my Momma's," Julie said as she fingered the short veil fastened to her hair by a crown of seed pearls. "Daddy wanted me to wear her wedding gown, but it didn't come close to fitting me. Mom was so much shorter than me, but Daddy wanted me to at least wear her veil. I love it."

"It suits you, Jules. You are so elegant and I am so jealous of your height. Sometimes I feel like a stubby little girl."

"Thanks, but being tall is not always an asset," Julie said as she took in her friend's blue eyes, stunning white-blonde hair, pert little nose and luscious, pouty mouth. "You know I would give anything to have your figure. I haven't seen a man, or woman for that matter, who doesn't turn around when you walk by. Well, guess we need to get changed and ready for the rehearsal," Julie said as she pulled a black and white paisley sundress from the closet.

"Is Tori meeting us at the church?" asked Carrie.

"Actually, she is going to swing by to pick us up," Julie said. "How do you think Tori is doing? How is her new doctor working out?"

"Great," said Carrie. "She told me she truly looks forward to her weekly visits with her therapist."

Tori Roberts, a former student of Mimi Bradley and currently, a First Grade teacher at Caradan Elementary School, had an abusive childhood. Psychological problems resulting from her early years returned after the death of her parents the previous year.

"That is terrific," said Julie. "Tori's had such a difficult life. It is about time things start turning around for her."

"I agree. Look, you finish up and I'll be in the kitchen. Would you like some sweet tea?"

"No thanks. You go ahead. I'll be there in a minute."

The two girls were roommates and had been since their days at Texas Tech University. Carrie was two years older than Julie and had graduated with honors from Tech, with a degree in Journalism. She was currently employed as an Investigative Reporter at The Caradan Eagle.

Julie, also a Tech Honors Graduate and formerly, a local Homicide Detective, was now the new Director of Trainees at the Caradan Police Department. This was a position she accepted when she became engaged to her previous partner, Devlin Ames.

Carrie headed downstairs and Julie slipped out of her gown and hung it and the veil on a satin hanger, which she placed on a hook located on the back of her closet door. She quickly pulled the sundress over her head, slipped on black strapless sandals, grabbed a brush from the dresser and pulled it through her long tresses. She briefly threw on a little eye-shadow, mascara, light foundation and blush. Julie glanced in the mirror and was ready to go. Just before she left the bedroom, her eyes strayed to the photograph of her parents located on her nightstand.

"Oh, Momma," Julie said. "If only you could be here today. How happy we would be."

She softly closed the door and went to join her friend in the kitchen.

2

THE REHEARSAL

The doorbell rang as Julie walked into the kitchen and Carrie rushed to the front door.

"Hey Tori," said Carrie opening the etched glass door. "Come on in and have a glass of tea."

"Thanks, Carrie," said Tori James. The tall, slender girl with a shy smile and sprinkling of freckles across her petite pug nose, had a mane of dirty blonde hair. It was pulled into a chignon at the base of her neck. She was dressed in a black leather mini skirt topped by a white tank top and sheer white blouse. Her black platform shoes added another two inches to her already lengthy form.

"Hey Julie," said Tori as she followed Carrie into the kitchen and accepted the glass of sweet tea Julie handed her. "Can you believe the day is here?"

"Kind of feels like a dream, Tori."

"I am so happy you are letting me be a part of your special day, Julie."

"Oh Tori. You have become such a good friend in the last year. I can't imagine not having you for a bridesmaid and you know how thrilled Mom would have been."

"All I could think about this morning was she should have been here. It's not right that she isn't."

"I know, but it is what it is," said Julie. "I am wearing her veil tomorrow and I know she is watching over all of us every day."

"Okay. Okay," said Carrie. "Tori…Jules told me earlier we have to let the past go, so starting right now, we are only going to have happy thoughts on this delightful day."

"That sounds like a plan to me," said Tori, finishing her tea and placing the glass in the sink. "Are you ready?"

"Yes, Ma'am," said Julie.

"Right behind you girls," said Carrie. "You go on out and I'll lock up."

Julie and Tori went out the front door as Carrie set the security alarm.

The three climbed into Tori's blue Honda and they headed for the church.

"I think it is so neat that you are getting married at Mt. Olive's Primitive Church," said Carrie.

"Back when Mommy and I discussed weddings…you know…when I was engaged to the Butthead? She really wanted to have my wedding in the Primitive Church. We even had it planned."

Julie had been engaged to the local District Attorney, who she learned was having an affair with a married woman. He told her he just wanted to have a final fling before they got married. Unfortunately, or fortunately, depending on how you look at it, Julie found that her future husband was not the person she thought he was and returned his ring and called off the wedding. It had been devastating at first, but God had a plan for her and his name was Devlin Ames. She found herself smiling as she thought of her good looking fiancé with chocolate brown eyes that she could get lost in.

"Tonight, after the rehearsal, we are going to Andy's for dinner. Raul has closed the restaurant for the night. It is a wedding gift to Dev and I. Isn't that sweet?"

"Yup. That ole Raul is a sweetie," said Tori.

"It really drives Dev crazy, you know," said Julie. "He wants to know why the restaurant is named Andy's instead of Raul's.'

"You know what Raul says?" asked Carrie.

"Jus always bin Andy's," said the three girls in unison laughing happily.

"So what is happening after the dinner?" asked Tori.

"Well, Dev and his groomsmen are going to Dad's and he and the Chief are entertaining them," said Julie.

"What are they doing?" asked Carrie.

"Do you really want to know?" asked Julie. "I sure don't."

"Know what you mean. What are our plans?" asked Tori.

"I thought we'd go back to Carrie's and my place and put together some bows for the pews and make some goodie and rice bags for the guests at the reception and well, drink some wine and watch some old chick flicks."

"Whoo hoo. I can hardly contain my excitement." said Carrie.

"That sounds great to me," said Tori. "We could maybe fix each other's nails and roll our hair in curlers and hey, we could put our jammies on and have a sleepover."

"Very funny," said Julie. "What do you want to do?"

"We are just teasing you Jules," said Carrie. "I can't think of anything else I'd rather do than spend the evening with my best friends."

"I like the sound of it myself," said Tori as she pulled up to a white-framed church surrounded by a white picket fence. Two huge Pecan Trees stood sentry on either side of the building's entrance, towering over the simple steeple. Colorful flower beds filled with a variety of petunias edged the walkway to the building.

Julie's Father, Mack Bradley, pulled into the parking area adjacent to the church. The gray-haired gentleman stepped out of the vehicle and turned to wave as his passenger unfolded his leggy frame and exited the car. Chief Matt Holden, Mack's best friend and Julie's boss, also gave the girls a wave as he joined his friend. He twirled the ends of his handle-bar mustache with one hand and then placed his other hand on Mack's shoulder.

"She sure is a pretty woman, Mack," the Chief said.

"Yup. That's my girl," Mack said through misty eyes. "I can't believe this day has finally come. God, Matt. How pleased Mimi would have been."

"I'd like to believe she is smiling at all of us right now," his friend said.

The two men joined the girls and the group walked into the church.

"Good Evening Pastor Witten," called Mack. "How are you doing this fine evening?"

"Hello Mack," said the Pastor. "I'm doing quite well, thank you. Julie, your husband-to-be just called to tell me he is running a little late. He should be along soon."

All eyes turned to the front of the church as the doors opened and a tall, blonde giant strode in. He paused at the end of the pews and looked around, taking in the cluster of people at the front of the church. Julie quickly walked toward him.

"Kristian?" she asked.

"Yes, Ma'am," he said.

"I'm Julie Bradley. Dev has told me so much about you and I am so glad to get the chance to finally meet you."

"Well, Ole Dev told me about you, but he didn't come close to tellin' me how pretty you are. It is my pleasure to meet you."

"Thanks," Julie said with a small smile. "Dev just called and he is running a little late, but he should be here any minute. Let me introduce you to everyone."

Julie took his hand and led him down the aisle toward the crowd. She introduced him to the Pastor, the Chief, her Father, Tori and then Carrie. His eyes lingered on the petite fairy with the gorgeous eyes for a long moment and she stared at him, almost as if mesmerized. Finally, she realized that her small hand was still encased in his large one.

"Nice to meet you," she said as she tugged it away. "I didn't realize you were so big."

"And I didn't realize you were so tiny," he said with a smile.

Just then, Devlin Ames walked in with his partner, Detective Roberto Gutierrez.

"Sorry everyone," he said as he gave Julie a hug and began shaking hands.

"Is everything okay?" asked Julie.

"Yes Babe. Just had to stop by the travel agency to pick up our paperwork. It took a little longer than I thought it would. We are all set. We head to Austin for the night right after the reception and then we will be on a plane for San Francisco Sunday morning. From there, we get on another plane and Tahiti…here we come."

"I am so excited," Julie said.

"All right, ladies and gentlemen," said Pastor Witten. "It's time for us to rehearse for tomorrow's ceremony."

Julie, her Father, her Maid of Honor Carrie and her bridesmaid Tori walked to the back of the church. Chief Holden took a seat, because he was just along for the ride to give his friend some moral support.

Dev, his Best Man Kristian and his groomsman Roberto walked to the side of the lectern.

"Hey Man," Dev said quietly to Kristian. "I'm glad you made it."

"No problem," said the big man. "How come you didn't tell me your lady was such a fox?"

"Do you have to ask?" laughed Dev. "I know your reputation as a ladies man."

"Awww. That's a cheap shot," Kris said. "But why don't you tell me about the tiny blonde. Is she available?"

"Would it matter if she wasn't?" Dev asked.

"Well," smiled Kristian.

"Gentlemen," said the Pastor. "I need you to follow these instructions."

They completed the practice ceremony and everyone congregated out front. Mack and Matt asked if anyone needed a ride to the restaurant and Gutierrez said he would ride with Kris if that was okay. Dev wanted to take Julie with him, so Carrie and Tori said they would follow in Tori's car.

With everyone's travel plans arranged, they got into their vehicles and followed one another onto the blacktop, with the Pastor close behind.

When they arrived at Andy's they were met by Jerry Steelman, Carrie's parents, and a few other good friends.

Just before getting out of the car, Julie turned to Dev and asked, "Wasn't it great of Raul to give us his restaurant for the evening?"

"Sure was, Babe. Life is good."

"Just another day in paradise," she said, hopping out of the vehicle and joining Dev and their friends inside the restaurant. "Just another day in paradise."

ABOUT THE AUTHOR

Mistakes and Opportunities is Myrna's debut novel. The author is a retired Elementary Teacher with first-hand knowledge of children who are damaged as a result of physical, emotional, or medical abuse. Myrna lives in the great state of Texas and is currently working on her next effort in The Caradan Series...*Another Day in Paradise.*
Visit her online at myrna@MKBooks.net
Visit her website http://www.MKBooks.net

Made in the USA
San Bernardino, CA
30 September 2014